SOMETIMES GOOD
THINGS *ARE TAKEN*

Claimed

M. L. MARIAN

EPIGRAPH

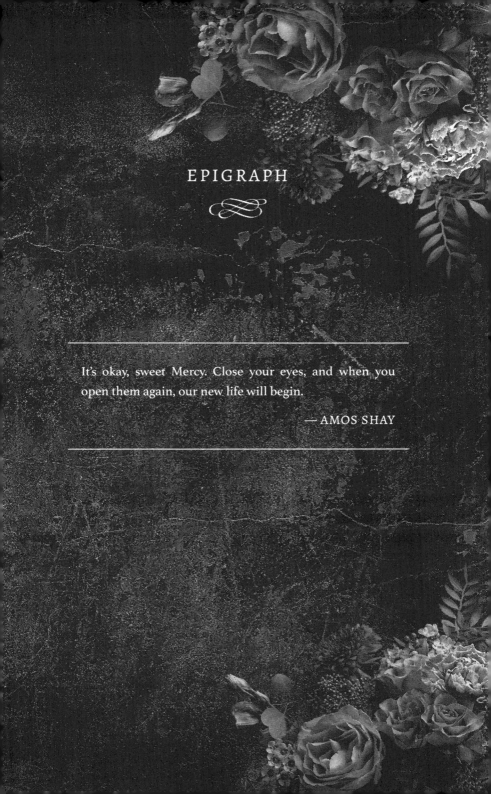

It's okay, sweet Mercy. Close your eyes, and when you open them again, our new life will begin.

— AMOS SHAY

INTRODUCTION

The Shay family has a tradition, one inspired by the story of the Roman soldiers and the Sabine women.

When a Shay sees the woman meant for him, he's not above a little...ahem...*persuasion* to convince her they belong together.

Hot loving every night.

Forced cuddling.

Steamy kisses.

Happily ever afters.

This is what it means to be a Shay.

This story has a bit of sweet bite to it with themes that may be disturbing to some readers. For a content warning, please visit the author's website at mlmarian.com.

CHAPTER 1

MERCY

17 HOURS EARLIER

The obnoxious blare of my alarm clock jolts me awake. Ahhh—the joys of waking up before 7:30 to go to work. The highlight of everyone's day. But a single woman has to do what she must in order to survive. Rent doesn't pay itself. I groan and throw a hand out to hit snooze, but miss my phone and land on an unfamiliar shape. Well, not entirely unfamiliar, but it certainly doesn't belong *here* on my night-stand, of all places. A sleep-crusted eye cracks open to glare at the misplaced object—my perfume bottle. It's been moved.

Again.

And it wasn't me doing the moving either time.

I think.

A growing thread of uncertainty cramps my stomach. I'm absolutely sure I didn't leave it there last night. Why would I? I only wear perfume when I go on dates, and since I haven't had one since I moved to Providence Falls a year ago, it should have been collecting dust on my bathroom counter. The other time happened last Saturday. I was brushing my hair when the bottle caught my eye. The bottle's position, rather. I have a thing about angles and object placement being equal and proportionate. Not enough of a quirk to be a disorder, but enough to get on my nerves when I notice something out of place. My perfume *should* have been in the corner so the back-splash equally hugged its sides.

But it wasn't like that anymore. It had been rotated a quarter turn to the left. Such a minor change that I wouldn't have noticed it if not for my weird idiosyncrasy.

Staring at the nightstand now, I have no idea what to do. I have no one to call for advice. I'd aged out of the foster system, having been shuffled through way more sets of foster parents than a young orphan should have gone through.

So here I am. An orphan still, but an older one. No parents, no one close enough to call *friend*, and all on my own. And an introvert, at that. It's a proven fact that working as a receptionist is a living nightmare for an introvert. Having to answer phones and greet clients who want to stand too close and flirt...ugh. At least I get paid a decent amount to do it, though.

Since I'm the only one I can count on to do anything around here, I grumble to myself and roll out of bed. Grabbing my robe, I take a quick look through my house, paying extra attention to the doors and windows.

Nothing out of the ordinary there.

Same thing outside. Still nothing. No footprints in the grass or any obvious sign of someone having been there last night.

Frustration causes my teeth to clench. I can't prove that someone broke in and messed with my things. The police would laugh me out of the station if I walked in with zero evidence of anything.

And now I'm doubting myself. One of my foster parents complained that I sleepwalked, but I never knew for certain if that was actually true. Maybe I should set up a camera just to make sure. Would I actually move the same object two times? Or more? Why just my perfume bottle?

Can't say for certain, but I don't think so. At any rate, if I don't get to work, I won't even *have* a house for anyone to move things around in. Which reminds me—I need to pay the rent since the first of the month is just a few days away. Worrying won't solve anything at the moment, so I may as well get dressed and focus on making it through today.

Fridays are pretty good at Shay Construction because we close at noon, giving everyone a much-appreciated head start to the weekend. Today is also the owner's last day of work, so a little party is on the schedule.

Ex-owner, I guess I should say.

And by little party, I mean donuts and kolaches that *I* have to pick up on my way to work. If there's anything else I hate more than talking on the phone, it's going in anywhere there's people.

Like the donut shop that stays open every day of the year and is always crowded with customers because they have no drive through.

Joy.

JUGGLING MY PURSE AND SIX WARM BOXES OF BAKED GOODS, I blindly grab for the door.

"Oh, good morning, Mercy! Let me get the door for you. That's quite the handful!" The words come from my right. Eliza's smiling eyes meet mine over the stack in my arms. She's about my age, but much more outgoing and friendly to strangers than I am (which is good for an office manager). My complete opposite in looks, too. Tall where I'm short, thin where I'm thicker, and blonde hair to my black.

I've got to give her credit—she tries every day to engage me in conversation, but it's just so difficult for me to talk to people. I still appreciate her effort, though.

"Thanks, Eliza. Yeah, my car is going to smell like a bakery for days."

Walking through the open door as she holds it, I head to the break room right off the entrance and ease the food onto the counter. A mixed box for each of them because growing boys have to eat. I only got enough for the foremen because the crew never really come here on Friday, anyway. Especially on the last one of the month, because that's when the foremen discuss and plan the current and upcoming projects.

"How are you today?" I ask politely over my shoulder as she follows me.

As far as managers go, Eliza is pretty great. Jobs were scarce when I moved here last year, but I lucked out when she hired me at Shay Construction and started my pay at a figure higher than advertised.

An incentive, I was told.

Apparently, all the women who had the job before me quit unexpectedly. One eloped, one just didn't show up, and one got pregnant. Since I don't plan on doing any of those things, I'm here for the long haul. Especially at this pay rate.

Eliza flashes a grin. "Girl, I'm counting down the minutes until noon. So beyond ready for the weekend. Here—let me get that."

Between the two of us, everything gets set up on the break room table in short order. She may not have a need for things to be straight and at specific angles like I do, but she's certainly efficient. Eliza nods toward the paper plates and boxes laid out in a row. "How much do you want to bet they'll all come running as soon as you open those up?"

My lips curve a bit because it's true. These guys have the noses of bloodhounds. Sure enough, within moments of the first box opening, they traipse in one by one, each with a *mornin', ladies* mumbled towards Eliza and me.

All except the last one. Amos Shay, owner of Shay Construction. Devilishly handsome man with blue eyes and inky black hair flecked with silver. He's so ruggedly beautiful that it almost hurts to look at him. My heart thumps in anticipation the closer he gets. Almost goes into cardiac arrest at his deep voice when he stops right in front of me and rumbles, "Mercy."

That's all he says. Just my name. His voice is gravelly and deep. So deep. The depth that sends chills down my spine and tingles to my nipples.

Yeah. That *good* kind of deep.

"Mr. Shay. Got your favorite kolaches. Boudain. I put your b-box on the other side of the drinks." *Gah, why did I stutter?* I don't, normally. There's just something about Amos Shay that makes my heart flutter and my throat dry up.

His icy blue gaze catches on my lips before traveling upwards. "Thanks, Mercy. That was...sweet...of you."

My breath stutters as an awkward reply catches in my throat. Did he just emphasize *sweet?* We stare at each other in heavy silence, a bubble forming around us as the conversation in the crowded break room fades away. It's overwhelming having him this close to me with his cologne that's intoxicating enough to send a flood of hormones rushing through me. If he keeps climbing into my soul like this with his masculine scent drowning my senses, I'm going to faint. His eyes drop back down to my lips and stay there. Oh, God...I have something on my mouth, don't I? My tongue nervously darts out and does a quick pass, just to make sure.

Amos inhales sharply. "Mer—"

A hairy arm thumps across his shoulder, breaking our bubble. Rapidly blinking, I take a small step back and try to recover from that weirdly intense moment.

It's Wyatt, good old country boy with a country drawl that saturates every word. "How 'bout it, old man? Retiring at fifty? Gonna be time for your first knee replacement soon. Hope you got some money stashed away for that!" A hoot of laughter falls out of him at his own slapstick joke.

"Fifty?" Amos scoffs lightheartedly, smirking as he grabs a boudain kolache from the box I'd angled perpendicularly to the refrigerator and biting into it. "Still a few years away from fifty, and nothing wrong with my knees, either. Any more jokes, *old man*? Better get all your cracks in now 'cause today's the last day. Next week, you'll have to pile them all on Garrick."

"Yeah. That Garrick's a good fella. Got some mighty big shoes to fill, though, coming after you. Well, better grab me one of them cream donuts before they run out." With another friendly slap to Amos's shoulder, Wyatt heads to the boxes, leaving our bubble to slowly form again.

Okay, I'll admit my curiosity is piqued. He must have done extremely well for himself if he can afford to retire already. He doesn't look fifty, but he's no teenager, either. His face is too rugged and weathered with the kind of tan that only comes from working outside in the heat of the sun.

Sexy, if you ask me. Which he didn't. But still.

Being 6'5" and ripped doesn't hurt, either. Top it off with those arctic eyes and a thick head of hair, and he's quite the catch. *I wonder if he's dating anyone?*

Nope. None of my business.

Now that it's just us again in the corner here, my awkwardness comes full force to the front as he finishes his kolache. *Say something, Mercy. Small talk. Something. Anything.* "So, Mr. Sh—"

"So, Mercy—"

We look at each other in shared amusement as our words clash together. Having his soul-piercing gaze focused solely on me once more makes my heart dive-bomb into my stomach again.

"Hey, Mercy—wanna meet up with us tonight?" Another interruption comes in the form of Garrick, my soon-to-be boss. I swear, the universe is conspiring against us. I can't get more than a few seconds alone with this man. Not that anything could ever come of it because I'm sure I'm not his type. "A couple of us guys are gonna go to Midnight Blues."

Garrick's invitation makes Amos tense up, but I don't know why it would. One of the foremen—and the newly appointed boss—Garrick is always trying to get me to expand my social borders. He means well, I know. And he isn't bad looking, either. I've always been a sucker for a man who can work with his hands in more ways than one.

Of course, all six guys here fit that description—even Wyatt, if a person were in the market for a polar bear. They're all hot and actually know their stuff when it comes to taking care of the clients. Even if they hadn't been blessed in the looks department, their woodworking skills alone would be enough to tip me over the edge. Self-sufficiency is a turn-on at any age.

Not that I've *been* with any of them. Or anyone, for that matter.

I'm a virgin still. Practically a unicorn in this day and age, but moving in and out of foster homes meant not getting attached to anyone. The friend made today may be left behind tomorrow. Or worse—move on without you. Apparently, my habit of detachment carried over into adulthood, too, because I've never been able to be emotionally vulnerable with a man, let alone physically.

But I really don't feel like watching a bunch of grown men getting drunk and trying to land women while I sit awkwardly on the bar stool and get ignored. Count me out. So, I answer as I always do. "Oh...thanks, but I think I'll pass." I soften my rejection with a small smile, noticing that Amos looks almost relieved at my answer. *Why would he even care?*

"What about you, Amos? You gonna come with us this time?"

Amos leans back against the counter, long legs looking oh-so-fine in his well-worn jeans. "You know I have better things to do than getting wasted. I'm a retired man now. Too old for that crap. Besides, I have special plans of my own." He turns and directs his stare straight at me. "What are you doing tonight, Mercy?"

Now I'm the center of attention. *Great.* "Oh, just hanging around the house. Maybe baking a dessert or something." Exactly what every one of my weekends looks like. Doing nothing, that is. Baking is something I absolutely have to be in the mood for. I don't even know why I threw that out there. Must have been because the question caught me by surprise.

"Dessert sounds amazing. I like sweet things. Especially before bed."

His stare melts me on the spot. *Does he mean...* I wish I had more experience with men because I truly can't tell if he's flirting or throwing out a random fact about himself. This is part of why I'm perpetually single. Can't read innuendo to save my life.

"Amos, what do you think about doing this for the Henderson project..."

Amos reluctantly drags his eyes away from me and answers Garrick's question. I zone out when they start talking construction lingo. After years of being ignored, I've perfected the art of blending into the background, even in a room of only eight people. Instead, I watch everyone else. People divulge so much about themselves when they're watched unawares. Actions are real, without posture; hidden emotions are revealed.

"Are you okay, Mercy? You seem even more quiet than usual."

Eliza's voice startles me. How do I answer? Does she really want to know? I have a tendency to overshare at the most inopportune times, not knowing when people are asking to be polite or because they really want to know. It's only when their eyes glaze over that I realize my mistake. I don't want to make this blunder with her so I shove down everything that comes to mind and simply say, "I'm okay, thanks."

And, as is the usual reaction to that, Eliza accepts it at face value. "What you need is a nice relaxing weekend, huh? Don't we all? All right, boys! Take the rest of the food with you," she calls out. "Time to get this day started so we can get out of here."

"That's what I'm talking about!" hollers one of the guys as he suggestively grinds his hips. "Party at Midnight Blues, baby!"

Parties never appealed to me. Staying in my own little nest that I've made just for myself is a much better way to relax. For me, at least. Internally shaking my head, I walk back to my desk in the open reception area, stopping to adjust the sales tax exemption certificate on the wall. Just a smidge to the right. *There.* Someone keeps moving this—and *only* this—off-center every day and I haven't been able to catch them yet. It's driving me nuts, but at least it's one constant thing to look forward to when I get to work. I'd have fixed it earlier if I hadn't had the boxes of food in my arms.

Eliza's already emailed me some tasks to work through. Should be a breeze to get through them before noon, especially if it stays slow like it is right now.

One down, about fifteen more to go. Then the *ding!* of the front entrance interrupts my roll. Of course. I have all the luck. Holding back my sigh, I paste a somewhat friendly smile on my face. "Welcome to Shay Construc—"

Oh. It's *him.*

Flynn. A smarmy guy who hits on me every time he picks up the water cooler bottles to refill them. I'm sure lots of women would be attracted to him, but there's just something about him that rubs me the wrong way. Not to wish ill will on anyone, but I truly hope he finds another job or Eliza finds another water company.

He folds his arms across the top of my tall reception desk and leans down, eyes flicking down and pressing an almost tangible leer against me. "Hey, babe," he tells my chest. "Did y'all move the empty jugs or am I just overlooking them?"

Ugh. I may not be able to read innuendo that well, but I understand this loud and clear. My shirt isn't even tight or low cut, but he makes me feel as if it is. Crossing my arms over my chest, I glance down the hallway to the left, desperately praying Eliza can hear this mess from her office and rescue me. I know I should be able to stand up for myself, but I don't like conflict. My shyness is a curse and makes me seem younger than my thirty-three years. It's pathetic, but I blame my social anxiety on my childhood.

"Flynn," I start nervously, "you know where they—"

"The water cooler's in the break room, dickwad. Does this look like the break room?" Amos's hard voice from behind me is a welcome interruption. How did he get here without me hearing him? *Stealth ninja.*

"All right, all right, my man. I hear ya. Leave the fine chick with the hot legs alone and do my job. Water cooler in the break room. Got it." Flynn's hands raise in surrender as he backs away.

When he's out of sight, Amos softens a bit as he steps closer to me. Close enough that his delicious cologne threatens to wreak havoc on my cognitive abilities. "Does he always do this?"

I grimace. "Yes. Well, almost every time."

"Mercy," he chides, "I want you to tell me if this ever happens again. You shouldn't have to put up with this from other men."

"Tell you? But...you're retiring." And *other* men? As opposed to just *one* man?

A muttered curse flies from his mouth. "I mean, you can tell Garrick. Tell Eliza, even, but don't feel like you have to listen to any of that. He needs to do his job and nothing else. Coming on to you is not part of his job. Neither is dealing with unwelcome attention part of yours. Especially from him."

My heart stutters a bit at his attention. Twice in one day. This is the most he's ever talked to me.

"Got 'em all. See you next week." Flynn keeps his head down and shuffles out the door, lugging the empty water bottles while Amos stands watchful guard with clenched fists.

"Dickwad," Amos mutters under his breath again as he stares daggers at the door. Giving me a cursory nod, he walks away, scent lingering in his wake. "See you later, Mercy."

I fall back against my chair in giddiness, a stupid smile stretching my lips as I greedily inhale before his essence goes away. Amos Shay stood up for me. Sure, it was only because someone was messing with his employee, but still.

Amos Shay. I hold his name quietly inside my heart and instead breathe out a sigh. Dreaming's free, right?

CHAPTER 2

AMOS

$\mathcal{I}$ stand in front of my office window, blood boiling as I watch that worthless son of a bitch drive off. He stood outside for a good ten minutes after he loaded up the water bottles, just trying to get another glimpse of Mercy through the lobby doors. I need a good kick in the ass for not realizing how uncomfortable he's been making her, but today was the first time I saw him in action. He'd taken over our regular guy's route about two months ago, but I had no idea he was hitting on her.

As if my sweet kitten would ever lower herself to the likes of him. I don't deserve her any more than he does. But what separates a harmless worm like Flynn Woodrow from a man like me is that I take what I want. While he might stand there and crudely flirt with her, that's about the extent of it. With me... Well, nothing stands in my way in business, and nothing will stand in the way of me getting Mercy.

Not the constraints of society.

Not even the woman herself.

A normal man would pursue her in the expected method

Flowers. Chocolate. A lukewarm kiss on the cheek at the end of a lackluster date.

A normal man would also take *no* for an answer if a woman politely rejected him. I've seen it happen with Mercy, the way she casually declines invitations to do things. Like she did with the offer to go to Midnight Blues.

If she won't accept a simple invitation for social interaction, why would she accept a date?

But I'm not just any man. I'm a Shay. I won't give her the chance to tell me *no*.

I'm not ashamed to admit part of the appeal is Mercy's vulnerability. Her shyness. Does it make me a predator to be turned on by that? Maybe. Isn't that the circle of life, though? There's always an alpha at the top of the food chain, and in this neck of the woods, it's me.

Sometimes good things come to those who wait, but sometimes good things are taken.

Claimed.

Claimed in the way the Shay men have been doing for generations. As my father did with my mother, and his father before him, and so on. When a Shay sees the woman meant just for him, she becomes his, whether she knows it or not. And if she's, shall we say...*hesitant*, a Shay is always too happy to persuade her.

In these modern times, though, it's a bit difficult to plan our courtship. Social media, cell phones, security cameras... All the latest wonders of technology hinder our ability to elope with our women. Not to mention bribing a judge to officiate a wedding with an unwilling bride is next to impossible.

My dad had it easy in that respect. He caught my mom and didn't hesitate to immediately lock her down in holy matrimony when he brought her home to me. A wry smile forms when I think of all the marriages Judge Peterson performed for us Shays over the years before he passed on. Too many to count, really.

Those types of weddings died out when he did, though. The judge we had as backup wasn't as eager to blur the lines as his predecessor was when push came to shove, even for the money he was offered.

No, the good old boys and the good old days are long gone. Now we have to woo our women thoroughly before marriage. Not that it's a hardship, because I'm extremely looking forward to *wooing* my Mercy.

I've been with my fair share of women over the years, treated them nicely and let them go. Never felt the urge to claim them, though. None of them called to me the way Mercy does.

Now it's time to take her.

Take her and keep her with me until she gives in. I'm not above a little forceful seduction. Far from Providence Falls, the house my family helped me build this past year will be perfect for us to get to know each other.

Perfect for us to free ourselves, shedding the inhibitions that society forces us to dress in and just be as we were intended to be—a man and woman in the wild, claiming each other.

Just have to get her there first.

A knock sounds at the door, making me jolt. Stepping back from the window, I lean down and force my computer to sleep with a quick key combination. "Come in."

Garrick pops his head in. "Is now a good time?"

I hate when my ruminations of my unclaimed woman are interrupted, but I do still work here for the next few hours so I have to put them aside. "Of course."

He sinks down into my chair and stacks his feet on the desk. "So, this is my chair now, huh? Very comfortable. I approve. Quick question—how many times have you farted in it? If it's more than once a day, I gotta get myself a new one."

"Dude...not answering that. Not yours yet, so get your ass out of it. And get your feet off of my desk." Jerk. He knows I can't stand dirt there. Always finds its way onto important plans and contracts.

His feet thud as they hit the ground. "Seriously, man. Are you absolutely sure you want to retire this early? I'd be bored out of my mind."

As far as everyone knows, I'm retiring completely, but I still have a partnership I'll be keeping on the side. A man who stays idle is a man looking for trouble.

We've already discussed this, but for the sake of getting him out of here, I tell him again. "My mind's made up, Garrick. I'm doing this. Shay Construction is solid; it can stand on its own two feet without me. It took off so quickly when I built it twenty-six years ago, and with the way business has steadily been creeping up every year, I've been able to build up a nest egg in addition to making out like a bandit on the stock market."

Also because I had a nice sum of money bestowed to me when I turned eighteen, as did every Shay male, and I used it to build my own business so I could provide for my woman when it came time to claim her. I could have followed tradition and worked the family farm, but I've always preferred the satisfaction of building things with my own hands. "And no, I'm not going to be bored at all. I just want some peace and quiet. Even though Providence Falls is a small town, I'm dying for some open country air and the ability to walk around naked outside if I feel like it. Just need freedom."

"Oh, yeah...the new place. You still haven't told me where it is yet. Some secret compound out in the middle of nowhere?"

He laughs, but he has no idea how right he is. Well, it's not quite a compound, but I suppose that's objective. Mercy certainly might think so. At least for a little while.

"I know you. If I give you the address, you'll probably try to surprise me with a visit." He'd better not. I don't want anyone interrupting our courtship.

"You know you're gonna miss my ugly mug." Garrick slaps his knees and stands. "I know we've already hashed this out, but I wanted to make sure one final time that you were ready to do this. It's a big change for you."

You have no idea. "I've never been more sure of anything in my life."

"Keep in touch, man."

Not likely. "Sure thing."

At his exit, my thoughts revert back to my sweet kitten. Even though she's leaving at noon, I won't be taking her just yet. No, I need to wait for the cover of darkness. She doesn't have close neighbors, but the last thing I need is for someone to see my truck anywhere near the vicinity before Mercy Callahan disappears. All it takes is being in the right place at the wrong time to screw everything up and have the course of my life forever altered in the wrong direction. She's too precious to risk because of a lack of self-restraint, so I'll just have to be content with the knowledge that she'll soon be mine.

Slowly sinking into the chair that will soon belong to Garrick, I wake my computer and go over the plan once again in my mind.

Wait for nightfall. Let her go to sleep. Break in and sedate her. Take her.

Why sedation? Because my mom almost caused a wreck when my dad took her. No, safest thing all around is for her to sleep through it. It'll be quite the drive to get to the house in Pleasant Plain, but with the sedative knocking her out, I should be able to catch a few hours of sleep once we get home.

Home. Our new home. Built in a clearing in the middle of the woods, there's no one around for miles. And I do mean *miles.* If she even managed to escape the house, the forest is raw and untamed. She could get hurt too easily. Just one more reason for me to make sure she can't leave.

I'm the only animal who gets the privilege of chasing her.

Logging into the company email server, I enter my webmaster credentials for the last time and find Mercy's account.

Click.

Select *new email.*

Click.

Schedule it for 4:00 pm on Sunday.

Click.

Compose a message to Eliza.

"Eliza, I'm so sorry to do this, but..."

My fingers fly over the keyboard as I type Mercy's resignation.

Almost done.

Click.

CHAPTER 3

AMOS

The weight of my tool belt is a familiar heaviness around my waist as I climb the steps to the front door, noting the wobble in the handrail, the peeling paint on the trim, and the crooked line in one of the window panes. This house has good bones; just needs a bit of work done on it. Once it's flipped, it'll be just right for a family with four or five kids. Maybe even throw in a dog or two for the yard that's definitely big enough for a neighborhood cookout.

This is one of the investment houses my dad and I own. And since I need something to occupy my brain until it's time to get my woman, how better to pass the minutes than with repairs I could probably do blindfolded? Can't allow myself to get too excited because time always drags before something big. So I busy myself fixing the small, easy things while I let my mind wander.

Ever since I saw her, my thoughts have belonged solely to my Mercy. My dad always told me a Shay is never complete until he finds his woman and makes her his own, and I've certainly found that to be true.

It's worked for our family for all these years, so why knock tradition? My great-grandfather passed on before I was born, but I remember seeing my grandpa, father, and uncles always doting on their woman. Always making their woman's plate at family gatherings because of their "if my woman breaks her back in the kitchen for me, I sure as hell can fix a plate for her" mentality. And when the eating was over, husbands and wives worked together to clean the dishes before saying their good-byes to the other family members.

Of course, it wasn't always like that for my father. When I was six or so, I remember being at one of those family events. Even at my tender age, I noticed things. Things like my uncles getting out of their cars, each with a woman and sometimes with a woman *and* kids, while my dad and I always came alone.

I tug at my dad's pants leg to get his attention as I watch one of my uncles pull up. "Daddy, why can't we have a lady with us like Uncle Oliver and 'em?" I'd noticed this before, but it was only just starting to bother me. Was something wrong with Daddy and me that no one wanted to love us?

Daddy looks at me funny. Why are his eyes wet?

"Are you sad, Daddy?"

He drops to one knee to get on my level. "No. Just...something got in my eye and made it leak a little. Do you remember what I told you about your momma?"

"'Course I do! I'm six and I 'member lots of things! You always say I got a membry like an elephant."

"That you do, son. That you do. And what have I told you about your momma?"

I recite what I've heard time and time again. "My momma was the most beautifullest woman in the whole wide world, and she loved me bigger than the moon." My arms fling out in exaggeration.

Daddy smiles down at me. "She sure did. She loved you more than anything."

"But not more than you, right?" I love him lots and don't want his feelings hurt. I could pretend that Momma loved us both the same,

even if I was secretly proud that she loved me more. "You and me the same, huh?"

"Yeah, boy." He laughs and chucks my chin. "Pretty sure she loved us both equally. I was her sun and you were her moon. I kept her warm and you were the light of her life. She'd spend hours looking at you at night, just watching you sleep." His voice fades off as he stares over my shoulder.

I don't know what he's looking at. There's nothing behind me except some trees. I smush his cheeks with my dirt-stained fingers and make his lips poke out. "But then she got sick and couldn't take care of me anymore."

He tugs my hands down so he can answer. "Yep. Your momma got really sick and had to go away."

He'd told me before that she'd died, but I still don't know exactly what it means. Is it like when my cousin's cat wouldn't wake up and they buried it in the ground? I don't like to think about Momma being stuck in the ground.

And that's why I don't like it when my dad leaves me. It makes me scared that he'll go away just like Momma did. "And she can't come back, right?"

"No, Amos. She can't come back. No matter how much we want her to."

If she can't come back, does this mean I'll never have a momma? Can I only have one? I love her even though I don't remember what she looks like, but I want a momma of my own that doesn't have to go away. I kick my toes in the dirt, hesitating before asking, "Daddy, do you think Momma would be mad if I wanted another lady to be my momma? And...and maybe she could love you like she loves me. Both of us the same, just like Momma."

"He's right, Mitchell." Uncle Oliver walks up with a serious look on his face. "The boy needs a maternal influence in his life. And he'll have to learn our ways sooner or later. What better time than now to set an example for him? It'll be good for you, too. Five years is long enough of being alone."

Daddy's head jerks up. "He's already got our mom as a mother figure. Are you saying she's not—"

"Not the same, and you know it."

They stare at each other for a long time and don't say anything.

"You're right. You're right." Daddy hangs his head and grips my thin arms. "No, Amos. Momma wouldn't be mad at you at all for wanting someone to love you as much as she did. In fact, she'd probably be mad at me for taking so long."

I smile at the nostalgia the memories dredge up. After that day, I went on a drawing frenzy and soon our refrigerator was covered in my stick-figure pictures depicting the momma I didn't have yet but was hoping for.

Then a few weeks later, Dad told me I was going to spend some time with my Uncle Oliver because he had a big surprise for me and it was going to take a while to bring it back. I was so excited but nervous, too, because I didn't like to do sleepovers away from my dad. With my childish fears, I was scared he'd go away and leave me, too. Just like my mom.

That summer had my little stomach churning in knots every day. Some nights, I'd get to talk to him for a little bit when he called from a pay phone. Each time, I'd ask him when he was coming back and if my surprise was ready. Every time, his reply was, "Soon, and almost. Keep waiting."

The weeks flew by and one afternoon I saw my dad's truck coming up the long driveway while I was chasing bees in a grassy field of flowers. Typical boy, I'd quickly learned the hard way which kinds were harmless and which kinds would sting.

"Daddy! Look how long my legs got!" I yell out to him as I run beside the truck, determined to beat him to the front porch of Uncle Oliver's house. My uncle said I grew two inches taller this summer, so I know my legs are longer. That means I'm faster, too. I'm laughing my head off and spinning around in circles by the time he comes to a stop.

"I missed you so much!" I try and open his door for him.

"Hold on, Amos. Let me get out, Little Bit." Finally, my dad's arms wrap around me. I squeeze him so tight, so happy that he's back. He went away just like Momma, but he came back!

"Where were you, Daddy? You were gone forever!" My words are muffled against his shirt.

He pushes me back to look at me. "Remember your surprise?"

My surprise! I'd forgotten. "Yeah! Where is it? I wanna see it. Is it in the truck?"

"Sure is. Come on, let's take a look." We walk around to the other side of the truck. I can barely keep myself from running, but I know Daddy wants to be the one to show me. As we round the front, I think I see something inside.

"Is it a puppy?"

"No, not a puppy." Daddy opens the passenger door and reaches inside. "Come on, Corina. Don't be shy."

Corina. That's a pretty name. Peeking under the door because I'm tall but not tall enough to see through the window, I freeze as I see a foot with light pink toenails step to the ground.

My dad's strong hands grip a lady's waist and help her all the way down before closing the door. I'm gonna be as strong as him one day, but not yet—whoa. My jaw drops in awe as I stare at the most prettiest lady I've ever seen. "Geez Louise, Daddy! Who...who's she?"

Daddy's hugging her close like he hugs me sometimes and he's holding her hand, too, his fingers all twisted up with hers. "This is your surprise, Amos. I got married and brought you back a momma." He smiles down at her and kisses her cheek. "This is my son Amos. Amos, this is Corina. Your new momma."

My momma. I burrow between them and give her the biggest hug I've ever given anyone. Even bigger than the ones I give my dad. She's stiff, though. I tip my head back to see her better. "Why aren't you hugging me, Momma? Don't...don't you like me? I'm a good boy, I really am." My voice wobbles. I want her so much to like me.

"I..." Lips turned downward, her voice is sweet and quiet as she looks between me and my dad. Just how my teacher at school is *always wanting me to sound. A good inside voice. Not so much for outside because I can't hear her very good.*

"Go on, Corina. Give him a hug," Daddy urges her.

Slowly, a soft arm presses me against an even softer body and a hand brushes through my dark hair. I bury my nose into her shirt and inhale, squeezing her so tight. "Momma, you smell sooo good! Thank you for my surprise, Daddy. She's just what I've always wanted!"

"It's the three of us from now on. You, your momma, and me."

"And she's not gonna go away and leave us alone?"

"No, son. I promise you, she's not going anywhere."

My new momma's belly shakes. I look up to see tears leaking from her eyes. "Why's she cryin'? Is she hurt?" I don't want her to get sick like my other momma, even if Daddy says she isn't ever leaving.

Daddy tucks some hair behind her ear and cups her chin, kissing her right on the lips even though her tears are all over them. Yuck. Grownups do gross things. "I think she's crying because she loves you so much already and is so happy that we're a family now. Isn't that right, Corina?"

Even more tears run down my new momma's face. Happy tears. I get those sometimes, especially when I get presents. Yeah, that must be it. I'm happy, too! I can't believe she belongs to me and Daddy. "I love you, too, Momma. More than...more than all the bees I caught today! I can't believe you found me a momma. How'd you find such a pretty one, Daddy?"

His big hand presses her head to his chest. She's so tiny against him, like the picture I saw of me as a baby when he rocked me to sleep. My new momma's hands grab his shirt and hold on tight as she cries. She must love him so much already, too, if she's hugging him.

"It took a while to find her, but now she's ours. You don't under-stand right now, but you will one day. It'll be your turn. This is what it means to be a Shay, Amos."

As I grew older, I learned more of what he meant, but never so much as I knew when I saw my woman. Four decades have gone by since then, and I'm no longer an innocent boy yearning for the unconditional love of a mother.

I'm a man now, with a man's desires, and I'm going to claim my woman.

This is what it means to be a Shay.

CHAPTER 4

MERCY

The day passes quickly and before I know it, I'm pulling into my garage, cleaning the house from top to bottom, and cooking a lonely dinner for one from my meager pantry. I'll need to go grocery shopping soon. Should have stopped on my way home, but I'd forgotten all about it and now that I'm home, it's too late. I'm already here and not going anywhere.

I love my little brick house. It's just far enough away from town that I have the best of both worlds. Privacy and convenience. And as a bonus for my antisocial self, my nearest neighbor is about a mile away and hidden behind half a dozen abandoned warehouses between here and there.

When I first moved to Providence Falls, homes were almost as scarce as jobs, so when my realtor showed this one to me, I snatched it up. Both she and I were shocked that utilities were included in the rent, but, never one to look a gift horse in the mouth, the penny pincher in me was elated. Apparently the landlord, AMS Holdings, is some big company that doesn't mind spending a little money to make a little more.

What I don't love about it, though, is how empty it is. Don't get me wrong—there's furniture in every room. Well, every room except one.

The guest bedroom.

I can't bring myself to put anything in it because I like to sit in there, close my eyes, and envision things.

Things like a changing table with a stack of tiny little diapers. My raggedy blue stuffed rabbit, the only tie to my past, sitting on a glider in the corner to stand watch in the night. A husband hugging me from behind as we look down at our little one sleeping in the bed against the far wall.

But my rabbit sits on the floor all alone in that corner.

Those things are just empty wishes. And if wishes were horses, I'd have lost my virginity a long time ago. Isn't that how the saying goes?

Of course, I can't let myself sit in there too often or I'll wind up in a major depression episode. Still, it happens far more often than I'd like.

I never thought I would reach the age I am today and not have a family of my own. Just like all little girls, I daydreamed that a strong, handsome prince would rescue me and carry me off to his castle, where we'd live happily ever after with all of our children that would be named from the pages and pages of possible names I'd written down.

But it wasn't happening where I was in the big city. It was too big, I think. So I moved, needing this to be a fresh start.

And it was, but putting myself "out there" and meeting someone is *not* as easy as it sounds. Even here in small Providence Falls, guys on dating apps are so judgy and—in my limited dating experience—only after one thing.

Sex.

Like guys everywhere else, they'll go after it however they think they can get it. Sweet talk, dirty talk...only to turn into a jerk of epic proportions when you don't respond to their junk pics like they think you should.

Sorry the sight of your withered penis being strangled by a jungle of pubic hair failed to ignite fiery lust within my loins.

That's been my experience. No pretty penises for me. I'd like to think I'm an equal opportunist when it comes to the male anatomy. I mean, not every man can have the perfect package, so if my perfect man who is head over heels in love with me has a micropenis, it's not the end of the world.

Am I being too picky?

It may be a shot in the dark, but I still want to hold out for someone who loves me for me, not just for my body or what I can do to them. *Ahem*—blowjobs.

Not that I've done anything remotely close to that, either. No, just one experimental summer kiss with a boy I once knew. A sweet kiss with dry, closed lips behind a shady tree. I remember our shy giggles when we broke away from each other, promising to meet in the same spot at the same time the next day.

But more importantly, I remember how I felt when he never showed up. I've often wondered why. Was it just a game to him? Did he get grounded by his parents and couldn't leave the house?

I'll never know. I was moved by the State to a new foster home a few towns over the very next day. And that's a prime example of why I'm hesitant to open myself up to heartache. Illogical, yes. But it's all I've ever known to do. It's not true, what they say, that time heals all wounds.

No... It only builds scar tissue.

The oven timer drags me back to reality. "Life is what you make of it, Mercy, and you just made dinner. So eat your heart out, babe." Nothing like a self-pep talk.

Giving the stink eye to the pill bottle over the sink, I shake one out and take a swig of water. Plate in hand, I sprawl out on the couch instead of the empty dining room table and flip through the channels while my food grows cold. I do this *every* time. Maybe one day I'll learn and decide what to watch *before* I sit down with my food.

Maybe.

What's this? I flip back two channels. "Tarzan," I announce to no one in particular. "Sure. Why not?" I'm a sappy woman. Animated movies are the best. So sue me. I select "Watch from beginning" and settle back as I take a bite.

Before five minutes have passed, I regret choosing it. How could I have forgotten how emotional it makes me? It's all too much—parents escaping a fiery death only to be killed by a wild animal; the lonely baby crying for someone...*anyone*...to give him just a little bit of love; the mother gorilla cradling him and taking him as her own.

Right on cue, the bitter tears come. Our situations aren't entirely the same—mine and Tarzan's, that is—but I see enough of myself in it to trigger a depression session. My parents died when I was too young to remember anything about them, but I know all about crying out from the inside for someone to love me. *Please, just love me and give me a new mommy and daddy who'll push me on swings and read bedtime stories.*

Appetite gone, I let them stream hotly down my cheeks as I chuck the rest of my food in the trash and wash the dishes. Why do I do this to myself?

But it's too late. I've been through this so many times that I know the only remedy now is to let the episode run its course and cry it out in the shower. So into the shower I go. At least I get the weekend to claw my way back to happiness. Or neutral existence, rather.

The water beats down on me, washing away my tears. It doesn't help when I realize my birthday is in a few months. I try to forget about it when I can because every year serves as a painful reminder that another rotation around the sun has happened and I have no family of my own.

No one to hold at night. No baby to rock to sleep. No car seats to put in my empty car. No precious hugs from chubby arms or sticky kisses. I'd even take the sleepless nights staying up with a crying baby because it would mean *family*.

The pain cuts deep, like nothing else. I know lots of people have it worse than I do and it's not the same as having loved and lost someone, but it's its own brand of torture because it's the emptiness of what *could* be there but isn't. Pain is pain, no matter the cause, and it hurts.

I want a man to hold me so tightly that I can't breathe. To lay on top of me when life gets to be too much and just let his heavy weight comfort me. I want to surprise him with little love notes in his socks when he's getting ready to go to work, and to *really* surprise him by attacking him when he gets home from a long day of work.

I want a family.

Wiping the last of my tears away, I dry off and walk naked into my closet. If I weren't feeling so emotional, I'd begrudgingly admit that walking around the house in the nude isn't something I could do with kids running around the house. But right now I want to wallow in the pits of my self-despair, so wallow I will.

I pull on some panties, ready to sleep away my feelings. The closet door almost falls shut all the way when I wrench it back open to look at the mirror hanging on the inside. As if in a trance, I trace the outline of my reflection's lower abdomen on the coolness of the mirror. Then I move to my own warm skin, lips trembling as I try to imagine myself rounded with a small life growing inside of me and stretch marks radiating from my center.

But my womb is empty. No flutter of little feet kicking me. Nothing.

Without a doubt, there are things about pregnancy that aren't enjoyable, like morning sickness, swollen extremities, and bathroom issues, but to think that life could be created and incubated inside of a woman... The thought is so beautiful that I start crying again.

Unable to help myself, I go back to the guest bedroom and look at everything that isn't there. Nothing there except for my blue rabbit I always took comfort from the first months inside a new foster parents' house. Picking it up now, I squeeze it to my chest, hoping to draw strength from it like when I was a child. I hold it so hard, letting its shabby fur absorb my salty tears and snot.

Waiting...

Waiting...

Waiting for *nothing* because it's an inanimate object that can't hug me back. Inexplicable fury rises within me and I violently fling it where the baby bed would be.

"Why do you *do* this to yourself, Mercy?" I storm back to my room and climb into bed, pissed at my body and its failures. Yeah, it's not just my social and emotional skills that are lacking. My body felt left out and ever so kindly contributed to the pile.

In addition to having PCOS—polycystic ovary syndrome—I also have one fallopian tube, making what are already risky odds of pregnancy nearly impossible. Especially considering I don't have any prospects on the horizon and am not the type to just fall into some man's bed for a night.

So not only do I deal with depression brought on by my loneliness and PCOS, I also have everything that comes along with this syndrome—excess body hair (I have a nice patch right where a tramp stamp would go), thick black chin hairs that need plucked daily for population control, the occasional adult acne, and an increased struggle to get pregnant, just to name a few.

Not like I've actually *tried*, but the doctor told me it would likely be a difficult process. I resent having to take a little white pill that's supposed to improve my ovary function and help regulate my periods when I've never even had sex before. Between all of this and my relationship woes, I'm sinking deeply into the Mariana Trench of depression.

And just because I like kicking myself when I'm down, my brain starts thinking about the guys living it up at Midnight Blues right about now. Putting the moves on their lady of choice for the night. They might already be having sex right now. Right this moment, one of them might be wrapped all around a woman. Thrusting inside her.

What if his condom has a hole? Or what if she forgot to take her birth control pill? How many babies are being created all over the world at this very moment? I can't stop the random thoughts from racing through my head.

Then I think about Amos Shay. *I have plans of my own,* he'd said. If only I'd gotten the nerve to somehow get his attention before today. Now it's too late. He's retired and I won't ever see him again. Clenching my eyes shut, I try to go to sleep, but the sounds of my biological clock echo and reverberate inside my head.

Tick.

You don't have a chance.

Tock.

No man wants a woman your age with no experience.

Tick.

If you haven't lost it by now, you're not going to.

Tock.

The last of your bloodline is going to die out with you.

Tick.

Forgotten, all while the world passes by.

Tock.

Stop it, Mercy. Just stop.

My rabbit floats in front of my mind, abandoned and all alone in that room. Anger gives way to sadness again. I can't leave him like that—stuffed animal or no. Forcing myself out of bed, I pick him up from where he landed on his head and cuddle him against my naked chest all the way back to my room.

Under the covers once again, I squeeze him to me and apologize. "I didn't mean it. I just wanted to feel safe again. I don't know how you did it, but I wish you could talk back to me and tell me everything's going to be all right, just like when I was a little girl. Tell me there's someone out there who cares about me and wants me for himself."

A fresh wave of tears falls. "That there's *someone* who would hold me in his arms and wipe my tears away." I hold him tightly and turn my face into my pillow, silently sobbing into it.

Life wasn't meant to be lived like this.

Something's got to change.

CHAPTER 5

AMOS

Leaning against the door frame as I pocket my spare key, I stare. Nothing can tear my gaze from her. Her beauty turns heads without question during the daytime, but when she's sleeping...well, it's beyond words.

Moonlight shines through a gap in the curtains, beaming at just the right angle to caress her face, tear tracks from earlier drying. Like a spotlight, it highlights those thick, black lashes that hide the prettiest green eyes I've ever seen. A rosy mouth, resting slightly open in heavy slumber. A cute button of a nose. Long hair as black as night fanning over her pillow.

Can nostrils be sexy? Yes, they can. If they belong to sweet Mercy Callahan.

Thoughts of her always make my balls tighten. Just the mention of her name...*Mercy.* I imagine her begging me for mercy as I tease her, bound and captive to my desires. Even now my cock hardens, pleading for mercy of its own as it stretches against the crotch of my pants.

She lies there in her queen size bed, only the barest hint of her naked shoulders visible. Not one for lingerie, my Mercy. No, her tastes were more simple than that. Her preference was to sleep in just a pair of underwear, with the heavy comforter tucked underneath her chin.

I should know. I've been watching her for a long time.

Oh, Mercy—you won't be needing those covers much longer. Soon I'll be the one wrapped around you. I'll never let you go.

Her swollen eyes draw my attention again. Why was she crying? I saw her holding a stuffed animal and crying herself to sleep, but I got here too late to see why. And I couldn't exactly walk out from the shadows to ask her. It would have frightened her.

At any rate, it doesn't matter. I'll be the one wiping her tears away from now on.

Tonight's the night. I can't take it anymore.

The sedative-filled syringe feels like a boulder in my pants pocket as my bare feet take me to her bedside. The sound of my zipper lowering is stifled, lost in the droning hum of the air conditioner. *Ahhh...*nothing like the feeling of a heavy cock being set free.

But something's missing—got to set the mood. Dick swaying, I detour to her attached bathroom, using the dim light of my phone's screen to grab her perfume from the counter. There's also a prescription pill bottle I haven't noticed before. Picking it up softly so the pills don't rattle, I add it to my pocket, reminding myself to look at it later. I bring her perfume up to my nose and inhale as silent padded footsteps lead me back to her bed.

A smirk twists my lips as I remember Mercy's confusion when she found her perfume here instead of in the bathroom. She didn't notice me watching through the opening of her curtained window yesterday morning, but I could see every emotion cross her face, from confusion to worry and even a flash of fear. I didn't mean to scare her, but I just couldn't stay away. Luckily, the grass had just been cut so I didn't leave any trampled spots on my way back to where I'd hidden my truck.

The days of stalking her and breaking into her house are coming to an end, unfortunately, but I'm okay with that because now it's time to take her home where she belongs.

Away from dicks like *Flynn* who think they can look at what's mine.

A small spritz throws tiny particles of vanilla, crème brûlée, and sandalwood floating in the darkness before they settle on her pillow. *Mhmm.* Just inhaling that intoxicating aroma sends the blood pulsing through my veins and precum kissing the tip of my cock. I give myself a couple of squeezes to relieve the pressure.

Cautiously, I roll her onto her back. No reaction. She's a heavy sleeper, but I'm always a bit wary that she'll wake up to me in the room. This is the first time I've done anything more than jerk off in the shadows while watching her sleep.

Propping a knee onto the bed, I wait, feeling the thud of my own heartbeat thundering through my veins. Still nothing. Just a little snore here and there.

Perfect.

Up goes the other knee. I gingerly move until I straddle her blanket-covered stomach. Slowly, oh so slowly, I inch the covers down until her nipples are revealed in the shadows. Soft tips rapidly harden as they meet the cooler temperature of the room.

My mouth waters in anticipation, but I can't set myself loose on her. Not yet. Not here.

Instead, I stroke my hardness, wetting my fingertips with precum before gently smearing a thin layer of it on one taut nipple, then the other. Back to my dick for more fluid, then again to those luscious tips as her chest rises and falls in the unhurried rhythm of slumber. My fingers dance over those beaded nubs before falling away, sweeping over the soft sides of her breasts.

Bracing a hand on the headboard, I lower down until I feel

the soft puffs from her mouth warming my cockhead. A thrill of power rushes through me as I tenderly paint her pink lips with my arousal, dragging my glans over the perfect bow shape, cock twitching as her lips slightly purse at the unexpected pressure. My eyes can't get enough of the sight of her covered with me.

She's covered in my secretions.

In me.

I'm marking my territory.

Suddenly, she mumbles out a sleepy sigh, lashes fluttering. I freeze, my blood turning to ice. This would be a terrible time for her to wake up as I hover over her, bulging erection sticking out like a flagpole over her face. Reflexively, my hand grapples for the syringe.

Just in case.

Her eyes slowly open as my fingers dip into my pocket. It wasn't supposed to happen like this.

Too soon.

Too late.

Mercy looks at me sluggishly, no doubt trying to process exactly what she's seeing—a shadowy, brutish beast of a man straddling her, cock exposed in the moonlight. Exactly what every woman living alone wants to wake up to, I wryly think to myself.

Not.

It's apparent the minute it snaps in her brain. Her eyes widen and drop to my cock, then to her naked breasts. She gasps.

Here we go.

Before she can scream out the air she collects, my hand falls across her mouth and traps it inside while I fish the syringe out, popping the cap off with my teeth.

"Shh, Mercy. I'm not gonna hurt you. It's just me," I croon.

If anything, my reassurances make it worse. Her chest

heaves and she flails about, knocking her rabbit off of the bed. The sight of her breasts would grab my attention in any other situation, but the sheer terror emanating from her suppressed cries takes away from the moment. Screams of passion are one thing—pure and undiluted fear is another.

It's a bit of work pinning her arms to her sides with one hand and my knees, but I get it done before putting the bulk of my weight onto her thighs so she can't gain any traction.

"I didn't want to do it this way, baby. You were supposed to stay asleep so you wouldn't get upset like this."

Intravenously giving her the sedative would have been ideal, but that chance has been shot to pieces. Intramuscular it is. I try to keep the needle out of view, I really do, but even in her distress and the darkness, my sweet Mercy has sharp eyes.

Nasal exhalations puff against the back of my hand in rapid release before her hot breath caresses my palm in a muted scream. Her restrained thrashing increases at the sight of a needle heading her way.

Poor thing. She doesn't know this is a necessary first step to our life together.

"Shh, shhh. Don't move, baby...it's okay. Try to relax so your arm doesn't get sore." Using the strength in my knees to hold her still, I depress the plunger into her tense upper arm as quickly and humanely as possible, ignoring the pang in my chest—and cock—as she pitifully whimpers.

"There we go, baby. All in." Now to withdraw it and wait. With the sedative, she'll drift off to sleep, enabling me to move her without a fight. "Just go back to sleep and everything'll be all right when you wake up, baby girl."

Gently, I massage the injection site with my free hand. "It's okay, sweet Mercy. Close your eyes, and when you open them again, our new life will begin."

In a feeble effort to dislodge my hand, her teeth scrape my palm, but a quick press of my thumb under her chin clamps her jaws together. Her short nails scratch uselessly at the underside of my thighs, unable to tear through my pants. Tears collect on her lashes, green eyes darting back and forth as she realizes she is completely helpless and at my mercy.

My Mercy. Why couldn't you have stayed asleep just a bit longer?

Disregarding her flinch as my head lowers to hers, I kiss the short paths her tears make as they fall into her hairline, nonsensical soothing sounds involuntarily leaving my mouth as her shrieks hit my palm.

Time ticks by slowly, so slowly, as we both wait. The sounds of our escalated breathing fill the room, her muffled pleas dying out as our eyes hold each other captive. Both of us speaking a language with no words.

I'm scared, her eyes tell me.

It's alright. I'm here now, mine soothe.

Don't hurt me, she begs.

Oh, kitten.

Two minutes.

Three minutes.

Five.

I see the signs. Mercy's breaths decrease to a more normal pace and her muscles loosen, tension fading out of her bit by bit. Warily, I remove my hand from her mouth, wiping the excess drool and the remnants of my precum on the bedsheets. Her brow furrows and she licks her lips, but other than that, she lies there docilely. Keeping a wary eye on her, I open a packet of sterile gauze and blot the beaded blood on her arm before collecting all the evidence in a pile. I'll have to borrow a small trash bag from her so I can dispose of it.

The fifteen-minute mark is my target before I move her. Just to ensure the full effectiveness. After that, I'll take her to our new home and settle her in, but if I've timed it right, it should wear off in her sleep. Probably won't even remember a thing when she wakes up. Hope she won't be too nauseated. Unfortunate side effect, though. Happiness isn't bought without a fight.

Seven minutes to go. I slide my hands down her toned arms until I reach her hands. Drawing them up over her head, I link our fingers together before giving her more of my weight as I bend down and stretch my legs out atop hers. I drop my forehead, making contact with the gentle slope of her own, and breathe in her exhalations.

My Mercy. My head moves down, down, down to her neck, where I inhale her heady vanilla scent and spend long minutes trailing sucking kisses from one side to the other.

Ahhh. I stop and let her neck cradle my face, lungs increasing their intake as I try to calm myself. The struggle with her riled me up more than I thought it would, aggravating my already angry cock. Her vulnerability ignites the predator within me. Against my better judgment, my hips move a little.

Good God, her bare skin against my dick is paradise. I shouldn't, but I close my eyes and let myself thrust lightly against her stomach, hoping my open zipper doesn't irritate her delicate skin.

Unable to hold myself back even if it did.

"Mercy," I pant. It's no good; I'm too worked up. No way will I be able to drive four hours with this monster demanding attention. "Sorry, baby. Been waiting...so long. Forever—"

With a grimace, my speed increases, cock dripping as her skin teases and stimulates my sensitive tip. "Mercy. Mercy...sweet Mercyyyy—"

Fingers tightly squeeze hers as I bear down and press my hips for one final thrust. Belatedly, I notice her eyes have drifted shut and her breaths are more lethargic, but it doesn't stop me from grunting out a release as my cock jerks and spatters cum onto her naked abdomen.

Catching my breath, a modicum of shame fills me for what I just did.

That was too quick, I know.

Next time I'll last longer.

Sitting up, I take in the white ribbons of cum decorating her belly and indulge myself by dipping my fingers into one of the shallow puddles. Wiping her mouth clean from her saliva, I reapply what came off during our earlier struggle to her nipples and lips, taking my sweet time now.

Pushing her panties aside, I sweep through more liquid and insert it into the warmth of her pussy, relishing its tight clench around my finger. A groan escapes me when I imagine how tight she'll feel wrapped around my dick.

Almost done.

A quick massage of my leftover cum into her skin.

A gentle kiss to her tender little clit.

There. Time to take her and her rabbit home.

CHAPTER 6

MERCY

*U*gh. The pounding in my head is killing me. So is the ache in my stomach. Hope I'm not getting sick. I roll over, bunching my pillow up as my arms slide underneath it. My lips smack together. Chapped, judging by the crustiness flaking off. A few quick licks with my tongue take care of it for now as my pillow receives an indentation, courtesy of my face.

Mhmm...there's nothing more soothing than the scent of freshly laundered sheets. The way they feel ag—wait a hot second. My fabric softener is lavender and vanilla. This pillow smells like...like Amos Shay? I've got to be dreaming, but my nose swears it's real.

So thirsty. I moan and reach over to my nightstand for my bottle of water. *Why is my arm sore?* Instead of my familiar nightstand, my hand encounters a warm body.

What? A...warm body?

This...this is no dream.

Alarm rushes through me, almost making me lightheaded as my eyes fly open and make contact with blue ones. At the familiar sight in an unfamiliar setting, the adrenaline fades away just as quickly, leaving confusion in its wake.

"Mr. Shay? What are you—why am I—?"

"Afternoon, sleepyhead. Call me Amos—not Mr. Shay." I swear I feel the bass of his deep voice in my rib cage.

Propped up on an elbow and looking down at me is my boss, Amos Shay. Ex-boss, rather. Sleep-tousled black hair flecked with silver. Eyes an icy blue colder than the Arctic Ocean. Massive tanned shoulders. Hairy chest.

Shirtless hairy chest.

There's so much to take in at once. He said it was the afternoon. How in the world did I sleep so late?

And...this isn't my bed. Good Lord, this bed is at least three times the size of mine! Saliva pools in my mouth as dread fills my heart. "Mr. Shay, how—" *Ooooh, hello, full bladder.*

I frantically look around the—*his?*—room. "Bathroom. Where's the bathroom?"

"Right there." He points to a white door by a dark mahogany dresser.

"Umm...hold that thought." I throw back the covers, sighing in relief when I see my intact underwear—and a too big shirt that definitely isn't mine—and crawl for what feels like miles to get out of the bed. I hotfoot it to the bathroom, ignoring the heat of his gaze on my backside.

Accidentally slamming the door, I wince at the sound as I fumble for the lock.

There's no lock.

Why is there no lock?

Calm down, Mercy.

Why is there no lock?

Leaning against the frame, I try to think things through.

One—*Call me Amos?* I've never called him by his first name! Except for in my head.

Two—I went to bed alone last night.

Three—I woke up half a day later in Mr. Shay's bed. I go

from thinking I'll never see him again to being *in bed with him* and not remembering a single second of getting there!

Four—I'm wearing clothes that may or may not be his.

Five—What the heck? *What the actual heck?*

There's just no logical explanation. But as much as I need to figure things out, I *really* have to pee. No joke. And what a bathroom. It's absolutely gorgeous, decorated with a mixture of rich blacks, cool grays, and soft whites. There's a huge walk-in shower with a frosted glass door and way too many shower heads, a toilet with a bidet beside it, and an inset garden tub.

Toilet, my bladder reminds me.

After I get sweet relief, I wash my hands in the large farmhouse-style sink. Everything is so clean, it almost looks brand new. Absentmindedly scratching my stomach, I study my appearance in the mirror. It doesn't look like I spent the night having wild sex. Being a virgin, shouldn't I remember it? Wouldn't I be sore?

And what in the world is on my lips? I lean closer. Did I drool on myself? I've never known drool to taste so salty. Gross. A quick scrub with a little bit of soap gets it off. I eye the sink again. Maybe I'll take a fast rinse myself before I go back out there. But first...

Surely a bathroom this fancy has a toothbrush stashed away somewhere. I spot a brand new one by the cotton swabs and brush the filth from my tongue. My morning breath—or afternoon, according to Mr. Shay—is toxic enough to kill a dead animal. Yeah, an already dead one. Kill it twice. Bam.

I hope he doesn't mind me sneaking around in the drawers and cabinets, but I can't go back out there with my hair in such a mess. Quietly opening a random drawer, I cringe when I find a pack of ponytails. And makeup. And tweezers. And a brand-new bottle of the same perfume I have. It's somewhat odd that we have the same taste. Does...does all of this belong to another woman? I'm not touching her tweezers, no matter how much these stupid chin hairs are driving me crazy. I'll just have to ignore them until I get back home.

Silently asking forgiveness from the unknown woman, I steal a ponytail and gather my hair into a knot. But this stupid itch on my belly demands attention again when I raise my arms, so this time I reach a hand under the material for direct contact.

It feels weird, so I withdraw my finger and see dried whitish stuff on it. Ew. Disgust is written all over my face as I meet my own scrunched glance in the mirror. Hesitantly, I bring my finger up to my nose for a quick sniff. Smells bleachy and musky. Surely it can't be—my mouth drops open in shock. It's —*semen?* I think?

Oh my God. But whose? Mr. Shay's? Someone else's?

I haven't held onto my virginity for all these years only to give it up to some nameless man and apparently forget the entire event by the next afternoon. What is going on here?

My original plan for a spit bath won't work. I've got to get clean. *Now.* But without a lock on the door... Surely he wouldn't barge in here while the door is still closed. I'll just have to take that chance.

Clothes—I don't have any clothes. Doesn't matter. No way am I putting this contaminated shirt back on. Guess I'll be wearing that robe so conveniently hung by the towel rack when I'm done.

Two fingers peel my clothes off and drop them onto the floor. The dry patches on my stomach make me shudder. Was the crusty stuff on my lips semen, too? I gag, tasting the acidic bile creeping up my throat.

Shower. Get in the shower, Mercy.

Hot running water soothes all worries away in most cases, but not mine. Not today. I scour my lips and body, washing away all traces of whatever dried fluid was on me, and repeat what I told myself earlier.

"Calm down and think. *Think.* You went to bed alone. You didn't go to Midnight Blues. Did you? He's your ex-boss. You woke up in his bed, but your clothes were on. But were his? Ohmigod...Amos Shay. No, he definitely had his shirt off. What about underwear? He wouldn't—would he? You're in his house...where even *is* his house? Ughhh!" I close my eyes and tilt my head forward, letting the water from multiple shower heads rain down and drum on my neck.

Although I'm thirsty and need to drink something soon, my headache is a bit better after the pulsing jets of the shower heads. The water's still hot, but I don't know how big Mr. Shay's water heater is and if he'll want a shower.

Reluctantly, I finish, drying off with a thick fluffy towel and then don his thin cotton robe that thankfully hits right above my ankles. Must hit him just above the knees with as tall as he is.

I've got to give him the benefit of the doubt. This is Amos Shay, newly retired owner of Shay Construction, a very successful construction company in Providence Falls that does extremely well for itself, considering the extravagance of this house.

This is my ex-boss, who has never so much as looked at me the wrong way in the year I worked for him as his reception-ist. *Unless you count the way he looked at your lips yesterday.*

No!

Just Mr. Shay, I repeat to myself before throwing open the bathroom door, prepared to get some answers to my questions.

Surprise makes my limbs jolt when I see a still-shirtless Mr. Shay wearing gray sweatpants encasing what I'm sure are very muscular legs, if the rest of him is anything to judge by. He towers over me, arms resting above him on the door frame.

Whoa. Hot man alert. Cue rambling.

"Mr. Shay—wow, I didn't expect you to be so...so close. Do you need the bathroom? I'm sorry, but I just had to take a shower. I brushed my teeth, too. Oh, don't worry, though... it wasn't yours, it was one I found. Unopened. Hope that was okay, but I didn't want to kill you with my morn—" His grin steadily grows the more I nervously prattle on about stupid stuff, but a thick finger to my lips cuts me right off.

Okaaaaay, then. Shushing starts now. My eyes cross, I'm sure, as I look at his finger at the end of my nose. Yes, nose. His finger is that freakin' long. That beast of a hand has got to be as big as my face. And I'm no delicate flower.

"Call me Amos, sweet Mercy." His lips brush my forehead. I flinch in surprise and look at him sideways. Is it because he isn't my boss anymore that he's so insistent I be informal with him? And what's with the forehead kiss and *sweet* Mercy? "Believe me when I say that what's mine is yours. Come eat some breakfast. That'll go a long way in taking away your headache."

How did he know I had a headache? Did I get drunk last night and he somehow was there to take me home? That doesn't make sense. Nothing does. He places his hand on my lower back as he guides me out of the bedroom. I feel the singeing heat of his palm through the thin material of the robe. If I were braver, I'd push his pinky up so it's not resting on my pantiless butt. *Really, Mr. Shay?*

But I'm not. I'm weird like that. If a person does something embarrassing on accident, I pretend I don't notice it, thereby saving us both the embarrassment of having to acknowledge the elephant in the room.

So I deal with the ticklish itch I get when it ever so slightly dips inside my crack with each step I take. I'm able to catch a quick glimpse of the outdoors through the windows, but all I see are trees. Lots and lots of trees. Providence Falls doesn't look like this. *Where are we?*

"Is this your house, Mr. Shay?" And do I need to be on the lookout for a territorial woman? Oh, God...please let it just be us in the house. I can only imagine the conclusions his girlfriend would justifiably jump to. I was in his freakin' bed this morning, for crying out loud.

"*Amos*, Mercy. And yes."

"But where, though? In Providence Falls?"

He sidesteps my question as we enter the kitchen. "Let's get you that breakfast now. Does an omelette sound good?"

I suppose I'll think better with a clearer head, so I thank him and guzzle the glass of orange juice he slides my way.

"Now, one omelette coming right up." Opening cabinet doors at random, he mutters, "Pans...pans...where are the pans?"

Wouldn't he know where his own pots and pans were kept? This seems a little odd. But he finally finds what he's looking for, and before I know it, a plate is placed in front of me along with a fresh glass of juice. The entire time I'm demolishing this scrumptious breakfast, he silently drills holes into my head as he just watches me awkwardly try to avoid staring at his nipples. When I scrape the last bite from the plate, I daintily wipe my mouth with a napkin. "Okay, Mr. Shay. Give it to me straight. I've racked my brain trying to come up with answers to questions I don't even feel comfortable asking..."

My voice trails off and I squirm in my seat when I see his blue eyes narrowing in on my face. I meet his gaze and return the favor. Gosh, he's so handsome. A man that works with his hands is hot. A man who works with his hands *and* knows what he's doing with money? Utterly dreamy.

He wears his age extremely well, too. With his silver-sprinkled black hair, blue eyes, and facial scruff, he's got a mug worth a second glance or two. Or fifty. I may not have ever had a relationship, but I can still appreciate a work of art when I see it.

"Did you hear me, Mercy?"

No, must have zoned out. The angles of your jawline are too mesmerizing. "Sorry. What'd you say?" *Pay attention, Mercy.* He's possibly the only one who can explain last night.

"I brought you here."

Confusion colors my voice as my words slowly leave my mouth. "Yes, okay. I figured as much. But why? Where's here?"

"We're in Pleasant Plain."

Pleasant Plain? That's four hours from Providence Falls. "You and I were in the same place? I-I don't see how... I went to bed and didn't go anywhere last night. I didn't go to Midnight Blues. How did I get here...four hours away?"

He leans closer, encasing my soft, small hands in his callused, massive ones. *Gah, those veins.* His deep voice fills the room, its sound waves surrounding me. "My sweet Mercy. Has there ever been something that you wanted, that you yearned for so *badly,* but it was just out of reach? Something that was always on your mind, but you were hesitant to ask for it because the chance of rejection was too high?"

I don't answer him. Of course I have. I even had a breakdown over it last night, but what does this have to do with why I'm here?

"And then you realize that sometimes the only way you can get it is just to take it."

Wait a minute.

"You're mine, Mercy. From the moment I saw you, I knew you were the one I've been waiting for. Meant to be claimed. You won't be a Callahan for much longer."

What is he talking about? Does he mean—

"I'm gonna marry you and make you mine."

Marriage? We don't even know each other. Is he crazy? At least that answers my curiosity about another woman being here. I swallow down a hysterical giggle. *Surely not...*

"I know you don't remember much about last night. God, Mercy, you're so beautiful when you're sleeping. That's been one of my favorite things to do these past few months—

watching you sleep at night. I waited patiently for you...waited while my family helped me build this house for us. And last night was when I was going to take you and bring you here, but you woke up too soon and I had to sedate you. I didn't want to, but you left me no choice."

"What?" As if on cue, my arm tingles with the phantom sensation of a needle pricking me. My heart sinks like a lead balloon into my stomach with each word he speaks, but I mask it with a nervous laugh. "Very funny, Mr. Shay. Cut it out. W-what really happened?"

He arches an eyebrow and brings my hands to his mouth for a kiss, saying everything by saying nothing at all.

The food I just ate threatens to explode from my mouth. He *drugged* me?! *That's* the cause of my freakin' headache? Was that—my fingernails dig into my clenched palms—Mr. Shay's body fluid all over my stomach? On my lips?

My perfume bottle... It was him.

I didn't sleepwalk.

Sleep, sleep—he's been in my room watching me *sleep*. My blood runs cold, body limply falling back against my chair in shock, tethered to reality only by the shackles of his hands. I can't believe it. Never would I have thought that—

"A-a-amos?" I whimper as I search his eyes that light up in happiness at the sound of his first name leaving my lips. Did he rape me? I don't feel sore, but still. "W-w-why would you d-do that to me?" The break in my voice shames me.

"Because I'm a Shay. We take our brides, willing or not."

Be strong, Mercy. I belatedly snatch my hands away only to be scooped up into his arms and plopped onto his lap. "What about work? I have to go to work...y-you have to run your company. You've got to let me go!" Focus on the marriage part later.

A rough palm cradles my entire face, tilting my eyesight to his as he caresses my cheekbone with a warm thumb. "I heard you, you know. Heard you tell Eliza about how you grew up. I'm so sorry about that, baby, but you don't have to be alone anymore. Don't worry your pretty little head about a thing. I'm retired, remember? And you've moved to a job out of state. Last-minute thing, but the money was too good to pass up. Don't you see? I've thought of everything. You're mine, sweet Mercy. Only mine."

"No... Eliza expects me to show up. I can't just—"

"No, she won't. I sent her an email from your work account. You resigned. You no longer work at Shay Construction."

I...I can't believe it. He—he's completely isolated me and no one, not one person, even knows. "I...can't b-breathe..."

Hyperawareness magnifies my surroundings as my breaths come in pants and gulps that are too quick to properly distribute the oxygen my body needs.

I see and feel everything and nothing.

The curly salt and pepper hair on his chest tickling the corner of my mouth.

The beams of sunlight streaming through the french windows and dancing on the light gray walls.

The steady pulse in his throat carrying life to his villainous body.

The hum of the oversized stainless-steel refrigerator.

The manic look of love in his eyes as he peers into my soul and dips his head toward mine.

"Mercy," he whispers against my lips.

"No! No..." My protest is muffled by his mouth and my vision goes black as unconsciousness mercifully reaches for me.

CHAPTER 7

AMOS

My poor sweet Mercy. She weighs next to nothing in my arms as I carry her to our bedroom. I wonder how long it will take her to think of it that way—*our* bedroom. But it doesn't matter, really. She has all the time in the world to come to grips with it. She's not going anywhere. Now I understand why my dad was always dragging my mom to their room for *naps* in the middle of the day. My innocent mind couldn't find any logic in it then but I certainly do now. I can't wait to take *naps* with Mercy.

Laying her down once again and slipping my too-big robe from her limp frame, I sit next to her and admire how her ebony hair contrasts so beautifully with the pewter-colored bedding as I draw the covers over her naked form. The room was still too dark early this morning for me to fully appreciate it.

This wasn't quite the way I wanted her in my bed, but when life doesn't follow the plans you set, you have to go with the flow. Rest is what she needs. I'm sure her psyche has handled all that it can for the moment, but the reality of her circumstances hasn't truly sunk in yet.

It will, though. Especially when she discovers the biometric locks on the doors and windows to ensure she can never leave here on her own. Never leave *me*. Not like my mom did, although she didn't mean to.

And not yet, at least. Maybe in a few years when I know she completely accepts that she is mine, for now and always. And I will never let her be anything other than *mine*.

A mesmerizing lock of her hair escapes from her bun, begging me to touch it. Wrapping it around my finger, I think of what I still need to do. Her phone is safely tucked away— sans SIM card—as is mine. Her car and all her things in her house need dealt with, just in case someone goes looking. But I doubt they will. Mercy's a loner, and other than a little bit of shock and a lot of annoyance, Eliza will take her absence in stride and move on, looking for the next temporary receptionist.

I remember when I first saw her. It was her first day at Shay Construction, my company that I'd built from the ground up. Eliza had been looking for a receptionist to replace the three who had quit before and Mercy Callahan had appeared from nowhere to apply.

At least a foot shorter than my own 6'5", with jet black hair and mossy green eyes, she caught the attention of my dick first. Let's be honest. I'm a red-blooded man. But she caught the attention of my heart, too, and I knew she was the one for me within mere moments. Just like every Shay does.

When Eliza tugged me aside and told me Mercy was absolutely perfect for the position but was staying in a motel until she could find a house, the idea hit me.

I had several rental houses my father and I had bought and rented out under our partnership, AMS Holdings. Why not rent one of those to Mercy? I *needed* her to be in one of my houses. I'd keep the utilities in my name, say they were included in the rent. Anything to tempt her into choosing me.

And she did. She chose my house, not knowing I came along with it.

Mercy had only been working there a few weeks when I'd overheard Eliza asking her some trying-to-get-to-know-you questions. I'd hung back in the hallway, not wanting to interrupt because I wanted to know, too. It was like pulling teeth, but Mercy quietly mentioned the fact that she was an orphan who'd aged out of the system. And an introvert, to boot.

Vulnerable prey, helpless to the whims of vicious predators.

Good thing I'm here to protect her from scum like that.

It didn't take long to notice that crooked things drove her crazy. Like an itch that needed to be scratched, she would literally squirm in her seat until she got a chance to straighten whatever it was that was off-kilter. So I always made sure to push the exemption certificate's frame out of place, just so she'd have something to look forward to every morning. Same with her perfume. I wanted her to know I was there.

And now she's here. I gaze longingly at her, curvy limbs akimbo in my bed. It was a kindness, really, to reveal her future to her as I did. To let her hopes build and then be crushed would be cruel, and I cannot tolerate knowingly causing her unnecessary pain.

But we must start as we mean to go on. She's mine. Demonstrating that will be much more effective than mere words. Here on my secluded property, away from the rules and regulations of society, I can claim her, body and soul, as a woman was meant to be taken.

Primally.

Forcefully.

Finally.

Thoughts race through my mind, flashing previews of the fiery embraces my bed will soon see. My darker skin sliding against her paleness as our limbs tangle. The whimpers escaping her mouth as I pin her down with brute strength. The tightness of her pussy as I overpower her reluctance and breed her. Her thick hips forced wide by my bulk as I spray her cervix with my seed. Her ultimate surrender as she accepts she is defenseless against the potency of my passions. The explosive orgasms that will drain us both at our acceptance that I am the apex predator dominating his mate.

I want to chase her. Capture her. Claim her.

Blood rushes into my dick at the erotic visions. I'd rather her be awake so I can show her how good we are together, but she's entirely too tempting, naked and small in my Wyoming king size bed. The bed I bought just for us, wanting to have my sweet Mercy sleeping in something no one else has touched.

As I greedily run my eyes over her breasts, her breath hitches and a languid sigh leaves her. That does it. I don't like that she washed me off of her earlier, but that just means I'll have to put my cum back on her. If I could bathe her in it, I would.

I whip my thickening cock out. It's her own fault, really, for being so irresistible. A few pumps up and down and I'm rock solid. Ready to mark her again. But the feel of my hand won't do. Too rough. I need something soft.

Soft like Mercy's hands. Her left one is perfectly placed. Even positioned palm up, like she's begging me to put something in it. Or to wrap her softness around my hardness and drag it from root to tip, palming the knob in a circle. Like this.

Mhmm...feels so good. I manipulate her hand to form a fist and drill my shaft through it. Back and forth. In and out. Fast then slow. Good God, why does she affect me so?

My balls slap against her wrist and forearm with the rhythm of my thrusts. That feels amazing, too. What will it feel like when she's completely conscious? Maybe I'll be the one to black out as the sensations overwhelm me. I move faster, keeping my gaze on my sweet Mercy's face.

Closer, closer, closer...

Just as I'm about to erupt, a tiny sob escapes her in her sleep. I curse, faltering right on the torturous edge of coming. The battle between my mind and my dick is an agonizing one that I almost don't win.

But she needs rest. I can be reasonable. Just like my father was with my mother. After he brought her home to me, he spent countless hours just holding her on the couch. Constant reassuring touches throughout the day to reinforce that she was now his to comfort.

Instead of forcing Mercy to jerk me off in her sleep, I yank my sweats off and climb naked into the bed with her, propping up onto my elbow. She's finally mine, and I can't believe it. I just want to stare at her and drink in the sight.

But the heavy weight between my legs isn't easy to ignore. Still rock hard and dripping, I reach down to the wetness and swipe a finger through it. Bringing it closer to my face, I wonder at the small bead of liquid as the light hits it. This is me—and I belong in her.

On her, in her...either will do. As long as my stamp of ownership is all over her, I don't care which. Heat stirs within me as my eyes jump between my finger and Mercy's unconscious form. I've got to mark her *now*.

Grabbing her jaw with one hand and pursing her lips open, I spread my precum along her smooth gums and, after gathering more, on her tongue. I force her mouth closed, shuddering at the spike of electricity flowing through me as she smacks her lips in her sleep, tasting me. *That's it, kitten. Know my taste. Crave it.*

It's not enough. With my cock leaking like a sieve, I've got to do more. Another trail decorates her sweet little nipples, and when I'm done with those, I even leave some in her belly button, the small motion of going in and out reminding me that soon my dick will penetrate her pussy.

But for now, I'll settle for gently shoving more of me inside that pretty pink pussy. I swear, the sight and feel of my finger being clenched by her gorgeous cunt is almost more than I can take. At this rate, this river of arousal will never end.

I grit my teeth and turn us on our sides, my neglected cock nestling within the warm cradle of her cheeks. Drawing the covers up over us, I casually trace her nipples, not wanting to leave her to rest alone yet. I love the way those naughty buds harden even in her sleep.

This is sublime bliss, the feel of her in my arms. I brush light kisses against her dark hair that's so soft on my lips and smells like her shampoo. The rest of her smells like me, though. Like my body wash.

Shifting so her head rests on my arm, I take her hand in mine. We fit so right together. My gaze falls on the closed closet door. Inside are gifts just for her—clothes, shoes, and purses. Anything she might need, I bought, sparing no expense for my baby girl. She's worth every penny I spent and more. Yes, I know her measurements. Yes, it's creepy the way I obtained them. But I'm *her* creep.

Now that my plan is in motion, there's no turning back. She's here. I'll give her a bit more time, but when she wakes up, sweet Mercy Callahan will learn just what it means to belong to Amos Mitchell Shay.

CHAPTER 8

MERCY

*A*n insistent cramping in my lower abdomen brings me back to the land of the living. Wish I could have stayed in blissful unawareness, though, because this hurts. Hopefully, it's just my twisted emotions wreaking havoc on my system.

Reluctantly opening my eyes, I regret it as soon as I do. My blue rabbit has been ever so thoughtfully placed by my pillow. I can't think about that. I can't. I have to figure out what to do about right now. I turn onto my side and curl my legs up. I smell something funny again, like earlier. Did he—?

He did. He took off the robe I had, leaving me naked in his bed, and rubbed more of his...*semen*...on me. I've never shown my body to anyone besides a doctor before, and I hate that he's seen me naked at least twice. That he's done things to me when I was sleeping, completely helpless and at my most vulnerable.

A moan from both the pain and the overthinking of my brain leaves me. Amos kidnapped me after drugging me and marking me with his bodily fluids. His ejaculate. I still don't know if he raped me. And what does he mean when he says he's *claimed* me? That he's going to *marry* me? He doesn't seem to want to hurt me, but his obsession is borderline insane.

And it came from out of the blue. We didn't interact much at work, but never would I have expected him to do something this extreme. Unless I missed any signs, which is entirely possible. But surely I would have noticed something. Wouldn't I?

And now look at me. Abducted.

Four freaking hours away from Providence Falls and apparently in the middle of nowhere, no one even knows to look for me. I never made any friends here other than Eliza at work, if she even counts. And my many foster parents have no idea where I am. Probably don't care, either. I took off at eighteen and never looked back.

I didn't pay the rent. I don't know if my landlord will care, maybe just think I skipped out. Would a corporation care about one single tenant who skips out? Maybe they'll raise a fuss and look for me. I can only hope. Fear wants to overtake me, but I can't panic. I've got to keep a level head because I'm all I've got. Me—an introverted thirty-three-year-old who can't even act my age and will bend over backwards just to avoid any conflict.

It's okay, Mercy. Just need to keep a cool head and find my cell phone. Any phone.

Snick. The bedroom door opens and Amos stalks toward the bed, still sans shirt. "Feeling better, sweet Mercy?"

No, not really. I need to sit up because I don't want to increase my vulnerability by lying down. Not that it would stop him. Makes me feel just a smidge better, though. I jerk up, wincing and wrapping the covers around me as I do. Oooh, I regret moving now. A gush of wetness falls from my core, letting me know the cramping was more serious than I thought. It's my freakin' period.

Great. With my PCOS, I can go months without having a period, even when on my medicine, but to get one *now* of all times? It's probably going to be a heavy one, too. How am I going to get him out of the room long enough for me to clean up? And what'll I wear? There are no clothes, no underwear here for me unless he brought any of my things here.

Oh, God—the sheets. How am I supposed to stop him from seeing the blood on the sheets? *Please don't let there be blood.*

"Mercy? What's wrong, baby?" I never did have a strong poker face.

He rushes his last two steps to the bed, scanning me for injuries. My kidnapper has the nerve to ask me what's wrong? Freakin' clueless man. I don't want to antagonize him, though. That wouldn't be smart when he's staring so intensely at me. "I just don't feel so well."

"I'm sorry you're still feeling bad. Your system should have been flushed out by now." I internally scream as he casually glosses over the fact that he drugged me. "Do you want to eat and drink something? Maybe that will help. You slept so long, it's just about time for dinner."

"Sure." No, I don't. I want to leave. I want my own house, with *my* bed and *my* clothes. I slept so long because he freakin' *drugged* me. "Why don't you go make something and I'll meet you in the kitchen?"

There. Go away. If he leaves me alone, I can clean up. I don't remember seeing anything in the bathroom I can use. I may have to settle for wadded up toilet paper and his briefs.

Gross.

"No, come with me. I want to spend time with you, get to know you better. We didn't really see much of each other at work." Bulging biceps pluck me from the mattress. "Are you bringing the covers with you?" he says on a laugh.

Glad one of us finds this amusing. And yes. Yes, I am.

His chuckle cuts off, muscles tensing. Uh-oh. Guess he found the blood. "Do you need to tell me something, Mercy?"

Need, yes. Want, no. Hard no. But I think I have to. "Ummm..." My face is red-hot from embarrassment. I avoid his gaze and turn my head, blankly staring at the huge wall-mounted tv across from the bed. *Be nice. You catch more flies with honey than you do with vinegar.* "I-I think I started my period. Do you...have anything I can use until I can go to the store?"

Silence.

Oh, no—did I gross the bad man out? Apparently, the mastermind didn't think of everything a captive woman would need.

Risking a quick glance, I peek up at him. Mistake. A curious look burns brightly from his arctic eyes. Calling it anything other than pure lust would be a lie. Is he...turned on at the fact that I'm on my period? I've never in my life had such a powerful stare directed to me before. Other than yesterday, but at least we were both fully clothed.

He moves. I yelp at the change in gravity, suddenly finding myself flat on my back, still with the covers wrapping me like a burrito.

"What are you doing?" I hiss as he strips his sweats and briefs off to reveal a thick red cock. Crazy man snatches the covers from me with ridiculous ease, leaving me completely naked. My hands fly down to cover myself, but he grabs them and shoves my legs apart. *No! This can't be happening.* "Stop—stop it!" The scream involuntarily exits my lungs. "Didn't you hear me? I'm on my period! A-amos!"

Amos ignores my screeching and kicking, shackling my hands to the mattress with his as he nestles between my open thighs and crushes his weight and erection atop me.

Can't breathe can't breathe can't breathe.

"Do you think a little bit of blood scares me? It's part of you. Besides, you won't be having to deal with this for many more months if I can help it. Do you know why?" That manic look comes back into his eyes as he links our fingers together. "No answer? That's okay; I'll just tell you. You're gonna have my babies, Mercy."

No. No no no no no. My body trembles at his proclamation,

only to be repeatedly stopped short by the wall of massive muscle over me. "Stop—stop, ohmigod...stop! I'm a virgin! Don't rape me don't rape me please please ple—" I scream with what little air I can grab. Why did I tell him that? I didn't mean to—it just slipped out. But now that he knows, maybe he'll stop. Maybe he won't want someone so inexperienced.

He curses, disbelieving. "A virgin? Really, Mercy?"

"Yes," comes my shaky reply as hope blooms in my chest. *Is he going to let me go?*

His head swoops down as he falls upon me, his soft lips rubbing across mine and short-circuiting my synapses. He's...kissing me. Kisses that almost feel...sweet? "It won't be rape, Mercy."

I don't dare to breathe, not wanting to provoke him into anything else. Long seconds pass as his closed mouth feathers kisses over mine.

But I have to breathe.

With a harsh inhale, I drag oxygen into my starved lungs.

I don't know where to look. Not in his eyes. Not there. I focus on his hair instead. The gray flecks contrast nicely with the black strands.

Close your eyes, Mercy. Don't look. Don't look. Just feel.

Feel the slow trickle of blood dribbling from me.

Feel the unyielding power in his hands as they imprison mine.

Feel his bristly scruff rub my tender skin.

Feel the terror racing in my chest.

Sweet kisses turn into wet, open-mouthed sucking ones. Hips grind against mine, his cock splitting my folds.

"It won't be rape," he repeats, his raspy voice blowing heated breath against my ear as he takes an earlobe between his teeth. "It's never going to be that way between us. I'll make you want it, crave it. You're mine, only mine. My woman. My wife. The mother of our babies."

He groans and tugs our hands over my head. Grinding becomes full-out thrusting against my naked labia. "Can't wait to put my baby inside you. Gonna hold you real still and tilt your legs up after so we know it takes. Watch your belly swell with my seed. Gonna pop your sweet cherry so good...Mercyyyyyy..."

Even if I wanted to see his cock, I couldn't. Because he's so tall, his shoulders smother my face as he moves against me. It doesn't stop my ears from hearing the slick sounds, though.

Sshllp. Sshllp. Ssh-sshllp.

Or his grunts.

Ungh. Ungh. Ungh.

Time stretches into eternity as I fearfully wait for him to finish. Each upward slide forcing my breath from me and making me wonder if he'll miss, either accidentally or on purpose, and rip my virginity from me.

Please finish.

Please hurry.

Please stop.

A growl begins in his chest, growing and turning into a rumble against my cheek as he bellows *"Mine!"* and orgasms, cum shooting out of him and landing on my belly and underneath my boobs. He collapses, his heavy weight pressing me into the mattress, and brushes moist kisses against my neck.

It's over. It's finally over.

For now.

Bright red blood mixed with cum smears his cock and abdomen when he raises up. *My blood.* I'm speechless and in shock, hot tears threatening to fall. It's all too much. I had to go and get myself kidnapped, start my period, and get humped and ejaculated on. And he's going to forcefully attempt to get me pregnant and carry his spawn? My first time can't be like this! Not with him!

"Don't cry, Mercy." Amos drags a finger through the cum pooled on me and brings it down to my pussy.

"N-no! Don't!" My voice breaks and I flinch, closing my thighs as much as possible with him still in between them. It does no good because the big brute elbows them wide open and gently inserts the tip of his cum-covered finger inside me.

I weakly push his hands away, only to have him grab my wrists in one hand and hold them captive on my stomach.

"It's okay, baby. You and me now." More cum, another invasion. "Just a little deeper." His finger slides in again, lubricated by my blood, but my virgin cunt clamps down, not wanting to allow this foreign object inside. I stare aimlessly at the ceiling, belatedly noting that the fan isn't centered in the room. I think it's off by three inches or so. He needs to fix that.

Amos wiggles his finger before exerting a bit more pressure and force. "Let me in, sweet Mercy. Let me—ah, there we go, kitten." His digit smoothly penetrates me with a stinging pressure as it slithers down my resistant channel until his palm meets my clit.

I whimper, a choked sob leaving me as my eyes fly to his.

Lust burns icy-white in those arctic orbs.

Then it gets worse.

Grinding circles against my clit. A slow, deliberate thrust of a finger. Sweet words from an obsessed man.

"Let me make you feel good, baby," he whispers. His finger leaves, but two more take its place when he rotates his wrist and rubs my clit with his thumb.

His fingers feel ginormous and too big to comfortably fit in me. My first sexual experience with another person, and it's happening against my will. But it's also turning me on, no matter how much I fight it inside. That's the scary part.

I hide behind my eyelids again. Shame fills me as my body betrays me, my nerve endings telling my brain the sensations they detect are amazing.

Arousing.

Why am I reacting this way? I don't want this. *Do I?*

"Come on, kitten. Let your man give you pleasure." Amos strokes my clit, polishing it in little circles. Combined with the stroking of his fingers, my body has no choice but to surrender to his mastery. "It's okay to give in...let it feel good. You want this. It's not a bad thing to relax and enjoy it. Look at me, just look at me."

The heated fervency in his words escalates the tension inside me, and my breath stalls before leaving in a rush of emotion.

Then I do what he says.

I meet my captor's gaze, a slow river of tears leaking from me. Mouth agape, lungs crying out for relief. My orgasm silently blazes through me, no less intense for its lack of noise and all the more potent with the pure male satisfaction shining from his eyes.

"Good girl," he croons and slowly pulls his hand away from my throbbing core, wiping his red-tinged fingers on the sheets. Picking up my hand in his clean one, he reverently kisses the back of it. "We're gonna be so good together, kitten. You'll see."

Hold it together. Freakin' hold it together, Mercy.

But I can't take it. The pseudo tenderness contrasting with his assault of my body is the final straw that breaks the camel's back, and an embarrassingly squeaky sob escapes my lungs on an inhale. Blacking out earlier didn't stop me from processing my situation, only delayed it.

"Up now. A warm shower will make you all better."

"But—the bed!" I wail, staring back at it as he carries me to the bathroom. Don't ask why I care that there's blood and cum on my captor's bed. Stupid hormones, I guess. Or maybe because I have a woman's intuition that I'll probably have to sleep in it later.

With...*him.*

"Don't worry about the bed. It's just sheets. They can be washed." He adjusts the water temperature with one hand. "And so can we. In you go."

I don't even bother trying to cover my breasts and pussy—he's proven that he'll just snatch my hands away so he can see what's *his*. And when he joins me, I apathetically look at the red smears on him, my tears drying in the heat of the room.

It's useless. He's going to do whatever he wants with me and I won't be able to stop him. I can only hope that he stays as loving and gentle—from his perspective—as he has been. Maybe I can just play along and escape after I get him to let his guard down.

Amos rinses off the blood covering him and corners me, angling the shower heads for a full-body massage. The pounding stream feels amazing after the stress of that moment. I take a chance and close my eyes, trying to somewhat enjoy it, letting the water wash away the red streaks and cum staining me. Two baths in one day. I definitely need it, although I wish he weren't in here with me.

Unexpected warmth on my neck startles me. My swollen eyes flash open to see him focused on his soapy hands around the back of my neck. The strength in his grip is enough to set my heart to fluttering—whether in fear or arousal, I don't know—as he slowly squeezes and releases the muscles at the nape.

Please. Not now—I just gave you so much. I can't give you any more.

Amos pulls me to him. I resist, but my feeble strength is no match for his. I end up right where he wants me—breasts and pussy smushed against him. My breath catches when he moves to my shoulders. At his gentle urging, my forehead rests on his broad chest as his firm circular motions work out knots of tension I didn't know I had.

"Aghh..."

His hands falter at the moan I couldn't keep in before

resuming his massage. It feels so good. I hate that he has control over my body, though. Making me feel things against my will. But I would much rather him massage my shoulders than do anything else.

Much too soon, his kneading moves down my back, stopping at my hips, fingertips grazing below. The air instantly feels heavier, and not because of the steam of the water. Fingers twitch and dig in as he clenches my cheeks, his chest lifting and sinking on a ragged sigh.

He pulls back, a severe expression tightening his features. "Wash me, Mercy."

Playing along starts now.

CHAPTER 9

AMOS

I can't believe my luck. My soon-to-be wife is a virgin. Untouched. I don't shame her for it, though. There are all sorts of reasons why a woman her age might still be a virgin. Religion, personal preference, lack of opportunity.

Life happens. Or doesn't. But whatever her reasoning, my cock will be her first and only. The thought makes me swell, but I tamp it down.

This changes things, though. Blood leaking from her doesn't make me squeamish in the slightest—it's a turn-on, in fact—but I can't let her first time be now when she's bleeding and uncomfortable.

I'm not that much of a monster, but I also can't afford to back away and undo the progress I've made. Time to compromise.

"Wash me." My second command prompts her to action. Mercy purses her lips and turns to peruse the bottles, presumably to find the body wash. I run my eyes down her backside, stopping at the patch of hair just above her ass cheeks.

Interesting. She even has some on her arms and stomach, arrowing down to her pussy. Doesn't turn me off; just piques my curiosity. I don't mind body hair on a woman unless she has more than me. And since I'm hairy as a bear, I don't mind at all.

She's still standing there doing nothing. "This one," I point out to her. I'm aware she's stalling—she took a shower this morning and knows exactly which one it is.

Liquid squirts from the bottle into her palm. At the squelching sound, I flash my teeth. "That's what your sweet pussy did earlier."

An embarrassed blush flowers over her face, and my predatory smile grows wider. "Mercy, sweet Mercy. How prettily you blush."

"Um...can you grab a wash rag?"

"Use your hands."

"My hands? Please, don't make me do this..." Her blush deepens and travels down, coloring her breasts a rosy pink. *Gorgeous.*

"I know you aren't feeling the best right now. Probably cramping a little, huh?"

She timidly nods, her head dipping the tiniest bit.

"Thought so. Here's the thing—I'm not going to take you when you're bleeding." I wait for the relief to hit her face before I continue, "Not your first time, anyway."

Her face falls in disappointment for a split second before she unsuccessfully hides it.

"So, we're gonna get to know each other's bodies nice and slow. There's not an inch of you that my mouth, hands, and cock aren't gonna be intimately acquainted with. Same goes for me. You're mine and I'm yours, and the best way for you to learn my body and get comfortable with me is to just do it."

The water streams around us as I brace a hand over her shoulder and tilt her chin up. The descent of my head to her plush mouth is slow because I want to see if she'll back away. Part of me hopes she does, just so I can unleash the beast in me and devour her mouth. But because the other part of me wants to woo her, I also hope she accepts me, maybe even meets me halfway.

The tip of her tongue nervously peeks out and licks her lips the closer I get, until my mouth hovers above hers. To tease her, I moisten my own, letting my tongue briefly tickle hers in passing. She shivers.

Inside my head, I pound my chest in triumph. Mercy can fight her body all she wants, but there's no denying her response to me. Still I linger, our mouths almost touching but not quite. Hot water beating down on us, we stand there in silence. Almost cross eyed because of our closeness, just breathing in each other's breaths.

And I wait. And wait. And wait.

And she moves.

There.

She sways toward me. Just a fraction of an inch, but I pounce. Possessive is one word to describe my kiss. Claiming. Dominating. That works, too. I pull her lower lip out and suck on it. Bite it. Lick into her open mouth when she gasps at the feel of my teeth, her soapy hand lifting to lay on my chest.

Long, drugging, gasping kisses fill the silence until I reluctantly tear my mouth away from her swollen lips. Pride raises my cock at the wet sound of our lips separating. She didn't kiss me back, but dilated eyes and hard nipples tell me she's not unaffected.

"Mercy." I wait for her to look at me. "Wash me. Now. This starts now."

She doesn't move. Just stares at me with a pleading expression on her face, the twinkling of unshed tears silently begging me to change my mind.

My patience is wearing thin. "You'd rather I take you now? Back to bed, then. Come on." I bend down to swoop her up. I wouldn't, of course, not since I already told her we'd wait. She doesn't know yet that a Shay always means what he says.

But she will.

"No!" she yells, slapping at me with slick palms. "Stop! I-I-I'll wash you. Just...stop, please..."

My stare is hard and direct. "Last chance. Wash me."

Mercy blinks her tears away, sniffling quietly, and squeezes more soap, using her bare hands to wash me. She reaches for my shoulders, but that's too safe.

"No," I say. "That's already clean. Wash me here."

I drag her wrist down to my cock, wrapping her limp hand around my very erect and angry cock. It doesn't matter that I got off not even half an hour ago. It's my Mercy. She makes me hard. And this time she'll be awake when her hand's caressing my shaft. "Have you ever seen a man before?" Surely she has. Even if she *is* a virgin, because who the hell has never watched porn?

"N-no."

"Not in real life? How about in porn?" Poor woman embarrasses too easily. I'll take that deep, red blush as a yes. It seems uncommon to me that a woman in her thirties would still be so shy and introverted, but not everyone grows at the same rate, both emotionally and physically.

Her emotional growth will happen, though. It won't be all at once, but at some point all her shame and insecurities will be stripped away from her, revealing her hidden passion. And oh, what a tigress my sweet Mercy will be. "I'm sure you know, then, what a tight grip and pumping will do. But I don't want that yet. Learn my cock. Drag your hand up and down, up and down. Twist your palm on the head. Stroke the spot under the head and squeeze my balls."

At my words, Mercy's slightly watery gaze fixes on my cock held in her slack palm. A low laugh rumbles from me. Wait 'til she hears what I have to say next.

"Look at me." I wait for her red-rimmed eyes. "It may not be today, but soon, when you get a little courage, I want you to milk me. Tongue my taint. Take my seed from me. Taste it. Taste *me*. Like I'm going to taste you when your body's ready. Here...let me help you."

I encase her hand within mine, and together we slowly stroke up and down. "Up. Twist on the head. There you go, baby—nice and slow. And down. Feel how your fingers wrap around its shape. Got to make sure you wash real good right here. No, right here." She squeezes a groan from me. "Mhm...again, baby girl. Do it again. Keep going until I say stop."

I let her take her time, let her spend long minutes playing with me. The hot water will last for hours since I have a tankless heater. Even if it did turn cold, I'd stand in it and keep her warm. If only I could turn the resignation on her face to pleasure as easily.

"Down to my balls, kitten. Hold 'em in your hands. Yeah, use both. God, baby...so good. Squeeze 'em a little. Ahhhh...just like that. Now do my cock and my balls. Can you do that for me? Good girl. Harder—pump me."

Her lips pinch together as her hand slides up and down my pole while she massages my nuts. Quick learner, my Mercy. And she's about to get another quick lesson on the male anatomy.

"Mercy, I'm gonna come, baby." I'm torn between wanting her eyes on mine or on my cock, but in the end I decide she needs to see how weak she makes me. "Watch. Watch it shoot out of me." Holding her hand tighter around me, we work my cock together. Faster, faster, until—"Aghhhhh...Mercyyyyyy..."

Words won't form, only groans as white ropes of cum erupt from my swollen red tip and land on our hands. "Don't stop, baby. Keep...going..." My knees buckle as our combined strokes force the last bit of cum from me.

At the last drop, I tenderly wash the cum off her hands,

then tilt her face up to look at me. Slowly leaning down, my lips erase her tear tracks. "Good girl."

I don't like seeing her cry, but it had to be done. She's got to get used to touching me because she's mine.

Yes, she's the one for me. My sweet Mercy.

TOOK ME A MINUTE OR TWO TO FIND ALL THE INGREDIENTS AND pots tonight when I started to cook. Some of the women in my family helped out by putting all the kitchen things away, but they did so well that it's gonna take forever to learn where everything goes. I guess men just naturally think things should go in the wrong places.

Hope my mom doesn't get her feelings hurt that I haven't told her and my dad about my Mercy yet, but I want to surprise them. They've been waiting so long for me to bring my special woman home to them.

Bringing her plate to the table, I sit next to her and cut the chicken into pieces. A look of confusion crosses her face and she moves to get up.

"Where are you going?"

She freezes halfway out of the chair. "To get a plate."

"This one's yours." I stab a piece and lift it. "Taste."

"I can feed myself." That stubborn look is so cute on her as she reaches for the food.

"Ah-ah-ah." I move it out of reach. "Let me feed you. Open."

Gently, I brush the fork over her closed lips and cajole her with a singsong voice. "It's gooood. Orange marmalade chicken…"

She sullenly opens her mouth and accepts the bite. And the next. And the one after that.

A thought hits me. Should I…? I'm so terrible for doing this, but it can't be helped. Putting the fork down for a moment, I reach for the salt shaker. "Green beans need just a little bit more, don't you think?"

Smothering a grin, I shake a minuscule amount on the food and then put the shaker back, but about one inch further away and turned the opposite direction from the pepper. How long will it take her to—there she goes. Not long at all. Mercy glares at it before angrily turning it back and scooting it to where it was before.

This woman and her moods. The memory of her shocked expression as I unveiled the stash of feminine products and clothes still amuses me. Silly woman. She just watched me in disbelief as I moved her things to the bathroom and stored them away. As if I'd bring her here and not have anything for her.

She's here—really here. I don't know why I'm amazed; my meticulous plan ensured I'd get her here no matter what, but it doesn't feel real yet. And I don't think it will until I say my marriage vow to her.

I can't believe it. Can't believe we've shared our bodies like we did. Can't believe she's eating from my hands, albeit reluctantly. I stab the last sweet potato cube and watch as it disappears into her mouth.

God, that mouth. "Do you want more? More tea?"

She silently shakes her head and looks around. I'm not ready for the night to end right now, though. And since I'm not going to have sex with her tonight, a movie will have to do instead. A small chuckle leaves me when I remember the sweat that went into running coaxial cable all over the house. "Come on, baby. Let's get in bed and watch a movie. We can watch just about anything you want. Sound good?"

Her face tightens with the origins of an argument, but then she grimaces. "Ohhh—"

"What's the matter, baby? Are you cramping again?" And

there she goes with that blush. Another silent yes. "Let me get you some ibuprofen."

Oh—and she also needs these other pills I found in her bathroom. Metformin, I think it was? Said for her to take one pill daily with the evening meal. Naturally, I was curious as to what it was for, so I looked online while she was sleeping earlier. It appears my Mercy has diabetes. I'll need to be sure and cook the proper things for her.

"Hand, please." Her face pales, eyes darting to mine when I bring out her prescription bottle and shake a pill out. "There you go. And here's the ibuprofen, too." Trembling fingers bring the pills to her mouth. God, the simple flexing of her throat is so sexy. "Come on. Leave the dishes; I'll clean up in the morning."

And now time for some bedroom movie night snuggling. Plus an Amos Special. We'd already changed into our pajamas, of sorts, after our shower. I just pulled on a pair of briefs and she grabbed some shorts, a tank, and a tampon from what I'd shown her earlier.

Since the doors and windows are biometrically secured—they do have a hidden switch in the event of power failure—the nightly routine is as simple as switching off the lights and crawling into bed.

Well, not for Mercy.

She stands there at the side of the bed, nervously shifting from one foot to the other. "Can I sleep in ano—"

"No," I interrupt. "With me, Mercy. Always with me." I spread my legs and pat in between them. "Up you go."

Reluctantly, in between my legs she goes, dragging the freshly changed covers up over us. Fits so perfectly, so right, that I'm immediately threatened with a boner. People may scoff and think a man my age couldn't possibly shoot as many loads as I have today, but they don't know Mercy Callahan. She could bring life into a dead man's cock.

"You want to look for something or you want me to pick?" Never let it be said that I'm a control freak. I can bend on some things. Like this.

Tracing the pattern on the bedspread, she hesitates. "Umm...can we watch cartoons?" What? A grown woman wants to watch *cartoons?* Well, she also cuddles a stuffed animal, so I shouldn't be too surprised. At my skeptical silence, she rushes to explain. "I—never mind. Whatever you pick will be fine."

Oh, no. She can't leave my curiosity hanging like that. "I don't mind watching what you want to watch. But I want to know why that was your first choice."

Her fingers flex. "I never got to watch cartoons much growing up. All my foster parents never let me watch tv. They told me it was a privilege, not a right. Now I watch them when I...when I need to—"

When she needs to calm down. My fists clench. "They did that to you, baby? I'm so sorry you went through that, but you're not alone anymore. You've got me. And when we're ready, we're gonna have our own kids, and we're gonna love them like no kids have ever been loved before. Just you wait."

At the mention of children, she tenses, but I ignore it and lean her back against me. If cartoons help her wind down from stress, that's what we'll watch. "All right, then. Anything for you, sweet Mercy." *Except letting you go. Don't ask me to do that.* "Has the ibuprofen kicked in yet?" Her body seems to be giving her fits with the ache coming in waves.

"A bit." She's downplaying the severity. I can see the truth in her face and the way she cautiously moves.

"I'm sorry you're not feeling good, baby. Let me help you with those cramps." I use the remote to turn off the lights—high tech, I know—and soon a classic cartoon lights up the room. Time for the Amos Special. My body temperature has always been on the higher side, so I know the heat of my hands will feel good against her pelvis.

One thing, though...

Mouth to her ear, I whisper, "Forgetting something?" My lips curl up at her shiver. "I know you just sleep in your panties. Don't change that on my account. In fact, I insist. Let me help you."

She freezes, not resisting but not helping, either, as I lift her tank over her head. Sneaky girl clutches the sheet to her chest.

"Don't worry, kitten. I've seen you before. Not gonna do anything but try to help you feel better. S'okay. Lean back now. Good girl. Just gonna put my hands right here on top of the sheet. They're nice and warm and should help, just like a heating pad would." Mom always loved it when Dad took care of her like this.

It's hard not to tease her breasts through the thin material, but I told her I wouldn't. I'm a man of my word. And a big man, at that. I tend to forget how much of a giant I am, but seeing my hands completely cover Mercy's stomach and then some, the realization of how tiny she is compared to me hits me. I may use forceful seduction, but I'll need to ensure it's not too hard. I could never live with myself if I hurt my sweet Mercy.

I leave my palms on her, letting the soothing heat transfer, then gently palpate before rotating and massaging another area. It must work, because after about ten minutes, she slowly gives me more and more of her body weight until she's resting fully against me. I don't even bother hiding my triumphant smile. She can't see it anyway. But I make sure to nuzzle her temple with a rewarding kiss.

After five more episodes, my kneading declines, and I let my hands just rest on her soft stomach. I could seriously fall asleep right now. In fact, I think Mercy *did* fall asleep. Probably still feeling the residual effects of the sedative. Hopefully it'll all be gone completely tomorrow and she can get her sleep schedule back on track.

Quietly, I turn the tv off and curl on one side, taking her

with me. My little spoon. I couldn't ask for a better ending to her first day here. My arms wrap around her, my bicep her pillow. With my hand resting against her belly to keep the pain at bay, I link my free fingers with hers. My sweet Mercy's chest cradles my forearm, and my cock nestles between her ass cheeks.

If we weren't both so exhausted, I'd teach her more about what her body can do. Instead, I close my eyes and think about her next lesson.

After all, tomorrow is another day.

CHAPTER 10

MERCY

This is the third time I've woken up in this bed. The second day I've been in Amos's house. The first time I've questioned how I truly feel about my situation. The tiniest part of me is amazed at the astonishing success of his plan. I mean, I'm here, just like he wanted. There's also the person I keep hidden from everyone—the abandoned orphan no one ever wanted to keep. That part of me is so hungry for love and attention.

When I remember I asked him to watch *cartoons* last night, embarrassment floods through me and makes me want to curl up and die. I'm a grown woman, for crying out loud! I can only blame it on these stupid period hormones, my oversharing tendency, and this crazy situation I've found myself in.

I wasn't lying, though, about my foster parents. Multiple foster parents. Every child deserves the love and acceptance that a family can bring, and though I'm an adult now, the wounded girl inside me still craves that affection and fondness from someone. A family of my own. I just always thought it would be on my own terms.

And then the logical part of my brain tells me this is insane.

The night he abducted me, I'd whined and cried about how something had to change. Well, something changed, all right. But how can I give myself to someone who's torn me from the life I created?

Sure, it may have been a lonely life, but it was mine. *Mine.* Am I supposed to let him pressure me into marrying him? Just roll over and spread my legs any time he wants, spit out his babies that I don't even know if my body can create... Or should I try to escape? At the very least, I should look for my cell phone. If it's even here. But how to get away from him long enough to call for help? He keeps me practically attached to his hip every moment.

And if everyone believes his story about me moving out of state for another job, then he has successfully erased my existence in Providence Falls with a mere handful of words. No one knows to look for me. He's potentially made me disappear without a trace, my entire life erased from existence. And why would anyone question it? They didn't bat an eye at the three previous receptionists leaving them without a word, so why wouldn't they do the same with me?

I'd told myself yesterday that I would play along, keep him happy so he wouldn't hurt me, but I'm the one that wound up getting played. My captor made me orgasm, and I liked it. It felt good. Too good. I feel betrayed by my body, because it was at war with my mind and my body won. And not only did he make me feel things against my will, he also forced me to make him orgasm. I...I don't know what to think.

I must admit, though—my first night sleeping snuggled in someone's arms and I can't deny that I do feel wanted. It might be a mentally insane man wanting me, but at least *some-one* does. But will he still want me when he learns that I may not be able to give him children? He dug around enough in my house to figure out I take prescription meds. Does he know what I'm taking them for?

Gah! Why would I even care about him knowing? It's not as if I'm going to go along with this, right? Shouldn't I fight more than two days before giving up? I'd be betraying the entire female gender if I let him do what he wants with no fight.

Just because I was secretly harboring a crush on him doesn't mean I wanted him to kidnap me and have his way with me. Regardless of the fact that I spent way too much time at work daydreaming about him. And do I even want Amos to take my virginity? Heaven knows there'll be no getting away from him after that.

But he also hasn't raped me. He'd said my first time wouldn't be when I'm on my period. And the way he massaged away my period cramps last night?

I'm conflicted. It's not the snap decision I thought it would be.

As if he heard my thoughts, his warm lips drag over my naked shoulder. "Morning, baby girl," he mumbles, giving me the gentlest of squeezes. Good Lord, his morning voice is so rough. Almost as gravelly as when he issued those commands to me last night. *Wash me, Mercy.* "Sleep good?"

Just like that, my wariness comes back as I wrap my arms around my chest. Much easier to talk a brave game than it is to act it out. "Yes, thank you. I need to go to the bathroom."

"Me, too. Let's go. We should probably get up, anyway. You want anything special for breakfast?"

In the bathroom...*together*? Umm, not exactly what I had in mind. I pee like a horse first thing in the morning. Not to mention I have my tampon issue to deal with. "Uhh, not really. But can I go first? I'll be quick. Plus, you know..."

It's written all over his face, the debate on whether or not to let me go by myself. I hold my breath as tightly as he holds me, but eventually he reluctantly nods. "Okay, baby. You can go first. And quit hiding from me. You're beautiful."

I have no idea what to say to that unexpected compliment,

so I ignore it and dash to the dresser to snag a shirt and shorts. Closing the door that doesn't lock behind me, I grab a tampon and head straight to the toilet to relieve myself, shrugging on my shirt as I do. A quick pull disposes of the old and a swift motion tears open the new wrapper. I part my legs and reach between them to—

Rat-a-tat-tat. "Kitten, you done? I need the bathroom, too." Without waiting for an answer, he opens the door and saunters in, sporting a huge bulge in his briefs.

"Amos!" Quicker than lightning, my knees knock together as my thighs close in surprise. "Get out! I have to—" My words die out the closer he gets.

His eyes fly to what I'm holding. "You have to let me watch. I've always wanted to see."

What!? "Are you crazy? No."

Amos drops to his haunches and brushes his lips over my kneecaps before leveling his stare on me. "Yes. I want to watch. It's just a little bit of blood. Show me."

How am I supposed to let him watch me do such a private thing? But he's got the advantage, being in front of me as he is, and I can't stay sitting on the toilet forever.

"Come on. Let me see." He wraps his hands around my calves and separates my thighs with his relentless pull. I'm clean, but I hate being on display like this with his gaze zeroed in on my core.

Just do it, Mercy. Humiliated and embarrassed beyond belief, I close my eyes and bring my arm down to part my folds while angling the other to insert the tampon and throw away the applicator. "There." I push his hands away and close my legs. "Now you've seen it. Will you let me up, please?"

"Hold on." He reaches for my panties and drags them slowly up to my knees. "Up."

I stand and hurriedly reach down to finish.

"No. I'll do it." His incredibly warm hands slowly work my

panties up the rest of the way, inch by creeping inch. When I'm fully covered, his hands cover my hips and pull me forward the scantest bit so his lips can press against my lower abdomen. "God, you're so beautiful, Mercy."

I don't know what to think with him looking expectantly up at me, so I rely on my stellar social skills and say the first thing that pops in my mind. "I need to wash my hands."

The cool water running over my soapy hands gives me something to focus on other than what just happened. That was...strange. I dry them off and turn to face him. I don't want to be in here with him like this. Too awkward. Maybe I can scope the place out and see if there's an unlocked door.

I inch toward the exit. "Can I go to the kitchen and see what there is to eat?" Just a few more steps. But then my wrist is grabbed, halting my escape.

"Hold up. I need you to help me with something."

Well. There goes that chance. Not that it was much of one, but still. "Help you with something?"

That smile looks entirely too devious, but he pulls me closer to him. My senses go on high alert. Is he seriously going to start something now? "What do you need?"

Amos drags me to the toilet and flips the seat up before placing my palm on his bulge. "Hold my cock while I take a piss."

"What? But—why?"

"I told you we were gonna learn each other's bodies. This is one of the ways. I want you to know what my cock looks and feels like when I'm soft, hard, or whatever. Take me out." Encouragement comes in the form of him squeezing my hand around him.

Of all the things to come out of his mouth, I can honestly say I never expected that to be one of them. Just like I never expected him to watch me insert a tampon.

But I have a choice here. Do what he says and don't rock the boat, or push back and see what he does. If he'll make me. If he'll...force me. *Shiver.*

In the end, I submit. *It could be worse.*

My hand spasms on the front of his briefs. "Take it out? Your briefs o-or..." Male underwear confuses me! Does he want me to take his briefs all the way off or pull him through? Do guys with small cocks do that? I mean, what if it's so short that they accidentally get pee on themselves? Though it doesn't look like Amos would have that problem. "I've never..."

Amusement dances in his eyes. "And I can't wait to teach you. Pull it down and tuck it under my balls."

It's not as easy as it looks, because his cock isn't pointing down. It's standing up. Well, as much as it can, being constricted by his underwear. How can walking around with that massive thing between his legs be comfortable? Hesitantly, I pull down the material and gingerly hover a hand over the area, not knowing what to do.

"It's not gonna bite." He's laughing at me. "You're gonna have to hold it, though. Remember yesterday when we jerked my cock together?"

Did he have to bring that up? I snatch my hand away, but he grabs it back.

"Come on, baby. I was just teasing. Here, come closer. Put this hand around my waist, and this one on my cock. Now point it at the toilet."

I'm squished up against Amos's side, practically hugging him with one arm as I hold his cock—a red, angry looking, *hard* cock. It feels nothing like I've imagined one would. Even in my fantasies, I always envisioned a smaller one, not one where my fingers barely meet. And I've seen my fair share of porn, but a penis on a screen doesn't even begin to compare to one in real life.

"Hold it harder. When I start to pee, it's gonna jump a bit at first, so aim the head lower than you think you should. There you go. Good girl."

Oh, God—this is so embarrassing! I don't even want to know if he's looking at me or his cock.

A twitch or two, and then he starts peeing. It's the weirdest thing. And I mean the *weirdest*. I can feel the force of the stream as his whole shaft jumps like he said. If I hadn't aimed lower, there would be pee all over the toilet rim. Twenty seconds later, and he's still peeing full force.

The longer I hold him, the wetter I get between my legs, strangely enough. This is actually pretty arousing, holding him while he pees. I feel...*empowered*. Like I'm making him do it, even though he's the one making me hold it.

Amos's voice grounds me. "Give it a shake, then put me back in. There you go, baby girl," he praises as I awkwardly shake it up and down and stuff him back into his briefs.

God, that was weird. But electrifying. He picks up the hand I used and brushes a soft kiss across the palm while gazing deeply into my eyes. He seriously gets off on this.

And who am I to talk? I kinda liked it, too. But I can't give in so soon.

I can't.

PULLING HIS SHIRT DOWN SO IT PROTECTS MY THIGHS FROM THE coldness of the chair, I settle in and sip my coffee as I watch Amos make breakfast for us.

"Cutting board... Where's the damn cutting board?" he mutters. Shouldn't he know where he keeps it? Oh, wait. Of course he doesn't. Because he only just finished building this place with his family. "There you are." Palming an avocado, he gives it a firm squeeze before placing it on the wooden board.

The man must either not trust me around the knives yet or

he has a cooking fetish. At this point, I'm not sure which is the better choice. I normally don't eat anything for breakfast that requires me to do anything more than open a wrapper to get it ready for consumption, so to have two homestyle breakfasts back-to-back is surprisingly nice. *If* I don't take into account the fact that I'm stuck here because I'm too chicken to try to run from a man who says I'm his and he's going to marry me.

A kiss to the corner of my mouth makes me flinch. I must have drifted further off into my thoughts than I realized.

"Breakfast for my Mercy. Just let me know if you want more and I'll get it for you."

Looking at the square plate as it slides in front of me, I internally grimace. The eggs are over easy—not my favorite way of eating them. One single poke and all the yolk is going to run out like a golden river and contaminate the wheat toast and avocado slices.

On the plus side, it seems as if he's going to let me feed myself, so I tuck away my annoyance. Turning the plate so the sides are straight, I cut a piece of egg white and bring it to my mouth.

"Do you like it?" Amos watches me like a hawk as he sits beside me with his own plate. Couldn't he have sat across from me? The heat radiating from his body is enough to make me combust.

I stop, egg piece dangling on the fork. His tone is eager, as if he'll be disappointed if I don't. I shove it in and hurriedly swallow it down. "Yes."

Head tucked, I focus on carving the whites away from the yolk without puncturing it. I can still feel the weight of his gaze on me. Awkwardly, I eat as much as I can, not knowing whether to drag my feet or not. Not knowing whether it's safer to stay here at the table or try to explore the house.

"Too salty?"

"No."

"Would you like some more coffee?"

"No." Can't I simply eat in peace?

"Juice?"

I stare at him in reply. "Aren't you going to eat?"

His eyes drop down at his plate as if he'd forgotten it was there. With a little tug of his lips, he digs into his with gusto. It's easier for me to finish my own with his attention off of me. The silence is almost companionable, oddly enough.

After we finish and he loads the dishwasher with the dirty dishes, he takes my hand and drags me back down the hallway. Worry instantly creeps up my spine the closer the bedroom gets.

"No, please..." I try to pull my hand from his but he only grasps it tighter. Surely he's not going to—

"Here you go, baby." He leads me to the closet and opens the door. "What do you want to wear today?"

He's actually going to let me wear something other than his shirt? I'm shocked, but I don't say anything. I don't want him to change his mind for whatever reason.

Staring at the mountain of material in front of me, I feel overwhelmed. Is that a...cocktail dress? Everything I see so far still has the price tag attached. From the quality of the material, I don't have to see the tag to know it's a higher amount than I've ever paid for any piece of clothing. I'm not a flashy person. Not at all. Give me jeans, t-shirts, and cotton panties and I'm a happy camper. I don't even know if any of these will fit me.

And don't get me started on the rows and rows of shoes. Several of which have red soles. *Red soles*. I've never bought any, but I know of them. What woman doesn't? But why would I even need those out here if he says he's never letting me go? *Unless he wants to dress me like a doll.*

Since I want the comfort of actual clothes on me instead of

just underwear and a shirt, I pick something blindly and head for the bathroom.

"Where are you going?"

I stay facing the bathroom door. "To change into...this." Whatever *this* is. Oh—it's a sundress. Not my favorite, but better than what I have on now.

"No, do it here."

I bite back my frustration. *Don't rock the boat, Mercy.* Fine. If he's going to watch me undress, I don't want to see his face when I do.

Keeping my sleep shirt on, I step into the dress and slide it up underneath. No peep show for the bad man. Pulling my arms inside the sleeves like a turtle hiding his head, I look like a little kid now that my arms are swallowed up by my shirt. But that's okay. Not a single inch more of me is on display than was before, and with a little fabric fighting, I manage to get my arms through the arm openings.

Still facing away, I pull off his shirt and let it fall to the floor. *There.* But now there's a cool draft on my back. What? God, I must have grabbed a dress with a zipper. *Mercy, you have the best worst luck ever.*

Twisting my arms behind me, I get it zipped up as far as I can. Which isn't as far as it needs it to be for me to finish fastening it from over my shoulders.

It's stuck. God, I hate zippers. I am *not* asking him for help. He'll just turn it into another opportunity to get his hands on me and start something that I don't have the emotional strength to go through right now.

He hasn't said anything, but I can just picture him back there holding in his laughter while he waits for me to give in and ask. No. I won't give him the satisfaction of turning around to see.

Gritting my teeth, I bite the bullet and do the dance every woman learns growing up—the Zipper Shimmy. A hop and

dance in a little circle while trying to zip things up. Very undig-
nified, but when I feel the catch release, I could almost cry tears
of joy. Fully zipped now, I compose my face and calmly turn
around.

Amos isn't here. He...left me by myself? Ohmigod. I should
make a run for it, but is this a trick? I'm not a fast runner. I don't
know how far I could get before he realizes I'm gone.

"Do you want sandals or cowgirl boots?" he calls from the
closet. Stepping out fully dressed, he holds a pair of each in his
hands. "Either of these will look nice with your dress. I like the
boots, though."

There goes my chance. What little it was, anyway. I couldn't
have gotten far with him still here in the room with me.

Still holding the shoes, he looks at me—really looks at me
—and his face softens. "Your beauty, Mercy... It takes my breath
away. You're so gorgeous, kitten, and so very much mine."

"Sandals, please." I can't respond to that. Are there any
etiquette guidelines for what to say to your captor when he
compliments you and then claims you in the same breath?

His lips tighten when I only answer his question and ignore
the rest. "Come on. I want to show you the house."

He slips some shoes on, too, and takes my hand—why is he
so touchy-feely with me?—to lead me from the room. It's
different looking at my prison when I'm not under the influence of drugs or being dragged to and from the kitchen.

I'll admit it's beautiful. Extremely so, and built out in a
modern farmhouse style with a family room, reading room,
ginormous kitchen, five full bathrooms, four upstairs bedrooms
and a game room that he says are for our nonexistent children,
and the master bedroom downstairs.

But beyond the beauty of the architecture and style, it's
the high-tech locks on every potential exit that jump out at
me and cause my heart to sink in disappointment. It truly
looks as if there is no way out. Even if I had managed to run

just now, I wouldn't have been able to open a door or window.

I may as well make the best of it. As I told myself before, things could always be worse. I could have been kidnapped by a serial killer or a sadist.

He definitely put a lot of thought into this house, security aside. It's like he picked all of my personal tastes and preferences out of my brain and assembled it just for me. Which he did, in a way. He just so happened to guess right.

I think. God, I hope he just guessed and didn't stalk me on the internet or something. At this point, I don't even want to know.

CHAPTER 11

AMOS

"Would you like to go outside, Mercy?" It's not good for her to be cooped up inside all day, even if all I want to do is keep her by my side.

A curious look comes over her face before she tucks it away. "Yes, please."

Probably wants to learn how the doors are opened. That's okay. It won't do her any good just yet unless she manages to cut my thumbs or index fingers off. She also needs to see how isolated we are out here so she won't try to run away. I wouldn't be averse to a quick game of *Stalk the Captive*, but I don't think I could stop myself if she roused the beast within me.

I tilt my head and tug on her hand. "This way." The closer we get to the front door, the more her breathing picks up. *Calm down, kitten. You're not leaving me.* She's actually taking everything in stride, considering the way I ripped her from her life. Her stare lasers in on the silver box on the door as my free thumb lightly presses on the reader. The cylinder whirs, and releases the lock.

The warmth of the sun hugs us as we cross the threshold. Such a gorgeous early summer day, eclipsed by the croaking of frogs and chirping of birds all coming together to create a symphony for the forest.

The landscape is beautiful in its solitude. Our house is built on a slope, and standing here on the porch, we can see the dark green shadow of the forest stretch out for miles in every direction. Mercy walks to the wooden porch railing and rests her elbows on it.

"I didn't realize Pleasant Plain had such a dense forest."

"Yes." I mimic her stance but face her. "It's such a rural area, you know. We're actually on the outskirts, so around twenty-five miles to reach town. About forty to get to the next big city."

At my statement, her gaze flits to my truck parked in the driveway. Better nip that in the bud, too. "The truck also has a biometric lock in addition to requiring a PIN before the engine starts." That's a new feature I installed on it a few weeks ago in preparation for this. It's worth the few extra seconds it takes to start the truck up.

Her expression grows pensive as she turns her head to take in the thick trees stacked in on each other. The saddest smile graces her lips. "Is it even worth asking you if I can have my cell phone? Never mind. Don't answer. I can already see that I don't have a chance."

The resigned acceptance in her voice almost breaks my heart. Almost. But she's right. "No. Not a chance. Even if you did make it out of the house, you couldn't start the truck. If you took off in the woods, you'd likely get lost very quickly. And I don't want that. I can't have you getting hurt trying to get away from me." I reach out a finger and trace her soft lips. Petal soft. "And Mercy, the last thing you want to do is run. Do you know why?"

Her nostrils flare and her eyes close but she doesn't say anything. *All right, then. If that's the way you want to play it, I'll play.* My hand slides down from her mouth to firmly grasp the sides of her throat. Not squeezing, just holding.

Green eyes fly wide open as she instinctively clutches my wrist, a gasp involuntarily escaping her. Through the thin walls of her neck, her pulse pounds rapidly against my fingertips. *There she is.*

Dropping my face to hers, I lick around her lips with my tongue, tasting her bitter nervousness. "Do you know why?" I repeat through the gravel in my throat as I flex my fingers.

"No, Amos. I don't—I don't know why. Let...let go. Please."

I capture her hands with my free one, forcing them to rest between us on my chest. "I'm not going to hurt you, Mercy, but I don't like being ignored. I needed to get your attention. Do I have it?" The frantic bobbing of her head causes the silky black strands of her hair to brush over me. "I can't hear you. Do I have your complete attention?" Another gentle squeeze.

"Yes—yes, Amos," she chokes out. My grip isn't tight enough for her to sound like that, but I loosen it a bit just in case.

"The last thing you want to do is run. Because if you run, I'm going to hunt you. And if I hunt you, I *will* catch you. And when I do, you'll be mine in every way. There'll be no more waiting until you're not bleeding anymore. So it's all up to you, sweet Mercy. Are you going to run?"

"I won't...I won't run. I swear."

"That's my sweet kitten. And do you believe me when I say that you're beautiful?" She didn't answer me earlier. I can't have my Mercy thinking she's anything less than absolutely stunning in my eyes.

Her lashes close as she hides her eyes from me. "Yes," comes her hoarse whisper.

"Look at me. Look me in the eye and tell me you believe me."

Her shiny gaze meets mine, wavering before holding strong. "I... I believe you."

"Good girl." I remove my hand and Mercy falls back against

the railing, softly rubbing her throat as she warily watches me. "Now, let's enjoy this fresh air."

I lower onto the nearby oversize hanging swing chair. Perfect. Big enough for me to hold my Mercy and get to know more about her. A pull on her hand sends her tumbling onto my lap where she stiffly sits, trying to touch me as little as possible. That will never do. Turning her sideways, I grab her legs and prop them on the cushions.

"What sorts of things do you like to bake?" I ask as I softly stroke her hair and draw her head to rest against my chest. Maybe feeling my heartbeat and the vibrations of my voice will help to soothe her. My dad held my mom like this day in and day out when he first brought her home to us. *Two things usually make a woman feel better,* he always said. *Food and hugs.* "You mentioned your last day at work that you might make a dessert, but it didn't smell like you'd been baking when I got there that night."

Calmly petting her, I don't miss her slight flinch at my reference to taking her. No use pussyfooting around it, though. It's over and done with and we're moving on as we were meant to be.

"Umm..." She inhales deeply. I almost feel jealous when I imagine her breathing in the smells of the forest over my own scent. "I...anything, really. Cookies, cheesecake, bread. Nothing with fruit, though. I don't like fruit."

That's interesting. Should a diabetic be eating those things? "So...fruit. Not at all, or not baked?"

"Mostly not at all. I don't mind apples or apple pie, but I don't care for any other fruit."

I pick up her hand from where she was tracing imaginary ninety-degree angles on the folds of her dress and bring it to my chest. "Do that to me."

More flaccid than a limp cock, her hand lies slack against my shirt. "What?"

"Draw on me with your fingernails. That looks like it feels good." At her hesitant movements, I resume the conversation while preening under her touch. "I'll never make you eat anything you don't like. Fruit's good to me, but I can't stand spinach unless it's finely chopped. What's your favorite number?"

"I don't know. I've never really thought about it. I guess any number that ends in a five or a zero."

"Any particular reason for just those two?"

Her fingers falter. "I like the completion it represents."

"Fingers," I remind her, tucking away her explanation for later. "I've never really had a favorite number but I do now. Three." The number of the tiny freckles on her neck. "Favorite color?"

"Ah...soft gray."

"Mine is—hmm. I need to look to be sure." I tilt her chin up. "Yep. Just as I thought. Green. Green with the faintest hint of gold mixed in."

A faint blush colors her cheeks. I'll wear her down one way or another.

I place a hand on her bare calf and creep inexorably upward as the swing sways ever so slightly. Her legs are very toned, but shorter than mine, of course. If she ever runs, I'll be sure to give her a head start to even the odds a bit. The muscles underneath my hand tense, and as I travel closer to the hem of her dress where it falls mid-thigh, her fingers jump from my shirt to my forearm.

"Please. Don't."

I stare at our connection for a long second and then flip my hand around to link our fingers. My eyebrow arches. "You don't want my touch?"

Mercy cringes, no doubt scrambling for the least offensive response. "Please..." she begs again.

"Have I hurt you?"

"You drugged me and—"

"No. In this moment, here and now, have I hurt you?"

"My throat. You squee—"

"I placed my hand around your neck, yes. But I didn't restrict your breathing in any manner. Now I ask again. Have I hurt you with my touch?"

"No," she quietly murmurs, the sweat from her palm transferring to mine.

I'm trying to be understanding, but frustration heats my voice. Does she not comprehend the fact that she's mine and I would never hurt her? "Did I not tell you when we walked out here that I don't want to hurt you? That's not my intention at all. Yet you recoil from me like I have the plague. That doesn't make me feel good, Mercy. And I can't make myself feel better the way I normally would, out of consideration for you. Can't stretch you out on that big bed of ours and fill your sweet cunt with me yet.

"That's fine, though, because I'm willing to compromise with you. I won't go any further than your knee if you give me a kiss. A real kiss. Not a little peck. I want one with tongue. You do this for me, then we'll just sit here and relax. But if you don't kiss me like you mean it, my hand's going to slide up a lot higher and play between your legs."

My ultimatum hangs heavily in the air. I wonder what her response will be. If she'll choose a short time of uncomfortableness for a perceived reprieve or if her inability to act on a decision will win out.

Either way, I win.

"Your favorite number is five, you said? Since you like it so much, I'll give you five seconds before I decide for you." I release her hand and watch her eyes dart back and forth at my countdown. "Five. Four. Three. Two. O—"

Mercy's lips smash against mine. I don't know how far she's

gone with other guys—and I don't want to think about her sweet lips on any other man—but she's unskilled.

Severely so.

Unless she's putting me on.

I push her back and lift her chin. "Is this you giving it your best, Mercy?"

A hint of tears shines in her gaze. "I'm trying!" she cries out. "I've only...only two people."

She's only been kissed by two people? Including me? Jealousy wars with surprise, pinching something deep inside me at the very thought of another man's lips on hers. But pride fills me, too, because there won't be any more men. *None but me.*

Our teeth clink together as she attacks me, awkwardly opening her mouth to stab her tongue into mine. I don't mind the excess saliva, but it's clear I'll need to take control of this kiss. Teach her to seduce me with her movements.

My fingers climb the back of her head and cradle her skull, tangling with her hair as I pull her back. "Slow down," I mumble into her mouth. "Taste me. Like this." I lap at the inside of her cheek, the underside of her upper lip. Small licks to tease and tantalize. "Now you."

At the first tentative movement from her tongue, my eyes roll back in sheer delight. "Yes. Yes... Just like that. Give my bottom lip a little suck."

Quick learner that she is, she gets better with every second, stoking the fire of passion that simmers beneath the surface. It takes everything within me to hold back and not take this further, but I don't want to betray her trust.

When I can no longer control myself, I give a little nibble to her bottom lip and reluctantly break away from her mouth. "Such a good girl," I praise, wrapping my arms around her as she buries her head into my chest to hide from me. "My good girl."

Placing a hand back on her ankle, I caress her bare leg all

the way to her knee, stopping there just as I said I would. The road to progress is never smooth, but once the destination is reached, the reward will be sweet.

As if she hears my thoughts, Mercy shivers within the prison of my arms.

So sweet.

CHAPTER 12

MERCY

I have to bite back my instinct of offering to wash the dishes when we finish supper. I shouldn't want to help my captor, but it's been ingrained in me since I was a child. *Make yourself useful so people will want to keep you around.* That's what all the social workers told me before I went to live with a new set of parents.

So I did. I was the most helpful little girl any parent could ever want. It didn't work, though. Nobody wanted me.

Until now.

Until Amos. He made me kiss him. Kiss him or let him run his hands all over me. I chose the slightly lesser of two evils, but it doesn't seem like it with my lips still swollen from his attentions.

"Let's go to the reading room. I forgot to ask you today what your favorite book was. Or books."

I can't tell him that! If he knew the dirty books I gravitate to, he'd probably want to role play some of the scenes.

Grabbing my hand, he pulls me behind him as he leads us to a shelf filled with books. He does that a lot, the constant touching. It's both comforting and unnerving.

"So, I have non-fiction, mystery, romance, the classics...just about everything you could want. What's your poison?"

Steering far away from that potential bomb, I tell him my other favorites because...*oversharing.* "I like poetry and the classics. Sometimes I'll dip into a mystery."

"What a coincidence." He aims a crooked smile my way while picking his way through the titles. "I like the classics, too. How about *Frankenstein*? I've been reading this one lately."

Frankenstein. A scientist who uses unorthodox scientific experiments to create a creature who can reason, to a degree. I'll take that over him offering me a romance book any day. "Sure. I'm good with that."

Book in hand, he collapses onto the oversized couch. All the furniture in this house is sized just for him, I suppose. I don't have to wonder for long where I'm going to sit because he gently yanks me down on top of him.

"*Oof!*" My head connects with his chin.

"Sorry, baby." A kiss drops on the tender spot. "I didn't mean to pull so hard."

I rub the soreness out. "It's okay."

"Here—turn this way."

Amos puts me right where he wants me, which apparently is in between his legs. "Grab my glasses, would you? They're in the drawer closest to you."

I do as he asks, pulling out a pair of thick, black-rimmed glasses from the coffee table.

"Thanks, babe. Do you want to start from the beginning or pick up where I left off?"

I can't look at him. I can't. Glasses on men his age are my weakness, and I can't afford any more chinks in my armor. "Where you left off is fine."

Dragging my stiff frame back against him, his arms rest underneath my breasts as he holds the book steady and begins to read in a soothing and melodic voice. If he weren't my captor, I'd totally listen to him on audiobooks.

Chapter after chapter, the words of the book crawl into my ears and settle into my soul. Frankenstein's poor, poor monster. He just wants a companion. Just...just like Amos. Just like I do. But...

"You ready for bed, babe?" His voice cracks on a yawn.

"Yeah, I am a little tired." Though we didn't do much, it was still a long day. The closer we get to the room, though, the more nervous I become. Is Amos going to do anything to me?

"I'm just gonna grab a quick shower," I say, awkwardly grabbing my stuff and darting through to the bathroom. Just as the door's about to catch, pressure from the other side stops me. Through the gap, I see his arctic blue eyes.

"Me, too," comes his reply as he shoulders his way in.

Okay. Guess that answers part of my question. He starts the shower and strips off. "Come on, Mercy. Nice and warm already."

I really don't want to get naked in front of him. Plus I have to take my tampon out and get cleanish before I get in the shower. My legs cross as I internally hem and haw over what to do before finally moving to the toilet.

"Whatcha doing, baby?"

I jump. Good God, he's right behind me! "I have to...totakemytamponout."

My words leave me in a rush, embarrassment washing over me. Can't the man let me have a moment of privacy for this?

"I'll do it. Take your clothes off."

First he wants to watch me put it in and now he wants to take it out for me? "Can I use one of the other bathrooms?" I doubt he'll let me, but I at least need to ask.

"Mercy, Mercy, Mercy," he tsks from behind me. My heart sinks because I know that means *no*. "Come on, baby."

I can't. I physically can't make myself do it.

Amos sighs, then undresses me like I'm a living doll, prying my arms up and legs apart. Once everything's off, his arms wrap around me from behind, chest flush against my back, and cross my stomach.

"Straddle the toilet." I have no choice but to obey because he bumps his naked lower body against mine, forcing me to stumble forward. Gah, this is so awkward!

His hand wanders from my abdomen to my pussy, lightly skimming my flesh. Fingers gently tickle my sensitive lower lips as he searches for the string, then slowly pulls it out of me and raises it in the air. "Do you know why I find this so sexy, Mercy?"

A bloody tampon?

"It's sexy," he continues as it sways in front of me, "because it's proof of your femininity. A sign of your potential fertility."

Ha. If he only knew. The blood on it means absolutely nothing except a defective egg.

"And do you know what the sight of this makes me want to do?"

Three guesses, and the last two don't count, that it's something sexual. "Throw it away and wash your hands?"

A throaty chuckle vibrates my naked back. "You're so funny. Besides that. Makes me wanna throw you down on that bed and fill you with my seed. Drown your cunt with it until I make you pregnant."

He tosses the tampon in the trash and frames my belly with his hands. "Can you see it, Mercy? Imagine this sweet belly swollen with my baby inside of you. Every morning, you'd wake up with my face between your thighs. For lunch, I'd massage you all over before sending you off to nap with an orgasm. And each night, I'd rub your sore feet. Take you nice and slow, nice and sweet. Unless you wanted me to be rough with you. Primal. Like an alpha taking his mate. Make you feel so good, baby."

My knees tremble and I collapse back against his chest,

trying to ignore his cock sandwiched between us. Good God, he's making me want the picture he's painting. To be loved by someone, to create a family. I'd never be alone again. I'd give my children every bit of the love I craved growing up and more.

If only I could get pregnant.

"I think..."—I pull away and face him, carefully clearing my throat—"I think I'm gonna take that shower now." Before blood runs down my legs. I can tell by his expression that he wants me to respond to his words, but I can't process that right now.

We silently get in the shower. I wish he'd go to one of those other bathrooms, but I know he wouldn't. Not even if I asked him. So I turn my back to him and try to stay on one side. Easy enough in theory since each side has its own sets of shower heads.

But as soon as I finish shaving, warm hands fall on my hips. I knew it. Can't even get two freakin' minutes to myself to think. "I'm going to go to the other shower. I...I can't even think, Amos!"

I grab the shower door, ready to walk naked to another bathroom if I have to—even at the risk of leaving droplets of blood all over his clean floors—and slide it open. It barely moves an inch before a hand on my arm whirls me around. Angry eyes meet even angrier eyes. He almost looks...offended. Hurt, even.

"Do you think I'm just gonna let you walk away from me, Mercy? I love you! You don't need to think when you're in my arms! You just need to feel...feel me and know that this is your life now. I told you, Mercy, told you you're mine! You're *mine!* I'll make you want me. Make you love me."

Amos spins me back around, pulling my ass against him and separating my cheeks with his hard cock. Strong arms imprison me as massive hands cup my heavy breasts. Callused thumbs rub over my hard nipples before tweaking them.

"Shhh..." he soothes at my flinch. Round and round he rolls

my tips before stroking down. His huge hands spanning my entire waist. Kisses trail down my neck. "You're mine, Mercy. Give in to me. Give in to us. This can be so good between us, baby."

I should have known he wouldn't let me go. Not after what happened on the porch. It didn't scare me, really. I just didn't know how to respond because I've never been in a situation like that before. And as much as I fight it inside my head, this is turning me on. My hips tilt, subconsciously seeking stimulation, and I have a sneaky suspicion the wetness leaking from my pussy isn't all blood or water from the shower.

Mere seconds later, Amos proves me correct when his fingers confidently split my pussy lips, forming a vee as they slide down both sides of my clit. "A-a-amos!" I tense, his name coming out on a girlish moan.

Silvery webs of my desire tinged with blood cling to his fingers as he pulls them closer to his face to inspect it. "Look at this creamy pussy. Are you needy, Mercy? Do you need your man to take care of you?"

I whimper at his words.

Amos curses. "Hold onto me."

Slave to desire, I obey even as I silently berate myself for giving in so easily, reaching for his strong forearms and holding tight. He squeezes me against him, using two fingers around my clit like a clamp, then flicks it back and forth with his other hand.

"Ohhhh, Amos." I groan, nails digging into his muscles. "That...feels..."

"I know, kitten." Teeth nibble on the back of my neck. "Gonna be even better when I get my dick in you." Lips suck on my earlobe. "And then you'll have no doubt that you're mine. Only. Mine." He taps my clit on his last two words, sparking an inferno within me. "You like that? Yeah, you like it a lot. I hear that moan."

His fingers work me hard, rubbing in fierce circles around my clit before tapping the sensitive flesh with unpredictable and varying force. Squeezing me tightly within his arms, his teeth suddenly latch *hard* on to the back of my neck as his taps against my clit turn into outright slaps, causing the sexual tension simmering inside of me to culminate in a powerful and inevitable orgasm.

I scream in bliss, clawing my fingernails into his forearms as he spanks my pussy through my release, legs dancing to an unknown melody as my cunt clenches around emptiness. "Ahhh! A...Amos!"

Amos picks me up and wraps me around him like a baby koala as he carries me out of the shower. He surrounds me, body and soul.

"Mine, baby girl. Mine."

CHAPTER 13

AMOS

Mercy's been quiet since I wrung that last orgasm from her sweet pussy. She wants time to think, she says.

What's there to think about? She's mine, and that's that. I don't remember my mom giving my dad this much trouble, but it looks like I'm going to have to coax her more than I thought. There's no doubt about it, though—she *will* give in to me. Starting tonight. Starting now.

We dry off in silence, but when she goes to grab a tampon, I stop her with my voice. "Leave it. Pull the covers back on the bed. Put a clean towel down and lay down on it."

She freezes. "You're not going to let me use a tampon?"

"That's not what I said. And of course you can use a tampon. But I'm going to be the one to put it in." I watched her do it earlier. Nothing to it.

"Bu-but..." Her jaw drops open in shock. "Amos! Is that why you—"

I chuckle. "Don't sound so scandalized. How many times do I have to tell you you're mine? I want to take care of you in all ways, and this is one of them. Now go." I punctuate my order with a pop to her butt, making her squeal. She doesn't need to be in her head all the time. That's how she's had to live her entire life. It's time for her to live in the moment and just be.

Grabbing a tampon and panties for her, I follow her to the bed, not even bothering with briefs for myself. She lies there stiffly, the edge of her tank top brushing the middle of her clenched thighs. Guess I didn't tell her *not* to wear one. Clever girl.

Mercy watches me with a nervous expression. *The fickle moods of women.* "Amos, please let me do this myself. You don't need to—"

"Nope." I force her knees apart, my strength much greater than her own, and push them toward her chest. "Hold your knees. Keep yourself open." I prepare the applicator and then bump it next to her entrance.

"Look at me," I order when I see her eyes tightly shut. "Be in this moment with me." Staring dead into her green eyes, I place one hand on her mound, thumb toward her clit, and slowly insert the applicator an inch or so before drawing it back out. Again and again, teasing her entrance.

"Amos—please..." Her lips tremble and shiny tears wait for permission to fall from her eyes.

"It's all right, baby girl." On my next upward movement, I press the applicator flush against her pretty pink pussy, simultaneously stroking her clit with my thumb while I depress the plunger with the other hand. With the abundant moisture from her earlier orgasm, it slides in easily.

A choked sob fills the air as I remove the applicator. Wrapping it in the towel and then scooching the bundle out from under her, I toss it all onto the floor and drag her panties up her legs. Then I stretch out on top of her, hoping my heavy weight comforts her. Take her hands in mine and place them against each side of her head. Mercy scrunches her wet eyes and turns her head away from me. Doesn't matter; she can still hear me. Feel me.

My mouth brushes over the softness of her ear, the deep rumble of my voice tickling it. "Wanna know what I was doing the night I took you?" She doesn't say a word, but I continue.

"I stood in the doorway and just stared. All I could think was how lonely you looked in your bed all by yourself, cuddling with that stuffed animal. You were beautiful, for sure, but withering away inside with no one to worship you, to adore you. I wanted to be that man, Mercy. I'm *going* to be that man." A squeeze for emphasis. "You don't understand yet how a Shay loves a woman, but you will. I love you for the lonely little girl you were. For the woman you are now. And the mother you will be."

Tears seep out of her eyes at my last sentence.

"The fact that no man but me has ever seen your body makes my cock so hard for you, baby. I swear I've never come as much as I have since you've been here. I don't know why you're still a virgin, and you don't have to tell me now, but deep down, you know you were waiting for me. You didn't know it was going to be me, but here I am. Here we are." I pause and kiss away the salty tears streaking toward her hairline. "I can love your body and make you want it, but I need your mind. That's what I want most of all. And you'll give that to me, too. As long as it takes, that's how long I'll wait. But don't ask me not to worship you. To love you. I can't go one more day living without you."

Another sob hiccups from her. I roll us to our sides to face each other, dick grazing her panties. "Let me see your eyes, baby. Look at me...there we go. Lemme see those pretty greens. You don't need time to think about it because that's just how it's gonna be. All you gotta do is feel. So this is what we're gonna do—you're gonna feed me with these pretty tits whenever I want."

"Wh-whaat?" she sputters, her eyes red rimmed. "Amos, that's not how it works. I don't even ha—"

"Hold on, just listen." Propping up on an elbow, I run a finger up and down the thin strap of her tank top, enraptured by the enticing way her nipples pebble and goosebumps pop up on her arms. "I know you're not producing any milk, but the more we do this, the more relaxed you and I will both be. Lots of women breastfeed their partners whether they're lactating or not. Sometimes it's sexual and sometimes it's just for comfort. This should be a nice way to ease you into this. Now, I want you to feed me and then we'll go to sleep."

"Please, Amos...don't—" Mercy's plea trails off as my finger drops and circles her taut nipple.

"Baby, I'm trying to give a little bit here. Do you want me to take your virginity or would you rather feed me with your tits? I'm not heartless, Mercy, but you've got to meet me in the middle. See my concession for what it is."

Silent seconds mix with elevated heartbeats as I wait for her answer. Maybe she doesn't even know how a woman says *yes* to a man. Doesn't matter her age. If she's never been in a sexual situation, she's not gonna know how to respond in one. In this respect, she's like a young inexperienced woman. "Mercy, give us a chance, baby. A real chance to make a go of this. I *need* you. I know it's only been two days for you, kitten, but in my mind it's been forever. Don't you want a family, Mercy? To fill this house and make it a home?"

"A family. I want that more than anything." Her tear tracks have dried and her poor bottom lip is swollen from the way she's nervously biting it. Reddened eyes search mine for long seconds before she gives the tiniest nod. "Okay, Amos. I'll try. But...be gentle—please, for the love of God, be gentle. And I've never done anything like this. I can't relax enough to—"

"Shhh...of course, baby girl," I soothe. "The last thing I want to do is hurt you. Sometimes I can get a little rough and carried away, but I'll never hurt you, baby. Never. Here, lean back."

She's so stiff that it takes a firm hand to push her back against the bed as she resists. True to my word, though, I'm gentle.

Gentle, but relentless. "You gotta loosen up a little, kitten."

My leg lifts to straddle her, but Mercy's small hand to my chest stops me. "Wait! Can...can you not be on top of me? It gives me anxiety. I'd rather sit up. Please, Amos."

With those sparkling green eyes imploring mine, how can I deny her this? "Okay, baby. You can sit on me if you want." I shift to my back and pull her on top of me, her legs parted on either side of my waist. "How's that?"

She shudders on an inhale, fists clenched on her thighs, and gives a slight nod. Good enough. I grasp each of her tits with my warm hands, letting my thumbs circle her areolae. The material of her top is so thin I can feel the heat of her skin. Each pass of my thumbs causes her thick thighs to squeeze me. Eyes tightly shut, she exhales in a rapid manner, her breasts lifting and falling in a mesmerizing rhythm.

"Slow your breathing, baby," I coax, edging my fingernails over her peaked nipples. I bet her areolae are all puckered and drawn up now that her buds are hard and poking through her shirt. Speaking of... "Time to take this off. Arms up—come on now, Mercy. There we go. Good girl. Now put your hands on my shoulders and lean down."

Rigidly, she falls forward, but not far enough to reach my mouth. I pull on her waist. "Further. Little more—there you go, baby. God, Mercy, your pussy's scalding my stomach, even through your panties. Relax your back; this is gonna feel so good."

I don't suck yet. Just bury my face in her bountiful tits and breathe her in, letting her get used to the heat of my breath and the feel of my scruff on her sensitive skin. Bet she's never been on top of a man before. Can't wait for her to sit on my face while I feast on her cunt. The mere thought hardens my cock like no other, but I force myself to calm down. There will be plenty of time for this once she's off her period.

Eat her tits for now, Amos.

I turn my head from side to side, making her little beaded flesh rub against my lips. The skin of her nipple and areola is so soft, even in its erect state. Back and forth, back and forth. On the next pass, I capture it and give it a soft, sucking tug.

"Amos—" Mercy gasps. "I—I..."

"Don't move away. Put it back in my mouth, baby."

She moans, obeying my order. Obedience deserves a sweet reward. Reaching up, I massage her tit as I tongue her nipple. Round and round my tongue goes, teasing her hard tip as her perfectly sized globe sits in the palm of my hand. Her breast might overflow another man's hand, but fits my giant mitt just right.

The desire to grab her ass and squeeze runs strongly within me, but tonight is about comfort, not arousal. Though I have a feeling from the wetness on my stomach that it's making Mercy feel *really* good at the moment. Even with a tampon in.

My tongue retreats into my mouth, pride filling me at the wetness glistening on her nipple. "Just imagine it. These big beautiful breasts, feeding our babies. Feeding your man. Comforting him after a long day. Mhmm. Calming him down after an argument. Calming yourself down."

My mouth latches back on, grabbing a mouthful. I place soft sucks on one tip, then move to the other. Mercy's mouth gapes open at the sensation, arms quivering with the stress of holding her weight up. Won't be long until she collapses onto her forearms.

And there she goes.

"Amos..." she chuffs, falling against me.

Now I can't reach her breasts. That will never do. "How about we lay on our sides? I want to fall asleep with you in my mouth, baby. Feel close to you all night long. That's all we're gonna do tonight."

Her beautiful green eyes pool with doubt, but she doesn't resist—much—as I hold her tight and roll us. Silly woman covers her breasts as she faces me. I'm about to turn the light off anyway, so it doesn't matter. I'll still be able to feel them. Taste them.

A stab at the remote turns the light off. It's dark now, but I can make out her shape as my eyes adjust. I scoot down so her tits are level with my mouth. "Let's get comfortable, baby girl. I want you to close your eyes and breathe deep breaths. I'm gonna hold you close and suck on this sweet tit until we fall asleep. There you go—you're breathing so good, sweet Mercy. Good girl."

Hairy legs entwined with her silky ones, I use my bent arm as a pillow and aim my mouth for the breast closest to the bed. I keep the sucks light but steady, and soft, slow circles of my thumb on its twin.

Comfort's the goal tonight. She's still a little stiff, but before too much longer, she'll have no choice other than to relax. My mouth isn't going anywhere, except maybe to her other breast if we happen to roll over.

Slow pulls, soft sucks, gentle caresses. That's all I do for long minutes until the tension in her body finally loosens by infinite degrees. If I didn't have a mouthful, I'd grin. I wasn't lying when I told her it would destress the both of us. As it is, I just roll my tongue under her bud and savor the moment.

When my sucks diminish in speed even more, she completely surprises me by tentatively resting a hand on my head and running her fingers through my salt and pepper hair.

That's my girl. I knew she just needed a push to accept this. Accept me. Accept *us.* My Mercy.

Everything hits us both at once: the darkness of the room; the emotions of the day; the stroking of my hair; the sucking of her tit.

All of it combined lulls us to sleep. Her breaths get slower and slower until I hear the teeniest snore. If I weren't so tired, it'd make me laugh. Instead, I close my own eyes, keeping my mouth close to her, and follow my girl into her dreams.

CHAPTER 14

MERCY

*T*eeth wake me up the next morning. Not my teeth, no.

Amos's.

Sometime in the night I'd rolled over onto my stomach. I tend to do that no matter what position I fall asleep in. And speaking of sleeping, I'm surprised I was able to drift off to sleep with him practically inhaling my breast. But Amos was right, as much as I hate to admit it. While his mouth felt amazing, the feeling wasn't overtly sexual. It soothed me, quelling my emotions. The warmth of his mouth felt like a sauna, and when he sucked, little electrical impulses made my hair raise.

Gah, it felt so good! I can only imagine what it will be like when it's done in a sexual way. Like what he's doing to me now.

Oh. My. God. The man is driving me insane and giving me emotional whiplash! I see his hands planted on either side of me right before his hot tongue licks a path from the line of my panties all the way up to my neck, straight up my spine.

"Mhmm." That tickles.

"Morning, baby." That raspy voice in my ear gives me the

A throaty groan is all that escapes my mouth again as his lips nip my earlobe.

Amos chuckles. "I agree. It's a *very* good morning, indeed. You just lay there and let me love on you. Let me thank you for giving us a chance." His tongue reverses its path, running down, down, down, my back until he's back at my panties.

His tongue veers to the side and traces my hip in slow circles. How did I never know how sensitive my skin was there? I've lived in it for all these years! I struggle to pick my head up from the pillow to see what he's doing when teeth suddenly latch onto the tender skin of my hip.

"Aggghhh! A—mos!" It doesn't hurt, but lightning bolts shoot from that one spot and electrify my clit and nipples. I swear my feet go hotly numb, too.

The pressure increases slightly before he sucks forcefully on the skin in his mouth. "Oooooooh," I moan. The tension ramps higher and higher before he releases the captured section. Then he's off to the other side, biting all over my cheeks through my panties on the way.

Lick. Bite. Suck. Release.

Repeat.

Ohmigod. What is this man doing to me?

Back up my spine he goes, using teeth instead of tongue.

Slow, teasing scrapes that make me shudder as I submit and give in to the feelings swirling inside of me. Over my shoulder blades they rake, tracing the delicate curves before continuing upward.

When he reaches the nape of my neck, he rumbles, "Breathe, Mercy. Can't have you passing out on me."

Was I holding my breath? I didn't realize. I soon understand that for the warning it was when he swoops down and grabs my neck in a harsh claiming bite.

"Aghhhhh!" I gurgle in surprise.

I'm surrounded by him. His thighs straddle me, his chest

a fire against my back as his mouth holds me hostage. A growl resonates through my neck as his teeth clasp me, a growl that causes arousal to trickle from my pussy and puddle in my panties. One more tight clench of his jaw, then he releases me, licking the marks he just made before he does it again a few inches over. My breath exhales in a rush.

"Mine, Mercy. Mine," he groans. Then the man goes crazy, raining stinging bites and nips all over my back, neck, and shoulders. Bites that I know will leave little bruises later but feel so divine right now that I don't care.

Down down down he goes, then travels back up up up to claim my neck again. Licking, sucking, biting...my back is a canvas covered with his artistry.

His mouth descends again until he reaches my panties. Hands that were so firmly planted by my head earlier now find a new home on each ass cheek, squeezing in confident caresses before yanking my underwear up together in the middle to bare each globe.

"What are you doing? Amos!" I yelp again.

The grin can be heard in his voice as he drawls out, "What, baby? You need lovin' here, too. Can't wait to mark your ass with my hand."

I freeze, completely and totally losing all arousal before I frantically kick my legs and scramble away from him, pulling the covers to my chest. "No—don't do that to me. Please, Amos don't!"

The teasing expression drops from his face in a heartbeat. "Mercy, what's the matter, baby? Don't what?"

"Don't hit me!" I hate how my voice quivers, mimicking the trembles of my body. "Please—I can take a lot of other things but not...that. I know I said I'd try, but I also asked you to be gentle. Please, Amos, please..."

Shocked, Amos stares at me, mouth open, before staring

accusingly at his gigantic hands as if they'd already struck me. "Baby girl, I'd never hit you. That's...not what I meant at all. I'm just talking about spanking done in fun, never in punishment. I'd *never* put my hands on you in anger or deliberately hurt you. These hands are for loving you and our babies. Never for hurting you."

At his fierce declaration, my heart thunders in relief, making me lightheaded as it rushes through me.

"Aw, come here, kitten." He drags me across the bed and into his arms. I bury my head in his massive chest, the crinkly chest hair comforting me as much as it distracts. His heavy hand runs up and down my naked back as he croons nonsense at me in an effort to calm me down. "Did...were you hit as a child?"

"Yes." Faces of former foster parents flash through my mind. Papa Jack when I was four. Daddy Gary when I was six. Mama Wendy when I was seven. Cruel eyes and harsher hands followed me from house to house, even until I was eighteen. I can feel them still to this day.

His warm hand cups my jaw as he tilts my face up to look at him. "I swear that will never happen to you or our kids. Not by my hand or any others, if I can help it. Do you believe me, baby?"

Amos is so earnest in his declaration that I can't help but to believe him. Or at least his sincerity. "Yes, I...think I do."

He rewards me by pressing his full lips to my forehead, the gesture so very tender. "That's my girl. We'll table the spanking for now, but I want you to know it'll be nothing like that, nothing done in anger." Another kiss. "But did you like how I woke you up this morning?" The words are muttered against the top of my head.

I did. I hide my smile in his chest hair.

"I feel your smile, baby." Satisfaction can be heard in his

words. "Good. And what about the way we went to sleep last night?"

That, too. The man knows how to work my body. But am I ready to potentially have children with this intense man? If he doesn't wear any protection, my body may not have a choice but to soak in his seed and make a baby. It would be something if he could control my womb as easily as he controls my body.

It's a complete one-eighty from when he first brought me here, I know, but there was something about last night when he put my tampon in for me. My tears weren't all sadness, though he certainly seems to think so. The sheer tenderness of his actions made me feel so...so *cared* for and the emotions were so overwhelming that they came out as a sob.

And when he told me he wants my mind in addition to my body? It's as if my heart has latched onto that bit of hope and refuses to let go.

Yes, it's only been three days—*three days*—but other than him drugging me, it seems like a dream come true. A man so head over heels for me that he couldn't stop himself from taking me? If I put aside the slightly traumatic experience he's put me through, it's...almost flattering.

But am I so desperate for love and a family that I would jump at the first opportunity? Marriages have been built on less, and at least with him so obsessed with me, I won't have to worry about him looking at other women. If he even leaves the house. If *I* even get to leave the house.

A tweak on my nipple breaks my thoughts. "Sorry...what were you say—? Oh, yes," I blush, "I...liked that part, too. It was like you said. Very calming once I got used to the...sensation."

"Sweet Mercy." Amos squeezes me tightly to his chest in a hug that is so ridiculously amazing it almost brings tears to my eyes. When a person goes without human touch, even touch as simple as a hug, it does something to them deep inside. I should know. "How about we get ready for the day, huh? Then

I'll cook you some breakfast and we'll read some more. Sound good?"

"Yeah," I say in a soft voice before turning in his arms to get up. It really does.

And that's the kicker.

"LET ME HELP YOU WITH THAT, BABY."

Innocent words, but not in this situation. He wants to *help* me with my tampon again. At this point it's not even worth arguing with him, so I dutifully hand it over. There's a faint hint of lust simmering in his eyes as he takes care of me. It's almost as if he loves anything related to the reproductive system.

Or maybe just my body in general. That's turning out to be the more logical explanation.

"There we go." With a gentle kiss to my lower abdomen, he slides my panties up. "How much longer do you think you'll be on your period?"

It's hard to say. With PCOS, it can be as short as two days or as long as ten—when it comes at all. It's not uncommon for me to miss one or two months, even with taking medicine. "I don't know. Probably a few more days, at least."

Just because I want to give this a go doesn't mean I want to have sex the minute I stop bleeding. But I wonder how I'll keep him from knowing. Maybe he'll give me more time.

He side-eyes me in the mirror the entire time we brush our teeth. *Who* brushes their teeth completely naked? Even I grabbed a sleep shirt on my way in.

Then he drops his request—command, rather—on me. "Dress me."

Dress him? *A grown man?* That's better than *un*dressing him, I suppose. "Okay..." I say dubiously.

The flexing of his butt as I follow him back to the bed is seriously fascinating. But not as fascinating as the shadowy glimpses of the cock and balls swaying back and forth as he bends and digs in the dresser for some briefs before disappearing in the closet for clothes. Amos truly has no shame in his body. And for good reason—the man is *built*. Even in its soft state, his shaft is a work of art.

Clothes drop on the bed. Just ordinary clothes. Briefs, jeans, undershirt, and a soft, thin button-down shirt. Nothing dangerous. Okay, let's get this man dressed so I can eat.

Gathering my courage and sitting on the bed so he can get his feet in the legs of his briefs, I studiously ignore the giant cock and nutsack bobbing in front of my face as I tug the briefs up over his calves, up his thighs...and—uh-oh. Now how do I get this massive dick in his underwear without touching it? I don't want to start anything that I can't carry through.

Stretching the waistband out as much as it'll go, I inch it up over his cock. All is working as planned until my hands suddenly weaken—for no reason!—and lose their grip, causing the elastic to pop back and smack his vulnerable tip.

"Agghhh!" Amos roars, flinching backward and cupping himself.

"I'm so sorry!" *Really, Mercy? Way to go.* "So sorry! I was trying to figure out how to...to..."

Explanations don't help in times like these.

After a few heavy inhales, he unclenches his jaw and throws me a pained smile. "That's okay, baby. But you have to make it right. Apologize."

I already did, didn't I? "I'm so sorry, Amos. I truly didn't mean for that to happen!"

"Thanks, babe, and I know. But that's not what I meant. I want an apology without words."

"Wha—how am I supposed to do that?"

"Kisses, Mercy. Or blowjobs. I'll take either. But

right now my dick needs a little tenderness to take away the pain."

A kiss? On his *cock*? My eyes must be as wide as saucers now because he laughs at me.

"Come on, baby. Just a little kiss to take the pain away." He points the head toward my lips. "Right. Here."

He really means it. Blood rushes through my veins, pulsing like thunder, and turns my face tomato red. This is much different from him making me hold it while he pisses!

I purse my lips, intending to give it the quickest and shortest of pecks, and lurch forward an inch or so. That's as far as I get. My body refuses to go any further, leaving about three inches between his glans and my mouth. I can't do this by myself. I look up pleadingly at him. "Help me."

"I see," Amos murmurs. "Still not there yet. All right, then." He reaches down to grab my hands, kissing the backs of each before placing one on each hip bone. "Keep them here," he orders.

"Okay." *Why couldn't I make myself just do it?* I wanted to. I really did, but I just couldn't close the gap. My fingers automatically curl, digging into his flesh and holding tightly. His hand threads through my hair before clenching against my head, making me gasp. He's not pulling hard, more like holding me still, but the tension ensures my focus is completely on him.

"Mercy, Mercy, Mercy," he tsks, looking down at me. "You could have gotten by with just one kiss if you'd done it on your own. Now it's going to be more. Don't worry, though. I'll go easy on you, kitten."

The last few inches between us seem an eternity apart as he slowly reels me in by my hair. I can't even see the slit on his cock anymore, but I swear the ghost of its heat singes me as it hovers there in front of my lips.

My eyes meet Amos's unrelenting ones as I peer up at him through my dark lashes. He pulls up a fraction more, turning my head to rest against his pelvis and butting my lips up to his downward hanging shaft. The skin is so soft and smooth, so silky. His balls sport finely trimmed hair, so hopefully I won't get any in my mouth.

One of the girls I met in a foster home told me a horror story of a time she went down on a guy and got pubic hair in her mouth. When she choked and tried to spit it out, he told her it was Mother Nature's dental floss.

Eww.

A nudge from his hips brings me back to the present. Oh...right. *Gulp.* He gently drags my head down the line of his shaft, causing my mouth to slide down the smoothness, right to the tip.

"Mhmm..." he groans. "Yeah, baby. Apologize to that cock with those sweet lips."

With his crown pressed to my lips, I purse them and give the gentlest peck to where the elastic popped him. That butterfly-soft kiss swells his shaft, sending blood to the tip and engorging it.

We both watch it twitch and grow. "Oh, you've done it now, Mercy. Open your mouth."

Alarm flashes through me. I can't do that yet. He's too big and I have a smaller than usual mouth.

He notices my anxiety. Of course he does—nothing escapes him. "Just the tip, kitten, I swear. I know you're not ready to do that yet."

Just the tip.

How many girls have been suckered in by that line? Hopefully, he means it, though.

Hesitantly, I open my mouth the tiniest of bits, but it's enough for Amos to push the head through. It shocks me enough that I almost reflexively bite down on the invading object in my mouth, but I catch myself at the last minute.

That's all I need. If I have to kiss his cock for hurting it with underwear, I don't even want to imagine how I'd have to apologize for accidentally using teeth. His dick is hard enough that he doesn't need to use a hand to hold it anymore, so his free hand interlocks with the other on my head, just resting and not pulling. Surrendering to instinct, I suck lightly on the tip.

"Yes, Mercy," Amos rasps. "Do that again, baby girl."

Stiffening my grip on his hips, I contract my lips again on his inflamed head.

"Harder. Suck...harder. Wait—" he pushes my head back, groaning in pleasure when he sees the silvery string of his precum and my saliva trailing from his slit to my lips. Taking my hands from his hips, he stacks them on his hard cock. "Squeeze me tight and suck the tip harder. Yes, just like that," he hisses.

It's easy to keep going since he's gotten me started. My hands barely wrap around his now fully erect shaft, but I tighten them as much as I can and suction my mouth, popping off and on his glans. Sucking that leaking head like I can't let one single drop escape.

Long moments pass as I nurse on his cockhead. The wet sounds as his shaft leaves my lips are so vulgar, but so arousing. I have no experience at all with any of this, but I'm pretty sure Amos likes what I'm doing.

He rumbles praise at me, fingers clenching in my hair. "Good girl, Mercy. Keep going. Yeah, baby. Yeahhhhh...al—most..."

His hips thrust a scant bit deeper into my mouth before he pulls back, saying, "Sorry, baby. I'm...about to come...keep sucking. Drink it all down. Drink—me. Aghhh—"

That's the only warning I get before warm liquid spurts into my mouth. I almost gag, completely unprepared for how far back it shoots into my throat, but keep a forceful suction around his crown and swallow his cum until his gasps die down and his hips still. Pulling back, I lick my lips, tasting the bitter and salty seed that came from his body.

"My Mercy," he pants. He grabs me by my upper arms and drags me up to devour my mouth, his tongue darting in and tickling the inside of my cheeks. There's no doubt he's tasting the remnants of his cum, but I think that just makes him hotter. "That's the best apology I've ever gotten."

CHAPTER 15

AMOS

*L*ike a kid, I milked that opportunity for all it was worth. That little slip with her hands was shocking, more than anything. But I couldn't pass up a chance to get in her mouth. Literally blew me away. I stood there stupidly with my briefs stretched around my thighs the entire time.

If I came that hard with just the tip in her mouth, I may actually die a happy man if she's able to fit any more of me the next time. I'm a big guy and her mouth is small, though, so I'll take whatever she can do.

But she needs to finish dressing me so I can cook her some breakfast. Not to mention, I have some special plans for her today. I don't want her feeling threatened every time I want to spank her, so I've got to teach her just what I mean when I say I'm going to mark her ass with my handprints.

Disbelief battles with ecstasy when I think of her words from earlier. *Okay, Amos. I'll try.* And that's why I gave her that little push—I could tell she needed that indirect permission to let go.

I'd thought about giving that sweet little pussy an orgasm,

but I think I'm gonna let her squirm in need. Make her hot and ready for me when her period ends in a few days.

"Here, baby. Finish dressing me so we can go eat something. This time just lift and tuck, please. And later, you're gonna feed *me*." I do enjoy making my baby girl blush. But she does as I tell her, lifting my cock and tucking it into my briefs. Even goes a step further by giving my balls a gentle pat.

Next are my jeans. I brace myself on her shoulders as I step in a leg at a time. When she reaches my zipper, her hands falter. "How do I... I don't want to accidentally hurt you like last time."

"It's okay," I soothe. "Just make sure you pull the material away from the sensitive bits so they don't get bitten by the zipper. I can tell you from experience that hurts way more than an elastic pop."

Mercy's lips tip in a worried smile as she works the zipper up.

"Good girl. Now my undershirt."

Standing, she beckons me to lower my head so she can pull the shirt over and get my arms through. Last item to go on is the shirt.

I specifically chose one with buttons because I want her hands to rest against me and learn my muscles as she buttons me up. Undressing someone in the heat of passion is hot, no doubt about it, but to *dress* someone...well, that is an understated form of eroticism.

I stretch out one arm, then the other, as Mercy walks behind me to get my shirt on. Her rotation complete, she begins buttoning the shirt from the bottom up, keeping her eyes down. That will never do. "Eyes up, baby. Let me see those gorgeous greens."

I can see the tremendous amount of courage it takes for her to lift her eyes with this intimate act, but her gaze fixes on mine as she fastens the bottom buttons. She needs some dirty talk to help her along.

"That dick you just popped? It's gonna pop your sweet cherry soon. Don't blush, baby—nothing to be embarrassed over. Just a fact."

I love the way her breath catches. Now she's up to my stomach, her pupils dilated. "You like these abs? They're gonna flex as I drive in and out of your cunt. Breathe, baby."

Her fingers fumble at my words. I cover her hands with mine, staring deeply into her beautiful eyes. "You feel these hands, these arms? They're gonna wrap around you and hold you down so I can breed you so hard. Let my cock spray deep inside you and make you pregnant with my kid."

"Amos," she breathes out.

There go her knees, buckling underneath her. Good thing my arms will always be here to catch her. I'm not done, though.

"Feel this mouth?" I lean down towards her mouth and drop a soft kiss on her lips. "It's gonna eat your cunt up every day. Like this."

Taking her hand, I tease the center of her palm with my tongue, swirling circles on the sensitive skin before licking up to the vee of her index and middle fingers where I mimic eating her out, letting the weight of my heavy stare hit her full force.

She doesn't know where to look, glazed eyes bouncing from me to my tongue before closing in ecstasy. The instant her lashes meet each other, I stop, amused at the way they flutter open in surprise, then I dive down to eat her mouth, peppering not-so-gentle nibbles on her bottom lip, then soft licks inside.

The lewd sound of our lips separating is almost enough to make me shoot my load again. "Patience, baby girl."

Now she has something to look forward to.

"More?"

I hold the fork up to her mouth, tempting her. There's

something satisfying about a woman unafraid to eat. And she didn't even balk this time when I told her I wanted to be the one to feed her again. A woman eating from her man's hand...well, it doesn't get much better than that.

Other than when I was in her mouth earlier. Maybe she'll be able to fit more of me with practice. I don't mind letting her experiment on me. Maybe I'd even let her bite me. But that's another kink for later. Something else is on my mind right now.

Mercy's a little antsy—it's plain to see by her fidgeting. I really got her worked up this morning, and without an outlet, all that nervous energy has no place to go but to steep inside of her. And I'm likely about to add to it. She still has to *feed* me, after all.

"No, thank you. That was so delicious, Amos. Can I help you clean up?"

Absolutely not. A real man cleans up a mess of his own making in the kitchen. So I don't get water on the sleeves, I take off the shirt that Mercy worked so hard to fasten. "Nah, baby, I'll take care of it. Why don't you get our book from the library and bring it to the couch?"

The way the kitchen is set up, I can see most of the living room from the sink, so I can keep a close eye on her. Not that I think she's going anywhere, but still. I don't like letting my sweet Mercy out of my sight if I can help it.

Doesn't take me long at all to wash the dishes and clean the table. I toss the dish towel on the countertop and walk up behind where she sits hugging her knees on the couch. She doesn't notice my approach, intently focused on the window a few feet away.

No, not just the window—the glaringly obvious deterrents I installed on all the doors and windows to keep her inside. Also to keep any bad guys, present company excluded, outside and away from my treasure. My Mercy.

I squeeze the nape of her neck lightly and begin massaging

my way down to her shoulders. Quiet reigns for a moment, then she softly speaks. "Amos, how long do you plan to keep me locked up in here, never letting me see anyone? Even when you know I want to give this a try?"

My hands falter before resuming. "It's not just to keep you here, you know. It's to *protect* you. If anyone were to get their hands on you, I couldn't live with myself. And I'll let you leave the house eventually, once you become mine and completely accept our new life together. When I can fully trust you."

When your last name's Shay and you're swollen with my kid.

"It's very apparent that you've put a lot of thought into this, with the story you've concocted about me moving away. But what about my house? What about my car and my things? I pay rent every month, and I still have a year left on the lease. Don't you think my landlord will try to contact me if he doesn't get paid?"

That's an easy answer. "No, he won't. Your landlord already knows you won't be paying him anymore. He's got no problem at all with you breaking your lease. Nor with your things still staying there for the time being."

"Do you know my landlord? Is that why he won't worry?"

My hands cease and rest on the back of the couch while I stare at the ottoman. Time for the complete truth. "I guess you could say I know him pretty well, considering I'm the one you've been paying rent to."

"*You?* I don't believe it! I pay some company called—"

"AMS Holdings," we say at the same time. Mercy's voice trails off as she swivels around to stare at me, stark disbelief in her eyes.

"Believe it. *Amos Mitchell Shay.* You didn't think it was odd that utilities and internet were included in the rent for a single-family home? I knew from the moment I saw you that I had to have you. Keeping the utilities in my name ensured the companies wouldn't need to talk to you to confirm cancellation or raise questions when you didn't pay."

Her brow furrows. "Rental houses were so hard to find. Was that why the house seemingly popped up out of nowhere?"

"Yes." I stare deeply into her green orbs. "And now you know what a Shay will do to get his woman, Mercy. I cared enough about you to plot and plan for an entire year to get you here. You're mine now, baby. All mine."

Mercy doesn't say anything. Just turns back around and wears a thoughtful expression. I don't want her to think too much on everything, though.

"You got the book ready?" At her nod, I walk between the couch and the ottoman. "Scoot to the corner, okay?"

When she's wedged into the corner, I sit and stretch out so I'm lying in her lap.

"What are you doing?" she nervously laughs.

This woman. "Don't you remember? I feed you, you feed me. You're gonna read to me, and I'm gonna eat from your sweet tits." I sit up a bit and take the hem of her shirt in hand, pulling it up. "Arms up, kitten. Come on, now...arms up."

Her breathing picks up, but she stays relaxed enough for me to get her shirt off and unhook her bra.

Once they're undone, I use a finger to slowly push one strap at a time off the gentle slope of her shoulders to expose her luscious breasts as I pull the straps down her arms.

"It's okay, sweet girl. We've done this before. You just relax and focus on reading the book to me. We're both gonna chill and enjoy ourselves, all right?"

When her chin dips in agreement, I settle back down and rest my head on the arm of the couch so I can comfortably reach her nipple with my mouth. "Grab the book. You can put it on my shoulder while you read."

Her voice rings out hesitantly as she picks up in the passage where we left off before. I let her get a few words out before I make my move, rubbing my mouth all around her nipple and areola while curving my hand around her waist. Every time my mouth touches her sensitive flesh, she stumbles over her words. It's the cutest thing. But I need to feed. Need her to soothe the beast inside of me.

I feather my affection over her nipple to get her used to my touch again, only halfway listening until her next sentences jump out at me.

"I have love in me the likes of which you can scarcely imagine and rage the likes of which you would not believe. If I cannot satisfy the one, I will indulge the other."

The words strike me with a stab to my heart. I've read it so many times before, but never has it had so much meaning to me as it does right here, right now in this moment.

Frankenstein's monster hungered for love, feeling there was no one in the world for him. Being denied doesn't stop the heart from yearning for more.

A weed is just as desperate for the warmth of the sun as the most beautiful flower is, and the love that I have for Mercy is unlike any other.

She's my sun. Like my biological mom was for my dad before she passed. Like my living mom is now for my dad. And, following in the footsteps of my father, whether I deserve her or not, I'm going to spend the rest of my days basking in the warmth of her rays.

I wrap my lips around her areola and suck, feeling her nipple brush the roof of my mouth. Mhmm, she tastes so good. Smells good, too. I don't know which is better—her natural scent, or mine overlaying hers.

Slow, wet noises fill the room, joining with the words from the book as I nurse from her and run my tongue around her areola. I'd planned for this to be a relaxing session, but I feel the monster within my own self rising with each word she reads. I need more. I need her to want me.

Popping off, I rub my stubble all over her poor little nipple, scraping it raw. I'm gonna have to get her some ointment so she doesn't hurt too badly. Mercy misses more and more words, squirming at the abrading intensity. God, her bud makes me want to suck it so hard. So I do.

Ravenous, I suddenly latch on, ferociously sucking as much of her tit in my mouth as I can and pulling hard on her nipple.

"Ohhhh..." she keens, book dropping as her fingers twitch on my shoulders. Let's see how she likes some teeth. If this morning was any indication, it's gonna drive her wild.

Moving my hand from her waist to her tit to hold it steady, I gently grab her nipple between my teeth then slowly pull back, stretching it from its base.

Her hands flutter, alternately pushing and pulling my shoulders at the sensation. "Agh!" she yelps.

When it's lengthened as long as it can go, my tongue flicks and teases the trapped head of her nipple. Long, swirling circles and lashes, then my teeth release it with a *pop* to spring back.

Yeah, she likes that. I move my mouth to the fullest part of her tit and rake my teeth down the thin, sensitive skin, lightly biting on her little bud when I reach it.

Bite. Suck. Flick. That elicits a shriek from her.

"Amos! Wha—?"

I pull back to encourage her. "Just go with it, baby. I need this...need you." My voice is raspy with desire. I bury my face under her breast, breathing in her scent where her soft globes meet her chest, then lick a curving path from one side to the other, relishing her moans and squirms as she throws her head back against the cushion.

Abs flexing as I crunch upwards, I turn her towards me a bit more, tonguing my way up the line of her cleavage and traveling to her other breast. Can't have it feeling left out.

If anything, I'm more aggressive in my attentions now,

pulling and biting harder than I did on the other side, enough so that Mercy flinches and tries to draw back.

I pull off with a pop and growl, "Gimme this tit, baby girl," and roughly scrub my facial stubble all over the tip of her breast, painting it a glowing pink. For sure gonna need some ointment. *Sorry, Mercy.*

The most arousing little squeaks escape her mouth as her hands spasmodically flex on my shoulders. I want those hands somewhere else. Reluctantly, I temporarily take one hand away and reach for hers. "My hair, baby. Dig into my hair," I mumble against her swollen bud, giving it a teasing suck. When I feel her fingers tentatively pulling, I grunt. Gives me goosebumps.

Putting my hand back where it belongs, I smush her breasts together so I can easily move from one nipple to the other, alternating stinging bites, hard sucks, and ticklish licks.

"Amos," Mercy hisses, squirming as if she's trying to get relief for the heat between her legs. I have a strong hunch that she's one of those women who could come with just nipple stimulation. But that'll be something we can test later.

For now, I really need her to understand that spanking—at least the kind of spanking I'm going to do to her—isn't anything to be afraid of. I want her to desire it, even crave the caress of my palm before it rears back and delivers pure ecstasy to her fleshy bottom. All designed to heighten her arousal. Never to hurt her or punish her.

Never.

When her breathing turns to pants and gasps, I pull off the nipple I've been sucking, the small noise barely audible over her breathing.

Time to teach my kitten that she has absolutely nothing to fear from my hands. That pain administered in the proper setting can indeed be pleasurable.

CHAPTER 16

MERCY

*W*hy did he stop? I stare down at him, stunned and unbelievably turned on. Arousal shines from his eyes as his deep voice rumbles, "Do you trust me?"

Trust.

Something I've struggled with my entire life. It's so hard to trust anything or anyone but myself.

Do I trust that Amos will feed and clothe me? Yes.

Do I trust that he doesn't intend to hurt me? Yes, I do.

But do I trust him enough to open up myself emotionally and allow him the ability to completely destroy me? To willingly place my vulnerable heart in his giant hand that could smash it to pieces, simply by pressing just one bit too hard?

Not yet. Not completely. But I want to.

His slow claiming is coaxing me more than he knows, making my mind and body inexorably crave this crazy love he's offering me. My trembling fingers smooth his hair away from his hairline that's still so full. "I *want* to. Does that count? The fact that I want to?"

Amos sits up and drags me onto his lap. "That means the world to me. Will you let me gain a little more? Show you the spanking I want to give is nowhere near the abuse you were given as a child?"

Will I or won't I? I turn the thought over in my mind.

"Growth doesn't happen by living in the past, Mercy. If you're always looking back, you can never see what's in front of you. Me." He places my hand on his chest. His heart booms steadily underneath my palm. "I'm right here. Wanting to love you."

My fingers spread across his nipple through his shirt, then trail down his muscled arm until I reach his hand. I pick it up, my own hand engulfed in its mass. He's strong. So strong. Working construction has given him some serious muscles. I trace the lines on his palm. His skin isn't the smoothest. In fact, it's a bit callused in spots, but the rough texture screams masculinity. These hands have done lots of things to me—some of them uncomfortable—but never have they outright abused me.

Not like the hands from my childhood. No, these hands have forced pleasure on me. Washed me. Caressed me. Fed me.

He's right. It's time to move forward. I lean forward and kiss his warm palm. "Yes, Amos. I want you to show me that it's not the same."

The kiss surprises him, makes his muscles tense. This is the first time I've kissed him voluntarily. But as illogical as it is, I meant it when I said I'd give us a try. What if this is my only chance to fulfill my lifelong wish?

Composing his expression, Amos tips his head to give me a sweet forehead kiss. "Thank you so much, baby, for being brave like this. I promise I won't break your trust with it."

He stands me between his legs. "Let's get these shorts off of you."

"Wait! What about my...you know?" My tampon.

"I don't mind a bit of blood. If any gets on me, it'll just be my pants. Now, back to you." Amos reaches for me with a hooded smile. Exposed, I cradle my breasts to myself and swallow a gasp as clothes hit the floor with a muted thud.

Shorts.

Panties.

His undershirt.

"Sit down. Lean on me and just relax. There you go. Now hook your legs on my thighs. Good girl."

The curly hair on his chest is rough against my naked skin when I press back and splay my legs over his thighs, opening up my center.

"Hold onto my belt loops and don't let go. Remember, kitten —I'm not going to hurt you. Just gonna show you how good you can feel."

My breasts hang heavily as I reach behind me to catch my fingers in the loops. *We're really doing this.*

His massive hand wraps around my throat, firmly clasping me in a dominant but reassuring way. My pulse flutters, my lungs working rapidly to disperse oxygen throughout my body.

I can do this. He's not going to hurt me. I can do this. I can.

"Calm yourself, kitten." Lips brush the shell of my ear. A hand holds my breast, flicks the nipple back and forth. "Feel me wrapped around you. You're safe in my arms."

Soft caresses soothe me as he subdues my body. Every nuzzle of his lips, every stroke of his hand stokes the embers of passion until down, down, down his hand moves. Down to my pussy. He cups me there, branding me with the heat of his hand. "What are some of the things your foster parents told you? Tell me."

No one wants you.

You're an ugly runt.

You're a worthless brat.

Good thing they're paying me to take care of you.

So many things that cut deeply into my soul and formed me into the insecure woman I am today. But it's hard to remember them while his thumb circles my clit with teasing motions.

"Oh...Amos," I moan. "That's so—no! Why did you stop?"

The hand on my throat tips my head back to meet his smoldering gaze. "I told you I don't like being ignored. Now tell me, kitten. Tell me what lies you were told as an innocent child."

I'm so out of breath with arousal that I don't know if I can form coherent thoughts.

"Tell me or I stop." The pressure against my clit lightens.

"They told me I would never get adopted because no one would want me. That I was worthless and only a paycheck to them." I throw the words out.

"My Mercy." His thumb moves again. "Anything else?"

How can I think with these feelings coursing through me? "That I was ugly."

"Do you still believe them?"

"I don't know. No. No, I don't think so." But I think I do to some degree.

"That will never do." A nip to the nape of my neck, a flex of his fingers. "I can't have you thinking these untruths about yourself. Get a pillow and put it on the coffee table. Good girl. Now I want you to lean forward and put your head on it."

His hands trail down my body as I lower myself, his muscular thighs supporting my torso. I rest cradled within his lap, arms and legs spread over his thighs and my face cushioned by the coolness of the throw pillow.

A moan escapes me when his strong grip forces the tension in my shoulders and back to dissipate. Working out the knots there, his rough palms inch their way down. Down to my lower back, so taut with apprehension. Down further still.

"It's just me. Not gonna hurt you." Spoken as he lightly massages my bare cheeks, his words settle me. "You were told nobody wanted you. That's a lie. *I* want you."

Pop! The first smack lands directly in the middle of my right cheek as his words hit my soul.

"Ahh!" I gasp and clench his legs with my hands and thighs, a zing of arousal shooting through me.

"You're all right, baby. Just surprised you, huh?" Amos croons. It did. I wasn't prepared for him to trick me by massaging me with one hand and spanking with the other. Cheater.

"Relax. You need to relax right here." He pushes down on the tensed muscles of my lower back and runs his hands across my thighs. "You're not worthless. I would give up everything I had in the world if it meant I could have you. You're everything to me, Mercy."

I am, aren't I? I *am* his everything.

Pop! My left cheek burns so good with the heat of his hand.

"Amos..." My moan fills the room.

He laughs throatily. "Good girl, letting your man show you how much he loves you. What's the last one again?"

You're an ugly runt.

"I'm...ugly."

"After this, I never want to hear those words leave your mouth again. Don't even think them. Never again. You're the most beautiful woman in the world to me. Do you hear me? You are beautiful. Every inch of you is gorgeous and *mine!*"

His third strike comes on the last word. *Pop!*

"Ahh!"

"Tell me you're beautiful."

"I'm..."—tears fall unexpectedly from my eyes—"...beauti-ful. I'm beautiful."

"That's right. You're my beautiful woman. And you look so gorgeous with my mark on your ass. With my bites on your back and neck. God, kitten, you don't know what it does to me to see you belonging to me, wearing my marks. But you know what? That was three. I know that's not your favorite kind of number. What do you say we go for two more?"

He doesn't even give me time to tense up again, striking me twice more scarcely before he ends his sentence. The last one is the hardest, but the force of it sends liquid arousal seeping from me.

My breath leaves me in a rush. It's over. I made it through without breaking down. The relief is so great that I tremble as my body releases the adrenaline that it didn't get to use in fight or flight.

"We're not done yet." Amos lifts me up and holds my hands on my chest as he stretches his legs out on the coffee table, my legs still hooked over his. His free arm reaches to my pussy, rubbing furious circles on my clit.

I cry out, twitching in bliss.

"There's my girl. Let me make my woman feel good. She's so beautiful. So precious to me. So loved."

Every word combined with every touch breaks down the walls of insecurity in my mind.

I'm wanted.

I'm valuable.

I'm beautiful.

"Let it go. Come on, give it to me, baby."

A powerful ball of emotion twists in my chest and exits my throat as a sob. This man, this crazy, obsessed man, loves me for *me*. My back arches, fingers reaching out to link with his as my orgasm forcefully rips through me, a raw and guttural cry leaving me.

I collapse against him, completely undone. His arms anchor me to him, his scruff abrading my neck as he nuzzles into me. "My sweet Mercy. Such a good girl."

I'm his. His sweet Mercy. "Hold me, Amos."

"I am, baby girl."

It's not enough. "Tighter. Please."

Amos turns me around, wrapping my naked legs around his waist in a sweet embrace. I bury my face in his neck and inhale his scent, trying to slow my racing heart as I battle the instinct to hide away.

"Shh... It's all right. You did so good, baby. So good. I'm proud of you. You were so brave to let me spank you." The deepness of his voice combined with his warm hands trailing up and down my spine calms me, little by little.

"Do you see now how that kind of spanking is different?"

The rumble of his voice through his chest is so soothing. At my nod, he tightens his arms, squeezing me so good.

"I would never hurt you like that, Mercy. But now you know a spanking can feel good, can turn you on. Like when I spanked your sweet pussy in the shower. Remember that?"

Do I ever. How could I forget that memorable orgasm? That burn and slightest hint of pain that served to escalate the pleasure?

"Yes," I finally get out in a whisper, curling my fingers in his wiry chest hair. "I was surprised by how good that felt. I didn't realize this would be the same."

"My kitten. Give me that mouth." Amos tilts my chin up to lay claim to my mouth, tongue dipping in and tangling with mine before retreating so he can suck my lips. "You have my heart in your hands, baby girl."

This man is relentlessly breaking through all my defenses with a gentle battering ram.

CHAPTER 17

MERCY

"**D**oes this feel good, kitten? You want it harder?"

I moan, toes curling.

Amos digs in deep. "That's the spot, yeah?"

"God, yes. Do the other one and make it even, please."

He'd picked my feet up ten minutes ago and, after a surprised, instinctive kick to his face—which he thwarted—started the best massage of my life. I never knew feet could hold so much tension.

The growling of my stomach breaks the moment.

"Are you hungry?" Amos chuckles and drops a ticklish kiss where my toes meet the underside of my feet.

"Starving, actually. I need sustenance." More than a few hours have passed since our big breakfast and the, erm... spanking.

He snickers and grabs the front of his pants, which, surprisingly enough, are still clean after what he did to me. "Sustenance, eh? I've got some *sustenance* for you."

"Amos." His eyes still light up every time I say his name. "I want *actual* food. Real food." The more I think about it, the bigger my craving gets.

"Well, let's go see what's in the kitchen and I'll whip some-thing up."

Not exactly what I had in mind. "Actually, I'm dying for a milkshake. Mhmm... Or a malt. Does Pleasant Plain have a place?"

"Yes..." The word is drawled out as he arches an eyebrow.

"Ooh, can we please go? And *then* we'll get real food after-ward. Let me grab my shoes and I'll be right back."

"Wait." He grabs my wrist and rakes a hand uncomfortably through his hair. "Mercy, I'm not taking you out yet."

He's kidding, right? "Come on... I'm hungry. Let's go!"

"No, Mercy!" *Why is he raising his voice at me?* "I said not yet. It's too soon. And you don't need it with your condition."

Too soon? And my *condition*? "What do you mean? It's lunchtime, maybe even later."

His grip tightens, his mouth sets in a straight line. "I told you on your first day here that I wasn't going to let you leave. I've got to be able to trust that you won't run off. And after just three days, I don't think we're there yet."

He's not kidding. My heart jolts, a strange pain lancing through my chest at the realization. "Amos, do you even hear yourself? You expect me to give in to you after only three days and yet you won't bend on something as small as this?"

His expression is resolute.

Trust. The hurt running through me morphs into anger, sending spikes of adrenaline to my extremities. Fingers trem-bling with the force of it, I scoff. "After what we just did this morning—after I let you *spank* me when I told you I was smacked around as a child—you say you can't trust me? I trusted you to do that to me and you can't extend me the same courtesy of believing me enough to take me somewhere to eat?" I yank my wrist from him, my blood boiling and pounding in my ears. "To *eat*, Amos. That's all I want to do—eat! But you know what? Let's get down to the root of the matter—why I'm here. This wouldn't even be an issue if you'd asked me out like a normal person."

The source of this new-found bravery unknown but not unwelcome, I throw my hands up in frustration and let my words spew out in a quavery voice. "But that's in the past—let's talk about now. You want to keep me in this house like a prisoner and I've gone along with it. I've given so much of myself to you. It's always *Mercy, give in to me. Mercy, let me do this to you.* Or *Mercy, do this to me.* It's all about you. What *you* want. What's best for Amos Shay."

His jaw clenches. Too bad. I'm not done yet.

My finger shakily pokes at his chest. "What about what's best for Mercy Callahan? Have you thought deep and hard about that, Amos? Sure, this weekend has been great if we don't count the rough start, but is this all I have to look forward to? All my life, I've been walked over. Hungering for every scrap of tenderness and affection I could find. I'm tired of not being good enough for basic human decency. Tired of it, do you hear me?"

Ohmigod. Am I really doing this? Is this really me? The high emotion of the moment brings angry tears to my eyes, and I furiously wipe one away as it escapes. "God, Amos... It's just like *Frankenstein.* Do you even remember what happens to the female companion the monster begs his creator to make for him? She gets destroyed. Destroyed by the scientist, just like you're doing to me. You can't make me love you, Amos! Just...just go!"

I don't mean to yell my last words, but it happens anyway in a long overdue outburst.

Amos's voice hardens. "You want me to leave? Fine. I'll leave. But you know what, kitten? I'll be back. And your sweet little ass will still be here when I do." He storms off barefoot down the long hallway.

Dazed, I put an unsteady hand on my heaving chest and fall

against the wall as I sniff and rub my wet eyes with my sleeve. Did I really do that?

I did. I yelled at him. I *yelled*. That spanking did more than just break down my insecurities.

Through my tear-blurred vision, Amos emerges from the bedroom with boots on. "While you're at it, make sure you think about *this*." He jerks me to him and devours my mouth before kissing away the wetness covering my face. With a harsh nip to my lip and a firm squeeze of my ass, he backs away. "I love you, Mercy. You're mine. And I *will* make you love me. Remember that."

When he gets to the front door, he turns around. "And be sure to eat something." The door slams shut behind him and soon after, I hear his truck start up.

I can't believe it. The wall is the only thing holding me up as the engine noises get further away.

I'm alone in the house.

I'm *alone* in the house.

I run to the front door and pull on it. Locked. Of course it is.

That's okay. Check the other doors, Mercy.

All locked. Even the windows.

Think, Mercy. Think.

I'm back where I started. Looking closer at the door handle, I see there's a keyhole just underneath the biometric plate. I'll bet just about anything the door can be opened with just the key. Otherwise, that wouldn't be safe in the case of an emergency.

The bedroom! Maybe there's an extra set of keys hidden there.

If I were Amos, where would I hide the keys? Hmm. The closet, maybe? I dig through his clothes, tossing them out on the floor. Nothing.

The sock drawer. How clichéd would that be? But just in case, I open it up.

There's something there, all right. Two somethings. My cell phone, minus the SIM card, and his. He must have forgotten to take it with him. My phone is useless because I don't have anything small and narrow enough to pop out his SIM card, so I press the power button on his instead.

Ugh! Of course it's locked. *Everything* in this stupid house is locked except for the bathroom door.

But emergency calls can still be made on cell phones without needing a passcode. The number pad on the screen stares at me, daring me. Am I really going to turn him in like this? I *should* call the police. It would serve him right. He abducted me!

With shaky fingers, I dial it out.

9...

I can love your body and make you want it, but I need your mind. That's what I want most of all.

I jerk around. I could have sworn he was behind me saying this.

I...

And you'll give it to me, too. As long as it takes, that's how long I'll wait.

He's not here. It's all in my mind.

I...

But don't ask me not to worship you. To love you.

My lips tremble. "Shut. Up. Amos."

There. Now to just press the call button.

Press it.

Press the button, Mercy!

Amos's voice whispers in my ear. *Don't you want a family, Mercy?*

My lungs stutter on an inhale. I can't bring myself to do the one thing that would change both of our lives forever. I can't do that to him, Stockholm syndrome or not. But I can't stay here, either.

I need the keys to the door.

Keys...keys...

In a fit of anger, I throw the covers off the bed and turn everything inside out. A wild grunt escapes as I yank all the drawers out and dump the contents onto the floor. "Where are the stupid *keys*?"

Screeching doesn't help, but it makes me feel better.

When I'm done, the room is a total disaster. It's been thirty minutes, and still nothing. He could be back any minute now. I collapse onto the floor, belatedly noticing my stuffed rabbit underneath a pile of shirts. I ignore it and draw my knees to my chest, resting my head atop them as my tears dry. With every beat of my heart, my ears ring with the river of blood rushing through them.

Calm down, Mercy. This is doing you no good.

Closing my eyes, I will my blood pressure to lower. I'm still hungry. And, surprisingly enough, feeling abandoned. Lonely. Why do I miss him?

The front door slams.

My heart jumps. *He's back.*

I hear his boots sound against the tile floor of the hallway.

Is he still mad? He hasn't said my name yet.

The footsteps are measured, deliberate, and steadily heading this way.

I've never seen him angry before.

He wouldn't hurt me, would he?

He might when he sees this mess.

Each beat of my heart pounds against my rib cage, my breath coming in quick bursts as the doorknob slowly turns, rotating degree by degree. Time decelerates, the seconds crawling by as I wait to see Amos's reaction. I don't think he'd hurt me, especially since he didn't lay a hand on me during our argument, but tension and stress make people act in strange ways.

I scramble to my feet, a short, involuntary scream leaving me at the sight of the male face that appears in the opening. He...he's not Amos, but could easily have been him if he were about twenty years younger. This man must somehow be related.

"Oh. Hello, Miss. I didn't mean to scare you, but what are you doing here? This is private property." He directs a stern look at me as he steps further into the room. I recognize that look. I've seen it on Amos multiple times before. His father, maybe? Or an uncle?

"I... Amos brought—" How am I supposed to answer a question like that?

A knowing expression covers his face. "Ah. I see. You've been staying with my son?"

That's one way to put it.

"Did he do this?" The Amos lookalike growls the words as he takes in the disarray.

"Mitchell, honey, who's in there?" An older woman with silvery blonde hair pops her head under his shoulder. "Well, hello there, sweetheart. Are—" Her gaze roams over the room before falling on me once again with worry. "Are you all right?"

Am I all right? No, I'm not. In fact, I'm the furthest thing from all right after these past few days. "I..." Tears collect again, threatening to fall at the slightest provocation. "Not really."

Compassion wells in her eyes. "What did that son of mine do now?"

These are his parents. That does it. My bruised heart reacts to the genuine concern emanating from these people, and the tears I tried so valiantly to hold back burst free as I choke out, "He...he abducted me and—" A sob claws its way from my throat.

The man and woman glance at each other before she speaks. "Oh. Let me in, Mitchell. Come here, sweet thing." Soft arms wrap around me in a motherly embrace and press my cheek against a cotton-covered shoulder. "Everything will be all right now, I promise. It'll get easier; you'll see. You just go ahead and let yourself have a good cry."

Her words liberate the torrent of hurt in me and the weight I've dragged around from childhood—the burden that steadily grew heavier with each passing year—washes away with the cathartic release that can only be found in a mother's arms. I soak in the silent strength this unknown woman freely offers me as the tears from my shuddering sobs saturate her shirt.

"There, there." A massive hand awkwardly pats my head as Amos's dad tries to comfort me, too. Surrounded in an embrace by a mother and father figure I never had, I cry even harder.

When my eyes stop leaking and my sobs become the occasional, quiet hiccup, I raise my head, surreptitiously looking for something to wipe my face with. *Oh, no.* I left a mess on her shoulder. A handkerchief presses into my hand, along with a gruff, "Here. Take this."

"Mitchell," Amos's mom scolds as she snatches it away, "you and your handkerchiefs. Don't give her that dirty thing; it's been in your pocket forever. She probably wants to wash her face. Go on, sweet thing. You wash up and we'll be right here when you come out."

My steps are unsteady as I walk to the bathroom and wet a washcloth, taking in my appearance in the mirror. Except for making the green in my eyes exceptionally vivid, crying does *not* do me any favors, that's for sure. I rest the refreshing coolness against my swollen eyelids before scrubbing the salty tear trails away.

I need to decide what I'm going to do. My abductor's parents are out there waiting for me. To be honest, I really just want to take a nap. Forgetting everything else, today has been extremely eventful. Monumental things, beginning with the way he woke me up this morning to our argument and every-thing in between, and it's a lot to take in.

Emotionally exhausted, that's what I am. Too exhausted to think clearly. But I know I don't want to stay here waiting for Amos to come back. And even if I had transportation, I don't want to travel four hours back to Providence Falls. When he took me, I only had a little bit of food left in my pantry.

No, I can't go back. I'd have to go to town to get food and risk running into someone who might start asking questions. I simply can't deal with that anytime soon. He still has my wallet, so I have no money or identification to get a hotel room, either.

Hushed voices filter through the door. Maybe his parents would be kind enough to loan me some money, but I don't know if I can get up the nerve to ask them. I can't hide in here forever, though, so I take a deep breath and walk out.

"—if she called the police?"

I couldn't do that to Amos. No matter how mad I am at him. I need to tell them. "No, I didn't."

At my interruption, their conversation halts and we all stare at each other. *Should I have?* My stomach is the first to break the ice, letting loose a growling sound so loud that redness creeps up my face.

"Well," his mother gently laughs. "First things first—let's get you something to eat."

History repeats itself as I let his mother lead me down the hallway to the kitchen. It seems all the Shays are determined to feed me before answering any of my questions.

"What's your name, dear?"

"Mercy. Mercy Callahan."

"That's a lovely name. I'm Corina and my husband is Mitchell. I'm sorry that we're meeting under such circumstances, but I can't say that we're surprised."

How could they not be surprised? I'm thoroughly confused now.

*A*lmost home.

Country roads aren't usually known for their smoothness, but the bumps on these go the extra mile. My lips twist in a grin. I'm surprised they didn't jostle Mercy awake when I brought her here.

I throw out a hand to steady the peace offerings—a milk-shake *and* a malt—in the cardboard cupholder so they don't spill on my leather seats. Even a diabetic can have sweets every once in a while, right? They're still cold and only melting a little bit, so I'll take whichever one she doesn't want.

Unless she chooses both. A grin tugs at my face when I think of my woman's appetite. I hope she ate something while I was out. Don't want her going hungry.

My Mercy.

As quickly as it grew, my grin falters as I remember the words she spat at me.

Do you even remember what happens to the female companion the monster begs his creator to make for him? She gets destroyed. Destroyed by the scientist, just like you're doing to me.

We both need to move on from this and chalk it up to a

learning experience. Relationships aren't always perfect, and this is a prime example that sometimes a little space away from each other is just the thing to bring things back into balance. I've practically kept her under my armpit the entire time she's been here and doing so made us both lash out in ways we wouldn't normally.

Turning down my long driveway, I decide that I'll take her out for dinner tonight. Woo her the right way. Yeah, that's exactly what I'll do, and let her pick a dress from what I bought for her. Then we'll eat a nice dinner and come back home to cuddle in bed.

Cold, sticky ice cream gets all over my hand when I jump out of the truck and grab the cupholder. Wiping it off on my jeans, I take the porch steps two at a time, so beyond ready to see my kitten. Hopefully she's calmed down a little now. With a quick press of my finger to the reader, the door unlocks. "Mercy? I'm home."

At the answering silence, I place the cupholder on the entryway table and glance around. Where is she? Could be she just didn't hear me. "Kitten? Where are you? I brought something for you."

Nothing. Maybe she's in the bathroom. I step lightly down the hallway to our room. I'm a little relieved to see the door shut. If she's in the bathroom, she may have closed the door by habit. I'll just let her know I'm here.

I poke my head in. "Mer—" *What? No... No.* My throat closes up at what I see. The bed is in disarray, the room a total wreck. Did someone break in and hurt my sweet Mercy? "Mercy! Where are you, baby?"

Is there any blood? It pains me to look, but I have to be sure.

No. No blood that I can see. Only slightly less worried, I search the reading room and kitchen. No Mercy.

I don't think she'd be upstairs in the empty rooms, but I

climb the stairs just in case, a niggling suspicion beginning to eat at me in a way I don't like very much.

"Kitten?" She's not upstairs.

Once I've covered every square inch, I go back to the bedroom and stare at the wreckage. Numb with disbelief, I finally admit to myself what I didn't want to believe before, the words resonating in the empty room. "Mercy *ran* from me. She swore she wouldn't, but she did."

But she couldn't have gotten far. If she somehow left right after I did, then she only has a head start of about an hour or so. Still too much of one considering the danger of the forest. I need to find her before she gets hurt.

Ring! My cell phone makes me jump. Surely it's not Mercy. She doesn't have my number. And what would she even be calling from? Not from *her* phone—I have her SIM card in the truck. I reach to my hip to answer it, but it's not there. A curse leaves me. Must have forgotten to take it when I left.

There's so much mess on the floor, it takes forever to find it. "My phone. Where's my phone? There you are, you little devil." Under some lingerie I'd bought for her.

Dad. I can't talk to him right now. Mercy's more important than anything. I silence his call and holster my phone.

The noise immediately starts up again. With another growled curse, I answer with a clipped tone. "Now's not a good time, Dad. I... I lost something and need to look for it."

A pause. "You know, Amos, the strangest thing happened to me just a little bit ago. Mom and I were in town and decided to drop off some jellies she canned for you."

No. It hits me like a bolt of lightning, making me groan inside. Dad has keys and access to the security system since he was helping to build out the house. Never thought he would show up after it was finished without a heads-up. No... I didn't want him and Mom to know yet. Not until Mercy was ready.

"This *thing* you lost," he goes on, "wouldn't happen to be a real pretty lady about 5′5″ with black hair and green eyes, huh? Goes by the name of Mercy?"

Dad has Mercy. That doesn't lessen my concern. "Dad, where are you? Where's Mercy? I need her." Roughly, I clear my throat when my voice threatens to crack. "She's... She's mine. I can't live without her."

His voice softens. "So, that's the way it is, is it? She's your special one?"

"Yeah." He gets it. "Just like you and Mom."

"That's my boy." Fatherly pride fills his voice. "Mom put Mercy in your old room so she could take a quick nap. Poor little thing was crying and starving to death when I found her. Mom and I grabbed some food in town for her since you didn't have anything cooked. You've got to take better care of your woman, Amos. She's a keeper, for sure."

Relief battles with shame. She's safe; she didn't get hurt running through the woods. But Mom and Dad are taking care of Mercy in my place. I should be the one doing that. Part of my question is answered, though—she didn't eat while I was gone. "I know. We...had an argument. Tempers were getting too hot, so I left so we could both calm down. Told her to eat something while I was out."

"That's no excuse, son. Should have made her something to eat before you took off. You never let your woman go hungry when it's in your power to feed her. You hear me, boy?" His tone is like steel.

She probably wouldn't have eaten it, but he's right. I've got to take better care of my sweet Mercy, especially food-wise since she has diabetes, starting now. "I hear you, Dad. I hear you. Though I could have done with a heads-up instead of the heart attack I got when I saw the bedroom. Thanks for that, by the way." Sarcasm laces my words.

"It's no more than you deserve, boy," he barks at me. Then he eases up. "But I'm proud of you. Took you long enough. Your mother and I were getting a little worried we wouldn't get any grandchildren before we died."

Children. Mine and Mercy's. My heart—along with my cock—swells. "Soon, Dad. Soon. You both have plenty of years left before worrying about that. And why do you only give me a hard time about it? Connor's old enough to claim a woman, too." My brother hasn't, though. Thirty-four years old and a veritable Dr. Doolittle with the way animals all gravitate toward him.

"You boys beat all I've ever seen," Dad dryly chuckles, "waiting as long as you have."

"But you know you wouldn't have it any other way." I pause a beat and continue. "Let me clean the house up and then I'll head over to pick her up." I don't want her feeling guilty over the mess she made.

"Now wait a minute. Mom's taken Mercy under her wing and she's not gonna want to let her go just yet. You'd best plan on spending the next week or two at the ranch with us."

I wasn't expecting that. Part of me is happy that my parents seem to love Mercy already—as I knew they would—but I don't want to share her when I've barely had any time with her myself. Unfortunately, what Mom says goes. It didn't take her long to get Dad all wrapped around her little finger once she became his. "All right, then. Does Mercy have anything with her or do I need to bring her some clothes and such?"

"No, she just had a little bag. Wasn't big enough to hold but one set, maybe two."

"I'm gonna get the house back in order and then head on over. Should be there about suppertime, I suppose. Think that'll give Mom enough time with her? That's about as long as I can stay away."

Dad chuckles. "I know the feeling, son. Yeah, by suppertime ought to be plenty long enough. See you in a bit."

When we hang up, I clear all the security push notifications from my phone with a swipe. I can't believe this happened the one and *only* time I left her alone.

I peruse the room again. My kitten sure did a good job of covering every bit of the floor with our clothes. But time passes quickly as I hang the clothes up, put socks and underwear back in the drawers, and make the bed.

Since we're going to be at the ranch, I pack some comfortable jeans and tees for Mercy. Boots. She'll need boots, too. Her medicine. Toiletries and tampons, for sure. Picking up her stuffed rabbit, I debate whether or not to bring it. It's old and worn with mismatched eyes. Fur matted a little in some spots and missing completely in others. Why does this mean so much to her?

In the end, I gently place it on the bed. If she wants it, she's going to have to come back home to get it. And if she needs hugs while we're at my parents, I'll be the one to give them to her. Not a stuffed animal.

With everything she and I could need for two weeks loaded into the truck, I start the forty-five-minute drive to reunite with my Mercy. Eighties rock blasts from my speakers as the trees whiz by in a blur. Long winding roads dip and rise to meet the sky. It really is beautiful country out here.

Refreshing and tranquil.

Unlike the gentle interrogation my sweet Mercy is likely undergoing from my mother if she's awake yet. But if anyone can pull any information out of her, it's Corina Shay. And she does it in a way that you don't even realize how much you've told her until it's too late.

I speak from experience. Mom always knew when I was telling lies. Sometimes because I'd painted myself into a corner and had no way out but the truth, but most times my confession spilled out of my mouth uncontrollably as soon as she gave me *The Look*.

Over the next rise in the road, the black iron gates to my

parents' ranch come into view, the sight familiar and welcoming. The bones of the house have stayed the same, but the inside was completely redone and modernized about seven years ago. Bedrooms were expanded and given bathrooms and the living room nearly tripled in size. I can only hope Mercy grows to love it here as much as I do.

Dad lazily pushes himself off of the porch swing and meets me at the truck, a knowing smile on his face. "She's still sleeping, but go on inside and see your Mercy. I can tell it's eating at you. I'll bring everything in and put it by the door in a bit."

"Thanks, Dad. Appreciate it." With a quick shoulder clap, I toss him the truck keys and ease inside. Quietly closing the door so it doesn't slam, I—

Whack!

I whirl around to see my mom glaring at me and tapping her foot angrily. Gingerly rubbing my shoulder from where I just got smacked, I give her a little pout. "What'd you do that for, Momma?" Calling her what I did as a boy usually softens her up. Doesn't work this time.

The Look settles over her face. "Amos Mitchell Shay..."

Ducking my head, I feel a little sheepish. A man's never too old to be reprimanded by his mother. I bend down and press a kiss to her soft cheek. "Now, Mo—"

"Don't you *Momma* me. That poor girl's been crying and heaven only knows what you've done to her."

I pick her up and swing her around in a hug as she reluctantly laughs and slaps at my back. Taking the hint, I stand still, her feet hovering as I hold her off the ground. "I love you, Momma," I murmur against her hairline. "Do you still love me?"

Exasperated, she leans back and cups my face. "You know I do. But you've got to be gentle with her—so gentle. She's such a sweet woman with fragile emotions, and if you've steamrolled her like your father did me, you may be doing more harm than good."

"I swear I've been as gentle as I can with her." Mom doesn't understand just how patient I've already been. And she's not going to know the details because that's between me and Mercy. "Supper gonna be ready soon? I'm gonna go wake her up so she doesn't get grumpy from sleeping too much."

"Amos..." she warns. "If you weren't my son and I didn't know you Shay men do these things with the oddly twisted but sweetest of intentions, you'd better believe I'd have sent her back to her home whether you liked it or not."

And I'd have taken her again. Because she's mine. "Don't worry, Momma. I'll be sweet, I promise." Another peck to her cheek and I put her down. "Dad told me you stopped for fast food. Don't know if she mentioned it to you or not, but she's diabetic. Can you make something safe for us to eat?"

Dad used to cook for us all the time, but Mom butted him out of the kitchen when the supper menu got too repetitious. *You stick to making breakfast, Mitchell,* she'd said with a raised eyebrow. *A person can eat the same thing only so many times before getting sick of it.*

"Amos, oh son of mine," Mom sighs. "Do you know if it's type one or two?"

Come to think of it... "Not sure."

"How old is she?"

"Thirty-three."

"And a grown woman?"

In all the right places. "Yes," I drawl.

"Then don't you think she's old enough to know what she can and can't eat, no matter which type?"

Her words are like a cold bucket of water to the face. "Of course she is! I just want to take care of her, that's all."

"I know you do, baby, I know you do. But be careful your concern doesn't cross the line and turn into dictating. Besides,

Dad and I have been eating a little lighter lately ourselves, so that won't be a problem."

Uh-oh. "Why?" I demand. "Did the doctor say something at his last checkup?"

"No, but you know he's not one to eat his vegetables, and the doctor just gave him a general warning about making his meals more colorful. I already told him mint chocolate chip ice cream doesn't count."

Relief settles in my chest. "You'll be sure and tell me if anything changes, won't you?" It's not often I reverse the roles and play the parenting card on her. They're still in the prime of their lives at sixty-five and fifty-eight, but it's a jolting feeling to wake up and realize that time stops for no one. Though I know my biological mom's passing was completely unpreventable, it's made me extra wary when it comes to their health. No matter how old a person is, they still need their parents.

"Oh, sweetheart." Mom gently squeezes my shoulders, knowing where my uneasiness stems from. "You've got to realize some things are out of your control and learn to be okay with that. Enjoy life, Amos. We only live once."

I know.

Time is short and life is fleeting.

That's why we've got to make it count and chase after what really matters.

CHAPTER 19

AMOS

*H*ere I am again, leaning against the doorframe and watching my Mercy escape from her emotions by sleeping. My heart twists at knowing I'm the source of her distress, but it's not easy for me, either. When a Shay loves a woman, he loves *hard*.

Pulling my boots off on the way to the bed, I climb in, gently dragging her into my arms. I'll wake her in a minute, but first I need to hold her again and know she's mine. Reaching to brush the hair away from her face so I can see her better, I almost wish I hadn't.

Her eyes are swollen from crying. From tears I caused. Things could have gone so differently today, and if she'd been hurt while running away through the woods, I'd never have forgiven myself.

Her body's safe and sound, though. It's her emotions that have been wounded.

By me.

Reverently, I press apologetic kisses to her forehead. "I'm sorry, Mercy," I whisper against the soft skin between her eyebrows. "I didn't mean to make you cry. Not when you were just starting to give us a chance."

Time slows down as I soak in the warmth and softness of her body and softly beg her forgiveness. A sleepy sigh hits my chin as she stirs, eyes opening in blurred confusion until they focus on me.

"Hello, kitten. Miss me?" My lips tug apart in a sideways smile. "I brought you back a milkshake. Malt, too."

Mercy doesn't say a word, just stares at me with those deep green eyes I could get lost in forever. After a few seconds of silence, her finger reaches up to trace around one of my shirt buttons.

"What flavor?"

"Vanilla and chocolate. They're melted now." I move her hand to my mouth and kiss those fingers, needing her to find comfort from me and not my clothes. "I'm sorry, baby. Sorry for not trusting you more, especially with everything I've been asking from you. Can you forgive me?"

The mattress dips as she pulls away and sits up. "What if I said no?"

"It would devastate me." No lie.

"What if...what if I said I wanted to go home?"

Dread forms a knot in my stomach and travels up to stick in my throat. But I'm not going to lie to her. I could never do that. "I don't think you'd like what my answer would be."

Resolution narrows her eyes. "What if I said I didn't care what you think?"

Kitten grew claws. "I—"

"Amos, what I'm struggling to wrap my mind around is *why*. Why did you take me like this?"

"I already told you the first time you asked. You're mine."

"That's not good enough—I need to know more. Why didn't you ask me out like a normal man? Why go to this extreme?"

History lesson time. I need to sit up for this, too. "I'm my father's son, Mercy. A Shay. And it's in our blood to hunt and capture our women."

"Hunt and capture? What the—how many women have you done this to? Or am I the only special one?"

"You're more special than you know." I grip her chin to kiss her, but she jerks away. My eyes narrow.

"Don't sweet talk me. I want to know, and I want to know *now*. It's probably no surprise that I don't deal well with conflict, but I can't keep going on like this, Amos."

My hand falls back to the bed. "All right. Every Shay male does this and has for centuries. My father, my uncles, my grandfather...as far back as I can remember. You're the only one I've taken." *The only one I ever will.* "It's likely they didn't teach this when you were in school, or maybe just glossed over it, but have you ever heard of the Romans and the Sabine women?"

Concentration furrows her brow. "Wasn't there a musical based on it...something about seven brothers in the mountains or something like that?"

Good. She knows a little, so it won't be that far of a stretch. "Sure was. Made in the fifties. The actual event had a bit more to it than what happened in the movie, though, and inspired our patriarch to follow in its footsteps to keep the Shay blood-line alive in the world. *Find a woman, keep a woman.* That's what we've always done, generation after generation. But we'd never hurt a woman. Might love her sooner than she wants, but never would we hurt one."

"And so you do like you did with me? Just pick one and kidnap her?"

"Oh, Mercy." Cautiously, I reach for a lock of her hair, elated when she accepts my touch. "That's not what happened with you. You're worth much more than that. So much more. From the very first time I saw you, you called to something deep inside me. One look at you and I could see our entire future together. You and me together with a little girl that takes after her momma and a little boy the spitting image of me. At least two babies, maybe more. Hopefully more."

A wince tightens her features at the mention of kids again.

That's it. I've got to know what that look's all about. "You've made that face too many times now. Tell me what's on your mind, baby. You don't want to make a family, or you just don't want one with me?" I don't know which answer to hope for because I don't like the thought of either of them.

Drawing her knees to her chest, she rests her head there for a moment, gathering strength. "Do you..." she starts before pausing. "Tell me the truth, Amos. Do you want me for who I am as a woman or are you looking for a broodmare so you can fulfill some kind of kink?"

I can't answer that with her tucked away in a fortress of her own making. "Come here." My hand extends toward her. "Let me hold you and I'll tell you."

"Amos," she sighs.

"Please?"

Giving in, she crawls onto my lap. I wrap her around me and hug her, caressing up and down the length of her spine. A finger pokes my side, making me flinch. "Don't think you're getting out of answering me just because I did what you said."

Hiding a smile in her hair, I hold her tighter and breathe in her scent. I love soft and submissive Mercy but I'm loving this feistier side of her, too. "You're no broodmare. I've waited all my life for *you*, Mercy. And it seems you've been waiting for me, too. And you may not believe me, but I love you." I need her to see me and know that I mean every word. A quick tilt of her chin and our eyes lock like a pair of magnets. "Not just because I want to make babies with you, but because I look at you and think, *Damn, I want to grow old with this woman. I want sunrises and sunsets with you. Every single damn one of them."

She sniffs and dips her head down, but I lift it back up and kiss away the wetness trailing down her cheeks toward her trembling lips. I've made her cry again, but I think these are good tears. "Life is short, kitten. Too damn short. And if you don't reach out and grab it by the balls to make it slow down, it's gonna pass you up and be over before you even know it's happened. And I don't want you spending the rest of your life alone. Not when we can do it together. Not when we can make a family."

Sorrow flashes in her eyes for a brief second before they clench shut, her mouth gaping in a silent cry that precedes the most despairing and guttural sound I've ever heard from a human being. With a *thunk*, her head falls against my chest, fingernails gouging my back as she fists my shirt.

These aren't good tears.

Panicking, I pull back to see her face, but she constricts around me like a snake, her gulping sobs breaking my heart. "Baby, what's wrong? Was...was it something I said?" I replay my words in my mind as her tears drench my shirt. Love. Babies. Sunrises and sunsets. Family.

Family.

I want a family more than anything, she'd said.

Because she's an orphan and deprived of love as a child? The beating of my heart picks up. "Oh, Mercy...I'll give it all to you. All the babies. The biggest family you want, that's what we'll have."

"*Stop.*" Mixed in with her tears, the word is too soft and I don't hear it.

"We'll add on however many rooms we need to. My family'll help out, too, because all of us Shays love kids. Connor can build a rocking chair—"

"*Amos. Stop it.*"

"—and my dad'll make a crib—"

"Stop it! Do you hear me?" Her watery eyes meet mine, filled with pain as she croaks the words in raspy anguish. "No more. I can't—my heart can't take it. Just stop."

"Tell me what's wrong, Mercy. Please." Reaching for the tissues on the nightstand, I tenderly wipe the mess on her face. "I can't fix it if I don't know where to start, baby."

Pitiful sniffs flare her red-tipped nose. "It's not something you can fix, Amos. I"—her gaze falls to my throat—"I don't know if I can have kids. Ever."

Stunned, I try to process what my ears just heard. "Mercy, what..."

"I have PCOS. Polycystic ovary syndrome. My body doesn't like to let my ovaries work like they should, and...and..."

She needs to catch her breath. "Breathe, Mercy. With me. In and out...there you go."

Shuddering inhales slowly smooth out. "I only have one fallopian tube, too. And yeah, there's a possibility that I can ovulate from the opposite ovary and have the egg travel to the other side, but it's small—so small—for it to happen correctly. And the older I get, the more I worry about it happening at all. I'm thirty-three, Amos." Her fist punches the bed in frustration. "Thirty-three and about to be a thirty-four-year-old virgin! Some women struggle for years, and they've all got a head start on me. Even with medicine to help regulate my periods, it still isn't completely effective."

She's throwing all this information at me—and I hear her, I really do—but my attention locks onto that word. *Medicine.* "That's what your pills are for? You don't have diabetes?"

A weak laugh leaves her. "Is that what you thought it was for? My *condition*, as you called it?"

"Yep. I looked up the name on the pill bottle." I see something else now. How my talk about making babies and a family with her must have been like a knife to the heart all this time. "Mercy, I want you to listen to me and listen to me good—I love you for who you are. Not for what your body can or can't do for me. Come here, kitten."

Turning her sideways in my lap, I lean against the headboard and tuck her head to my chest, loving the way she curls into me. "Families can be built any way they need to be, by blood or by choice. That's what my dad did with ours. I don't remember much about my birth mother because she died when I was one, but when I was six, Dad brought me a mother. Married her right before he picked me up from my uncle's and introduced me to her."

"You mean your dad and...and Corina?"

If her eyes get any wider, they'll pop out of their sockets. "He did. You ought to ask her after we eat. In fact, food's probably almost ready. Do you feel like going out there with me?"

"Oh, Amos." Alarm stiffens her muscles. "I can't go looking like this, and my head is killing me. Would your...Corina think me rude if I asked for a little snack or something to eat in here? I don't want to impose."

"You can call her my mom, baby, because that's what she is. And absolutely not. I'll bring us both back a plate. You just stay right here and I'll be right back."

She worries her bottom lip with her teeth. "I don't want them to think badly of me."

"Hey." My finger reaches out to her mouth. "This is my lip to bite." And then I prove it with a gentle nip. "Sit tight."

After moving our things that Dad placed beside the door into the room, I let the smells of supper lead me down the hallway and to the kitchen. "Mmm. Something smells good."

Mom dries her hands on a kitchen towel. "Lemon chicken, zucchini noodles, and roasted green beans. How's Mercy?"

Wearily rubbing the back of my head, I know I need to appease some of her curiosity, but Mercy trusted me with her heavy secret and it's not my place to mention it to anyone else. "I think everything's going to be okay, but she's got a terrible headache and doesn't feel up to socializing right now. We'll eat in my room and visit with you and Dad in the morning."

Her hand grabs my forearm like a vise. Mom means business. "Do you swear, Amos? You didn't break her heart more just now?"

"I swear. We both have a better understanding of each other and things can only get better from here. But she could sure use a mother. The fostering system didn't do her any favors, that's for sure."

Compassion darkens her eyes. "Her parents died? Oh, the poor thing. If there's anything I know how to do, it's mothering lonely souls."

I can't help the smile that sneaks up. "You sure do. And I love you for it. Especially since I know you love me more than Connor."

"You—" Mom scowls in amusement. "Both of my boys hold a special place in my heart. An *equal* place. And now Mercy does, too."

"Thank you, Momma. Supper ready?"

"Just pulled the last thing out of the oven, actually."

"Perfect. Can you grab some bottles of water for us while I fix our plates?"

"Of course. Does she need anything for her headache?"

I nod. The only medicine I brought was her prescription.

"And you be sure to run cool water on a washcloth and rest it on her eyes after she eats. That'll help with her swollen eyes."

"I will," I promise. "If you stick the bottles in my back pockets, I think I'll be able to hold the plates."

"Oh, I'll get you a tray so you can carry it all."

Even better. All loaded up, I head for the hallway.

"Wait—here's for her head." Mom stuffs a little bottle of pills in my shirt's front pocket. "You be sure and give her a hug from me and tell her not to worry about a thing."

"Thanks, Mom." Back to the room I go. Carefully balancing our food, I manage to open the door and deliver the tray to the bed. "Time to eat, kitten."

After passing her a plate and a bottle of water, I dig out her pills. "Here you go." We both must be starving because the food's gone in record time. "Want seconds?"

"Oh," she groans. "I can't eat another bite."

"Not even half of one?" I tease. Her puffy eyes narrow at me. "Okay, I hear you. I'm gonna take these to the kitchen. Why don't you get the shower started for us?" At the wary look on her face, I clarify. "Just to bathe, I promise."

Gathering everything, I make a quick trip to the kitchen and deposit it in the sink. When I get back and close the door, I strip my clothes off and join Mercy in the shower. Hair piled on top of her head so it doesn't get wet, her movements are sluggish as she washes herself.

"Can I do anything for you, baby?"

A weary sigh whistles through her lips. "Just...just hold me."

Angling us so the water falls down on her, I hold her so tight against me, letting her take what she needs from me. "Mom told me to hug you and tell you not to worry, but I don't think she meant while we were both naked."

Her drained laugh hits my chest. "I won't tell if you don't. God, I hate that I cried so much today. I'm just an emotional wreck."

"You cry as much as you need to. I'll always be here to hold you until the tears stop. And then I'll hold you some more, just for good measure."

CHAPTER 20

MERCY

$\mathcal{A}$ cat named Mouse is sleeping on my lap while Amos and I wait for breakfast. Oh, the irony, but her gray coloring suits her name.

That's not where the irony ends, though.

The man I'm watching whisk egg whites is a kidnapper, and the woman he took and married is buttering toast beside him. She looks happy and healthy. In love, even. Focused on his task, Mitchell still glances to the side every so often to throw a doting look down at her. When their eyes catch, gradual, knowing smiles that speak of years of intimacy spread across their faces. "Come here, woman. You can't be flirting with me like that and not giving me a kiss."

Feeling like a voyeur, I avert my eyes when their lips meet, the weight of Amos's hand on mine and the raw pureness of the moment too much to bear. Is their love real? I suppose it's altogether possible considering the way I'm falling for Amos despite our less than auspicious start. I'm beginning to believe over the top is the only way these Shays go after their women.

Normal is overrated, apparently.

Mitchell adds in cheese, chives, and seasoning before

scooping the stiffened egg whites onto a baking sheet and sticking them in the oven. "Almost done. Sweetness, you go sit with the kids. I've got everything under control here." With a pat on her butt, he sends her our way.

"Hey," Amos protests. "Keep it rated PG in front of the kids."

Kids. I smother a laugh. Even at our ages, that's what Amos and I are to his parents. He was so sweet to me last night after my breakdown. My well-deserved *and* overdue breakdown. But I'm feeling much better this morning now that my eyes aren't puffy croissants and I can breathe from both sides of my nose. Crying and sleeping away my stress maybe isn't the healthiest way to deal with things, but emotions can't be trusted to make the best of decisions.

A kiss to my fingers breaks me out of my internal monologue. "Ready to eat, baby?"

I look down at the food he places in front of me. Wheat toast, baked eggs that look like clouds, and—*grimace*—vibrant raspberries. Fruit. I hate it. My mouth already waters in a bad way at the thought of the pungent taste and the fine little hairs —a shudder involuntarily leaves me. I can't be rude, though. I'm going to have to choke these down somehow.

But first, I redirect as I gently move Mouse to the floor. "I've never seen eggs done quite this way, Mr. Shay." And I haven't. He put them in the oven again after dropping the egg yolk on top of the pillowy mixture that had firmed up. Luckily, the yolk isn't runny when I cut into it and chance a bite.

"Call me Mitchell. We don't stand much on ceremony around here." *They don't stand much on legality, either.* "As soon as I saw this recipe, I knew I had to try it the next time Amos was over. I know it's not melting behind the cloud, son, but I promise it tastes just as good."

Behind the cloud? Puzzled, I hazard a look toward Amos, but...are his ears turning red?

"Dad," he groans.

Now I'm truly confused. Corina takes pity on me and explains. "When Amos was just a little boy, he loved his eggs over easy. But he never could remember to call it that, so he always told Mitchell he wanted the sun to melt behind the cloud."

Ohh. Is that why he looked at me so funny and wanted to make sure I liked the eggs he cooked the other day? I see how a child would liken the whiteness to a cloud and the liquid yolk to a *melting* sun. The adorable image of a young and innocent Amos makes warm fuzzies tingle and sprout in my heart. That's actually way too cute, especially since he still likes them that way and it makes him blush.

"Mom? Dad?" A deep voice sounds from the front of the house.

"In the kitchen, Connor," Mitchell calls out right before an unsmiling man appears in the doorway.

Good Lord, is this another Shay? And why do they all have to be drop dead gorgeous? And muscular. Ohmigod.

Probably a few inches shorter than Amos, this Connor has massive shoulders. Thick pecs and biceps that wear his skin-tight shirt instead of the other way around. If he were Amos's height, they'd look the same body-wise, I think. But that's where the similarities end. Black tattoos snake up his forearms, disappear under the sleeves of his shirt, and reappear to circle his massive neck. A shaved head and eyes so dark they seem black add a menacing air as he moves closer.

"Did Mouse have babies? Toto found this when he jumped out of the truck." His huge hand unfurls to reveal a tiny black kitten that immediately squeaks out little mews. "Shh, Little Bit. Daddy's got you."

My fork drops to my plate with a clank as I choke on my bite and watch in disbelief as he cradles the little fluff of fur to his neck. *Daddy?* That's...insanely sweet. And hot. This slightly scary man can be brought to his knees by a kitten that weighs less than one pound. That makes him slightly less scary, but not by much.

The screech of my chair sounds in the room as Amos drags me closer and kisses my neck while rubbing my back. "You okay, Mercy?"

Someone feeling a little territorial?

"No, Mouse was spayed a few months ago, remember? Too many babies and not enough good people wanting to take care of them." Corina gestures my way, catching me as I awkwardly wipe my mouth with a napkin. "Connor, this is Mercy. She's here with your brother."

Having his focus completely on me is intimidating in a way unlike Amos. With lips tugged apart in a polite smile, he nods at me. "Mercy."

"H-hello." Needing to lessen the intensity of his gaze, I drop mine to my plate, intending to stuff my mouth so I don't have to talk. Just need to push those nasty pink things around so it looks like I'm eating some. Wait—where'd they go?

Amos squeezes my knee and winks at me, lowering his fork to a plate that now has a suspiciously large helping of raspberries.

That man. I don't have a sun, but something inside me melts a little at that. He remembered I didn't like fruit and sneaked it off for me.

"You stayin' for breakfast, Conman?" Amos throws a claiming arm around my shoulders, thumb lazily brushing little wisps of my hair, and directs a smirk to me. "Mom told me I couldn't call him Convict even though he has all those tats."

"Dick." Connor scowls.

"Connor..."

"Sorry, Momma. No, just dropped by to let you know I'd be going out of town for a few days to deliver some furniture in case you stopped by and I wasn't there."

"You boys." Mitchell shakes his head. "Guess I'm the last of the farming Shays on this side of the family. Glad you came out instead of just calling. Been too long since we've seen your face around here."

"I know, I know. I'll try to visit more often, but not today. Toto's not too happy I stuck him back in the truck. Nice to meet you, Mercy. Be sure and add some dye to his shampoo so he can cover up all those grays. See ya, dickface. Sorry, Momma." He kisses Corina's cheek, slaps his dad's shoulder, then drops a still mewling kitten in his shirt pocket that's so tight the helpless creature doesn't even have a chance of escaping. "I'll leave so I don't call him any more names. I'll just be taking little Bagheera with me since I didn't see any sign of his mother or siblings out there."

Aww, the black panther from the movie. Very fitting, and such a cute name.

"You know I'm not gonna call him that, don't you?" Amos taunts his brother.

"Oh, no? Enlighten me, *Amy.*"

Corina sighs and shrugs her shoulders as if to say, *Boys never grow up.*

"Baggy. Ole Baggy Britches."

"No. No, you're mixing them up. Bagheera was *Baggy* and Mowgli was *little britches.*"

"Yeah, but the kid was young like the kitten. So Baggy Britches, it is."

Connor scratches his nose with his middle finger. "Bye, Amy."

"Later, Conway Twitty." Amos returns the gesture.

I can breathe easier with him gone. One Shay man is almost too much. Two is definitely too much, and three? Well, there's no recovering from that.

"Believe it or not, Mercy, they really do love each other."

Amos shovels more raspberries into his mouth. "Of course,

we do, Momma. We just try to keep the love alive by adding a little spark every now and then."

Crunching through my toast, I think about what I just saw. Though they have unique ways and traditions, there's no denying the members of this family love each other. But isn't that what family is supposed to do? Love each other no matter what?

"You done, baby? I'll take your plate so Dad and I can clean the kitchen." Lips touch my forehead in a sweet kiss. "Why don't you sit with Mercy on the porch, Momma? It's such a nice day."

Shooting him an incredulous look, I almost grab for his hand and beg him to come with me as a buffer. I feel embarrassed for how his parents saw me yesterday and being alone with one of them is the last thing I want. But at the same time, I want to know more about Corina's story. What better time to ask her than when she's away from Mitchell and Amos?

"That's a lovely idea. Come this way, Mercy."

I follow her through the other side of the kitchen and into the living room, the clinking sounds of dishes trailing after us before disappearing as we move away. The house is very tastefully decorated in cool grays and dusky blues, but this room is a bit warmer with its golden mustard accent wall. And even though the vaulted ceiling opens the room up, it still feels cozy. I could definitely see myself taking a nap on that couch.

"Before we go outside, do you mind if I show you something?" Corina stops by a framed collage, softness overtaking her expression. "This is one of my favorite pieces."

Hesitant steps bring me closer. It's full of kid drawings. Stick figures and houses. "Your grandchildren did these?" That's pretty sweet of her to frame all—I do a quick count—ten pictures.

"No, no grandchildren yet." She sounds wistful. "These are all Amos. He drew them when he was six."

Six. I look curiously at her. "Amos said you married his dad when he was six."

"I did. And it all started because of this." She motions to the pictures.

They're old and faded, I can see that now. Blue-lined papers with ragged edges where they were torn from a notebook. "These are cute." But it's a little odd to frame forty-year-old drawings.

"They are, aren't they?" Corina traces the corner of a frame. "Has Amos told you about Allison, his birth mother?"

"He told me she died when he was one."

"That's right. An aneurysm. Long story short, Amos noticed their family was missing a woman. A mother. And he wanted one more than anything. He began externalizing his thoughts by drawing the family he wanted to have. Mitchell told me Amos wanted a momma to love the both of them so neither one of them would be lonely."

I can see him as a little boy. Tanned with a light spattering of freckles, maybe even a tiny gap in his front teeth that look too big for his mouth. Envisioning him drawing his wishes for a mom tugs at my heart and almost brings tears to my eyes. He and I are a little alike in that we both wanted someone to love us.

Looking a bit more deeply at the drawings, I see the story in them now. A crying boy with just his dad. A woman reading a book to the boy. A happy, smiling trio standing in front of a house. Three hands nested inside of each other, smallest to biggest. *Amos, Corina, and Mitchell.*

"Shall we go outside for the rest?"

I nod and she leads us outside where we settle in padded rocking chairs that overlook a rock garden. The gentle and monotonous motion of rocking relaxes my racing thoughts, but I'm anxious to hear this.

"So, after realizing just how much Amos wanted a momma,

Mitchell decided he was going to get himself a wife to be a mother to his son, by any means necessary."

Shock runs through me and must show on my face because Corina smiles wryly. "Believe it. It's exactly how it sounds. He drove hours away from here to go looking. Stopped at a little grocery store and saw me when I was babysitting two kids. Followed me to their house and waited for me to go home. Followed me again down a deserted country road and was right behind me when a flat tire forced me off the road."

"Did he..."

"He swears up and down that he didn't do anything to my tire, and I believe him. They were beyond needing to be replaced," she affirms. "I didn't have a spare and he said he'd take me home, so I got in his truck with him. Little did I know he meant *his* home, and then it was too late. Before I knew it, I was married and now the mother to a six-year-old boy."

Now I know shock is all over my face because my jaw hangs open. "No...no way."

Smiling hugely, Corina raises an eyebrow. "Yes. There's just something about these Shay men that makes it impossible to say no."

Tell me about it. "Did you have a family? What about them?" Did Mitchell make her disappear like Amos did to me? *I am my father's son,* he'd said.

"I did. Though he wouldn't let me go home, he let me write them once a week and sent the letters off with no return address."

"But how did that work? Surely the postmark gave the location away."

"Not in our case. Mitchell had a trucker buddy who'd drop the letters off at different stops on his route so they never came from the same place twice. The official story was when my tire went flat, my secret boyfriend in town picked me up and convinced me to elope with him and travel the state. A slightly different version of the truth depending on which of us you asked."

Can my mouth fall open any further? *Unbelievable.* But apparently it worked. "Oh my God. That's..."

"Messed up? Without a doubt. But now I have a perfect little family. My husband is head over heels in love with me, even after forty years, and I have two handsome boys."

"What about your parents? Did...did you ever get to see them?"

"Oh, yes, of course. After a year, we visited them and I got to show off my new little family. Dad was suspicious at first, naturally, but Mitchell and Amos just have that certain charm, you know? And when sweet little Amos ran to them and called them Grandma and Grandpa, that was it. They fell in love with him, and how could they not?"

Yes, he does have that way about him. That Shay charm. "Wait—you said your husband was in love with you, but what about you? How can you just be okay with what he did? The laws he broke...*forcing* marriage on you..." I'm not going to ask what else he did, but I can only imagine.

"Oh, Mercy." Corina's small hand covers mine on the arm of the rocking chair. "Love looks different for all people. In my case, it definitely took a while for me to fall for him. It wasn't overnight. And I'd be lying if I said Amos didn't soften me up towards the idea, but Mitchell just had this strangely sweet way of showing me he loved me. If I had it all to do over again, I think I'd still have fallen in love with him just the same. Even knowing the rough start we'd have. You have to understand these Shays think differently from other men. Complete gentlemen in their own minds, though others might disagree, and rightfully so. But everything they do is with the intention of giving all of themselves to the woman they love, wanting all of her in return."

She pulls her hand back before gently asking me a question. "But that's what I know and believe to be true. How do *you* feel about him? Say the word and I'll drive you home myself—Shay tradition be damned."

I can't stop the little laugh that breaks free. If there's anyone who would understand my conflicted feelings, it's this woman. And it sounds like she doesn't know that I live—*lived*—in Amos's rent house. I can't go home. Not that I really want to, anyway.

Not now.

"I...I think I could grow to love him very much, even with what he's done. Not with him smothering me like he has, though. Not wanting to let me leave the house, taking away my cell phone. Basically rewriting my entire existence. But...but I haven't really had much experience with relationships. My"—I trace little triangles on the arm of the chair—"parents died in a car crash when I was a toddler, and I've lived a lonely life ever since. How do I know I'm not just using him to get safety and security? That's just as wrong as what he's done to me. In a different sort of way," I hastily add.

"That's something you're going to have to answer yourself, Mercy. I can say without a doubt, though, that if you let Amos love you—completely love you—you won't regret it. You'll never find a man who'd cherish you more fiercely."

The sliding door eases open and Mitchell walks though, followed by Amos. "And what are you lovely ladies talking about?" As if second nature, both of them pick us up and take our places in the rocking chairs with us on their laps.

"How utterly stubborn men are." Corina tucks her head under her husband's chin.

They *do* look cute together.

"Stubborn?" Mitchell growls. "I'll show you stubborn."

"Dad, don't say it. Don't—"

"Time for a nap, woman." He tosses a shrieking Corina over

his shoulder and strides toward the door. "You kids behave out here and keep the noise down. Old people need extra sleep."

Oh, my. Are they going to do what I think they're going to do? Darting a quick glance at Amos's shaking head confirms it.

"He said it. Parents," he offers up ruefully before turning serious. "How are you, baby? Have a good talk?"

Squirming on his lap, I gather my fortitude and grab his cheeks. "If you want this to work between us, you're going to have to trust me. And I mean *really* trust me. I want my car. I want my phone. I want *my* clothes. I want to be able to go to town for food if I feel like it. If you can't give me that much, Amos, then you'll never have all of me. And don't you want all of me?"

Heat simmers in his eyes as his lids narrow. "You'd better believe I want all of you. All right, Mercy. You can have your things back, but only if you keep them at my house. *Our* house."

Compromise, but Shay style. As usual. "Deal."

Heat turns to outright flames of fire when his finger tilts my chin up. "It's not finalized until we seal it with a kiss."

When his lips meet mine, it's more than lust.

More than desire.

It's a new beginning.

CHAPTER 21

AMOS

The sunlight streaming through the trees flashes mesmerizing patterns as the lines on the road pass in a blur and lull us into a comfortable silence. We stayed a week and a half with my parents, the days spent watching sunrises and sunsets, holding hands, and stealing kisses when heads were turned.

Well, that's what my mom and dad did. Mercy and I did the same, but maybe just a bit more. Like some heavy petting against the barn door. And maybe even some grinding, but nothing further.

Now, after a final lunch with them, it's time for us to go home. I'd sent a text to my cousins asking for help in getting her things and car delivered to our house because I'm nothing if not a man of my word. She can have her car and she can have her phone, but not before I enable tracking on both of them. I love her and want her to be happy, but I want her to be safe even more.

And there will be no Mercy for me to keep happy if she isn't safe.

"You okay, kitten?" I can't stop myself from bringing her soft hand to my mouth for a kiss.

"Yeah." The light squeeze she gives my arm sends a jolt of electricity to my cock. These past few days have been a torment, not being able to touch her like I wanted, but the happiness glowing from her as she was completely taken in and loved by my parents made it all worth it. "I love Mitchell and Corina. They're pretty awesome. And your brother really seems to like animals."

"My parents are the best. And animals love Connor more than he loves them, believe it or not. Toto, his dog, is a huge German Shepherd and the biggest baby you've ever seen. Gets his feelings hurt if Connor goes on his delivery trips without him."

A yawn cracks her mouth.

"Sleepy?"

"No, just the sunlight and trees are making my eyes tired."

"Want some music?" With the push of a button, Rod Stewart comes on singing about tonight being the night. How fitting, because something very special *is* taking place tonight. Her period ended a week ago, but there was no way I was going to let our first time be somewhere other than our own bed. And though I held her in my arms each night, all we did was sleep.

But soon we're going to be in our own bed in our own house, and before this night is through Mercy won't be an almost thirty-four-year-old virgin anymore.

Ever so slowly, her head lowers to rest on my shoulder as she hugs my arm to her chest. There's something to be said for the small touches that come by surprise. They can hold more meaning and intimacy than all-out sex, and she's finally giving them to me. It means more to me than she knows. We ride with the music softly wrapping around us and when we get home, I stop her from opening the door. "Hands off, baby. I'll get that for you."

Walking around, I prop an arm up and block her when she moves to get out. As tall as I am, our faces are level, even with her seat being a good distance from the ground.

Puzzlement spreads on her face. "Aren't you going to let me out?"

"Not until you pay the toll."

"What toll?"

"A kiss. A kiss and then I'll let you out."

She nervously smiles, a blush darkening her cheeks and traveling down her throat. "Just one?"

"Just one." *For now.*

"I can't do it with you staring at me. Close your eyes."

Leaning in and doing as she told me, I wait for what feels like forever before I feel the sweet press of her lips.

Against my throat.

That's a surprise I wasn't expecting but greedily accept. Now just need those lips to move up and to mine so I can taste her.

"I'm done, Amos. You can open your eyes."

What?

Narrowing my gaze, I catch her smirk that she can't hide. "Come on, baby." When her hands land on my shoulders, I lift her out and slowly slide her down the length of my body. A quiet gasp tells me she felt more than just my belt buckle on her way down. "Let's go inside."

I lead her up the steps and when we get to the front door, I turn and lean against it. "Guess what, Mercy? You have to pay another toll."

A broken laugh stutters out of her as her eyes catch on everything but me. "Another one? Really, Amos."

"Yes, really." I crook a finger. "Step closer, kitten."

One foot nervously moves forward. Not enough.

"Closer." Another step.

"Closer." When she gets within reach, my fingers snag her pants' pockets and yank her to me. "Hello, kitten. I very much need a real kiss from you."

A slender finger reaches up to ghost over my mouth, making me twitch at the ticklish sensation. "Close your eyes again," she whispers, barely giving me time to blink them closed before her lips graze over mine in the lightest of caresses. When I feel her smiling against me, I almost lose it.

"Woman," I growl. "Kiss me right."

Mercy leans in and brushes her closed mouth over mine again. When my lips part, prepared to take what I want since she's not giving it to me, she surprises me by taking my bottom lip between hers and sucking gently on it.

"Mhmm..." she murmurs thickly, then completely short circuits my senses as her blunt teeth nip me. She moves to my top lip and gives it the same treatment, a suck and a bite, making my cock jerk at each stinging caress.

A glistening single string connects us when she slowly draws back. My dirty mind goes blank, imagining she's pulling off of my cockhead, a silvery strand of cum attached to her pretty lips.

"Good girl. Such a good girl," I rasp as my thumb wipes it away. "I can't wait to see that mouth wrapped around my cock-head, my cum spilling from the corners."

A chuckle rumbles through me as her head almost digs a hole in my chest with how deep she buries into me. But I love it because she's finding in me the protection she needs. "My sweet Mercy. Let's get you added on the security app."

Like a flower blossoming, she peeks up at me. With a few movements of my fingers and hers, she's granted full access. There's a pit in my stomach, though, and the urge to tell her one more time forces my words out. "Don't ever leave me. Please."

"I won't, Amos. I promise."

When my head lowers for another kiss, I remember something. "The bags. Be right back." I jog to the truck and grab our things. "Get the door for me?"

Tucking her lips to hide her smile, Mercy scans her thumb over the reader. I don't plan on her *needing* to open any doors without me, but it's important to show her my trust with this. I head to the bedroom with her close on my steps.

"Oh, I'll put those away, Amos." She jumps in front and blocks me in the hallway. "I...I need to clean up, anyway. From earlier."

My kitten. She doesn't know I already took care of it to spare her from having to do it. "I already did, baby." When embarrassment drops her head, I add, "Don't. There's no shame in what happened, because look where it brought us. Right here to this moment. Now, why don't you open the door for me and sit on the bed while I unpack?"

Dropping our things beside the bed, I take her phone and dig the SIM card from my pocket. Inserting it, I hand it to her. "Probably needs charged. You can use my charger until we get the rest of your stuff here. When you have a full battery, I'll add you to the family feature on it so we can both see where the other is."

Mercy connects it and sits on the bed, legs curled underneath her as she traces a hand over her stuffed rabbit's ear.

"How long have you had that? It seems very important to you."

Her fingers stall. "Yes. My parents died when I was two years old. I was in the car with them when they crashed, and God only knows how I survived when I slid free of my car seat. I was told when the ambulance arrived, the paramedics found me sitting on the side of the road holding this rabbit and sucking my thumb."

A thumb—maybe even the same one—reaches up to wipe away some suspicious wetness. "I either had no other family or no one wanted to claim me, so I was put into state custody. Luckily, I was able to keep my rabbit when I was passed around from home to home. It's the only thing I have from my time with my parents that's truly mine. I...always thought of how I couldn't wait to pass it down to my own children."

I can't stay away any longer. A quick tug and she's flat on her back, breath leaving her as I crawl over her and cage her in my arms. "Mercy, I swear to you that we're going to make a family. We won't let a little thing like biology stop us." Now to clear the heaviness from the air. "We'll start tonight."

Her limbs jolt in surprise. "You mean..."

"That's right, kitten. You got some extra time last week, but tonight you're mine." I nuzzle her cheek. "All mine. So here's what's going to happen. When I finish putting our things away, we're going to the reading room and you're gonna sit on one end of the couch and I'm gonna sit on the other. We're both going to find something to do until it's time for dinner. Then you're gonna pick out whatever you want to wear, get all fancied up, and we're going out to eat. So go ahead and get your nerves all worked out because when we get home, we're going to make love right here"—I angle my knee to graze her sweet spot—"in our bed."

I've never seen her pupils dilate so quickly. "Why did you tell me that? Now I won't be able to think of anything else."

That's easy. "Because I don't want to be the only one waiting with anticipation. I want that pussy so wet for me it runs down your legs while we're eating." I give her more of my weight, taking care not to crush her but needing her focused completely on me. "Want you thinking about my cock sliding in so deep when your legs are wrapped around me. Want you thinking about your fingernails clawing my back so hard I'll wear the marks for days."

She squirms underneath me with a quiet moan, but I swallow it with a hard kiss.

"Tonight, Mercy, we belong to each other."

IT TAKES GREAT SELF-RESTRAINT CONSIDERING IT'S THE FIRST
time we've been truly alone in the past week and a half, but I'm
managing to keep my hands off of her this afternoon.

For two hours now I've held a book, but I wouldn't know if
it's upside down or written in another language because all I
can see is Mercy. My hands may be safely preoccupied, but my
eyes? Those greedy things keep searching over the book and
catching on her. On her toes. Her thighs. Zooming in extra hard
at the vee of her legs, just in case a glimpse of the promised
land is revealed.

She's doing her fair share, too. I see the shy sideways
glances she throws under the guise of peering out the window,
but I know better.

"Is the window behind me your favorite one or is there
something else drawing your attention to it?" I shouldn't tease,
but the blush that floods her face is priceless.

"You...the...the wind keeps blowing and moving the
branches. The noise caught my attention is all." A shoulder
curves nonchalantly in a shrug.

"Hmm." The book in my hands hides my amuse-
ment. Sure it did. It couldn't possibly be happening in any of
the other windows in this room. The same windows that have
the same trees with the same wind blowing in the same
direction. "You want to watch some cartoons or something
else?"

"No, I'm good. All good," she breathes out.

"If you say so." Dipping my head back down, I pretend to
skim the words again, but a heavy sensation tells me to look up.
When I do, I know why.

Her eyes are glued to my crotch. If they stay there much

longer, something else is going to move and catch her attention. Clearing my throat makes her jump guiltily.

That's it.

Firmly closing the book with a snap, I lean over and snatch her crossword puzzle out of her hand. "Whatcha got there, baby? Oh, you haven't been able to solve any of them. This one giving you a hard time?" Innuendo drips from my voice.

Flustered, she lunges for it. Not expecting her sudden movement, I halfway fall on top of her, head landing on her stomach.

Now this is more like it.

No. Slowly back away and wait until tonight.

Back away. Back a—

My nose dips between her legs, inhaling deeply. *Too late.* "Ahh...divine." I nip the side of her thigh through her jeans. With no prompting, her leg falls open, silently begging for more. *She's killing me.*

"Mhmm," she softly whimpers.

"I think," I whisper against her as I come up for air, "an early dinner is just what we need."

CHAPTER 22

AMOS

Wariness sits like a rock in my stomach as I wait for Mercy to come back from the restroom. Surely she wouldn't leave me after the progress we made this past week and a half. I'd tracked her every step across the restaurant with my eyes, barely able to keep my feet anchored to the floor, but trust has to start somewhere. And now that I know how difficult it is to relinquish it, I admire her all the more for how much she's given me.

The relief that fills me as she catches my eye on her way back and smiles just for me waters the small sprout of trust and helps it grow. Rising to let her in, I can't stop my words. "Did I tell you how beautiful you are? No, don't hide from me. Look at me...there you are." A gentle kiss to the corner of her mouth. "And that dress looks gorgeous on you."

Technically, *I* picked it because she chose from what I'd bought for her. But she looks just as lovely in the lacy red skater dress as I knew she would. Paired with her dark tumbling curls and earthy boots, she's absolutely exquisite. And she smells amazing, too. It's the same perfume I sprayed that night in her bedroom.

"Thank you. You...you look nice, too."

Inching closer to her in our private circular booth, one arm wraps around her shoulder while the other reaches for her knee. As soon as my fingers touch bare skin, her own trace small patterns on the tablecloth. I give a gentle squeeze. "Nervous?"

Her shoulders dance with a shiver. "Just a bit."

I believe it. A blush has permanently stained her cheeks since we left for dinner. "Don't be."

"And here we are." Square plates appear in front of us with a flourish. "Medium rare steak with herbed butter sauce, loaded baked potato, and sautéed honey carrots for the gentleman. And same for the lady, but with the steak medium well. Enjoy." Our waiter departs as silently as he came.

Immediately, Mercy straightens her plate so the corners are, well, square. "Why do you do that?" I ask, cutting into my steak.

"Do what?" She's moved on now, making sure her napkin is perfectly folded in her lap.

"What you just did...making sure things are straight. The angles, patterns, all of that."

"Well," she circles a carrot in the honey drizzle, "I suppose it all started as a way to comfort myself as a child. To control what I could because I had no say in what was happening to me. Keeping my surroundings and the things that were mine in a state I created and could change kept me from going crazy and throwing tantrums when life didn't happen like I wanted."

That makes sense. "I noticed the way you kept your desk *just so* at work. The way you couldn't help but to straighten whatever seemed off kilter." I peer sideways at her. "Like a certain picture frame at work."

My arm tingles with the force of her light slap as soft laughter tickles my ears. "What? That—that was you? It drove me crazy that I never could catch whoever was moving it! Amos Shay, you did that every morning?"

"Every single one. My way of making sure you noticed me, even if you didn't know."

"Oh, Amos, I always noticed you. Maybe a bit too much."

Too much? "What do you mean?"

When her fingers move to trace random patterns on the tablecloth, I stop her. "No. Hold my hand and comfort yourself with me, Mercy."

Our fingers thread together, slender mixed with thick. "I have—had?—a crush on you. I'm sure you don't need me to tell you that you're a very handsome man."

A crush. On me. How can I feel love and lust at the same time? I encourage her to continue with a wordless squeeze.

"I was a bit devastated your last day at work because I thought I'd never see you again. Missed opportunities bring such a feeling of emptiness and regret that just weighs heavily on your shoulders. Or it does mine, at least."

"No more missed opportunities for you, kitten, because I won't let them pass you by. You're stuck with me. For good," I tack on, bringing our hands to my mouth. "Now, why don't we finish our food so we can get out of here?"

Mercy's already enlarged pupils dilate further at what I don't say, and she awkwardly stuffs a bit of potato into her mouth.

Tension curls in the booth and settles between us as we finish our dinner in supercharged silence. Nerve endings heighten. Every innocent brush of skin against skin becomes agonizingly sensitized.

Flagging down our waiter, I murmur thickly, "Check, please."

Time blurs as I pay and guide Mercy out of the restaurant into the brightly lit parking lot. When we reach the truck, her hand brushes against the door handle.

"No." I wrap around her back and grab her wrist, a

command lacing my voice as I bring it to rest on her chest. "Give me your other one." Mesmerized, I watch as our joined hands move up and down with the rhythm of her breathing. Lips just grazing her ear, I rumble, "You don't open doors. That's what I'm for. You also don't close doors. Not when I'm with you. And I'm always going to be with you." A stinging nip punctuates my order. "Now, up you go."

Our ride home doesn't do anything to calm me down because she's pressed against me. No bucket seats in this truck. And when she reaches for my hand and puts it on her knee to play with my fingers? I press the gas pedal just a bit harder.

Gravel crunches under the tires as the headlights illuminate our long driveway with their shine. Mercy's breathing picks up the closer we get to the house, and when I kill the engine, her shallow inhales are all I hear as we sit there in the dark. She flinches when my hand reaches for her seat belt and I can't help my low chuckle. "I'm not going to jump you, baby. I'm not an animal."

Not tonight. Tomorrow's another story.

Helping her down, I lead us inside and shut the door, trapping her against it and nuzzling her neck. "Will you dance with me, my lady in red?" Backing away to extend a hand, my heart skips time when her trembling fingers meet mine.

This is it.

No turning back now. Not that she ever had an option, but now her hand is in mine and she's giving herself to me. Satisfaction coursing through me, I pull up a playlist on my phone and cue soft music to play over the home theater system as I draw her to me. Even in heels, the top of her head still only comes to right above my armpit.

Staring into her beautiful green eyes, I wrap her arms around my neck and boldly span my massive hands across her ass, pulling our bodies so close I inhale her gasp of surprise. I can't help but to croon the first lines of the chorus in my deep baritone.

I bury my nose in her hair and breathe her in. "That was a hit song in 1980. 'Into the Night' by Benny Mardones. No matter the decade or the century, there's always been something about a woman that drives a man crazy, makes him long to possess her. Even if he has to bend the rules a little."

A shiver streaks through her as I nip her ear. "It's a tale as old as time. I want to possess you, Mercy. Make you mine in the way a man claims a woman."

She doesn't answer, but it doesn't matter. The sudden wobble in her knees answers for her. I hug her even tighter as we sway back and forth.

For mindless minutes, song after song, I bask in the sensation of feeling her softness contrasting with my hardness. The warmth of her breath as it hits my chest. The tingle in my nipple as Mercy nestles her face against my shirt, brushing against it.

But it's time for more.

Drawing back, I tilt Mercy's chin up so I can look at her. Our eyes silently hold each other, full of unspoken promises. "Come on, my virgin child. Tonight's the night."

"I'm not a child, Amos," she breathes out.

"No, but you are my virgin." Sweeping her up in my arms, I carry her out of the kitchen, the music growing fainter the further down the hall we go. I place her on her feet in our room and kick the door shut behind me, the *snick* of the latch cutting through the thick atmosphere. Mercy turns to face me, nervous as can be.

I prowl towards her, each click of my dress shoes on the hard floor signaling my impending approach. Her eyes meet mine fleetingly, then drop. "Stay in the moment with me."

She audibly swallows and closes her eyes. "Amos," she croaks. "I'm scared."

Going behind her, I hug her and cross my arms around her front to hold her hips. I run my nose from her shoulders to her nape, just breathing her in. "Don't be. It's just you and me. And once we get to the other side of your first time, you're gonna wonder why in the world you ever fought me. I love you, Mercy. Your quirks, your body, your mind...everything that makes you *you*. And I'm going to make you my wife."

The soft fabric around her hips bunches as my hands flex in anticipation. Slowly, I reach along her back to the zipper and pull it down, exposing her tense shoulders. The urge to see her bare almost makes me explode with need. I place my hands on her delicate curves and pull down. Mercy unfreezes, squeezing my wrist with her dainty hand.

"Wait!" she blurts out, still facing away from me. "Can I take a bath first? All I smell and taste is what we ate."

The remnants of dinner faded long ago for me, but I want her to be comfortable. "A bath is just what we need."

"We?" She spins around with wide eyes. "I didn't mean you, too."

"Come on." Sweaty palm in mine, I lead her to the inset garden tub where she stands awkwardly to the side while I run water and add scented oils. Something's on her mind. I can tell by her fidgeting with her unzipped dress. "What are you thinking?"

"I'm thinking I sound like a broken record, but you promise you'll be gentle, right? Because I don't think I can handle anything other than that. And just because I'm thirty-three doesn't mean I'm any less worried about my first time. I'm not a confident woman, Amos. Even if I were *fifty-three*, I'd still be nervous because no matter what I've read or seen, I've never experienced it for myself and you...you're so big that I don't know if it'll fit without hurting me and—"

If she weren't so worried it'd make me laugh. She needs to get out of her head. Stealing her words as I claim her lips, I dominate her mouth, tracing her tongue with mine and force-fully sucking one lip at a time before pulling away.

"Baby," I soothe as I cradle her face and smooth away her worry with my thumbs, "I promise I'll be gentle. I told you I would for your first time. I can't say there won't be any pain because that depends on how tense you are when I'm sliding inside you. Don't overthink things. Just feel and let me show you how I'm gonna love you."

"Okay," she whispers.

With a strategically placed nudge, Mercy's dress falls in a slinky pile at her feet, leaving her in just her bra and panties as she hugs her arms around herself. A breath leaves her as I grab her hair and work it into a messy bun that's not as cute as when she does it but functions just as well.

Shakily pulling off the rest of her clothes, she climbs into the massive tub. Her vulnerability almost triggers my instinct to claim her without regard for her timidity, but I shove it down for later as I undress. Now is the time for easing her nerves and calming her.

The water is hot and soothing as I slide in behind her and pull her resistant body to me. "Lean back so I can hold you. This will probably be the only time I tell you to ignore my cock." Horny thing doesn't understand that it's not time yet, but it doesn't stop it from seeking entrance against her back.

Spiced vanilla scents the air as the oils cling to our skin. Water dripping from my hand, it slides up and around her throat to massage the tension in her neck, forcing a low, quiet moan from her. "That feels so good."

"Anything for you." Smiling faintly, I rub out the knots and move to her shoulders. By the time I make it down her arms and to her hands, she's boneless and limp and the water chilled. "Do you want to brush your teeth, too," I tease, "or can I take you to bed now?"

Her head tilts back on my chest, green eyes unsure. "I do, actually. It's silly, I know, but it'd make me feel better."

I get it. It's her way of asserting what control she has over her situation. "Then that's what we'll do." In a smooth motion, I toe the drain and lift us. I gently dry my sweet Mercy before quickly toweling myself off and tucking it securely around her.

Our eyes can't stay away from each other as we brush our teeth. *You're mine*, I say.

Yes, I'm yours. But be careful with me, comes her reply.

Always, kitten.

Always.

When we're done, I carry her to our bed and lay her down and crawl over her stiff form, slowly easing my weight down and letting the warmth of my skin chase the coolness from her own as our foreheads touch.

"Don't tense up. I'm gonna take such good care of you, baby." My words from earlier echo against her mouth. Brushing sweet, minty kisses on those soft lips, I let her know with my touch that everything's going to be all right. "It's you and me." I drag my teeth along her jawline as I move to her neck.

She gasps before letting out a tiny noise of pleasure.

"Just a man and his woman." I nip the tender skin at the crease of her neck and shoulder and travel back up to her ear. "Wanna know what I'm gonna do next or do you want me to surprise you?" I whisper, loving the way she shivers.

"I...I don't know. It's almost better not to know, but at the same time, I can't stand *not* knowing. If that makes any sense."

"I won't tell you with words, then. Stick out your tongue."

"My tongue? Why?" Mercy's eyes narrow in suspicion. "What are you going to do?"

"Come on, babe," I cajole. "Stick it out."

When she tentatively pokes the very end of it out from between her lips, I swoop down to capture it with my mouth.

"Ahh!" Mercy yelps around my lips as I purse them and lightly suck on the tip before pulling off.

"That was a hint. Do you know what it was?"

Passion simmers on her face. "I'm assuming something to do with...sucking?"

"Good guess. You assume correctly." Keeping eye contact, I use a finger to slowly undo the towel. "Lift up." A swift motion and it's tossed haphazardly to the floor.

There they are. My sweet Mercy's beautiful breasts. With a harsh groan, I bury my face in them. I'll never get tired of rubbing little circles around her nipples and then tweaking the hardened nubs. Never get tired of the sounds she makes when I suck them hard.

Like now.

They're not my target, though. I've spent a lot of time with them, but now it's time to devote my attention to the pearl between her legs. Down her torso I go, decorating her gasping stomach with tiny kisses and easy nibbles until I reach the lady of the evening—her sweet, wet pussy. When I try to spread her legs, they stiffen, resisting me. "Mercy. Open."

She closes her eyes, sucking in a breath. "I'm trying, Amos. I swear, I'm trying. It's just so hard."

I can help with that. My hands run up her thighs, lightly squeezing before forcefully prying them apart.

"Ahh!" my kitten cries as her legs fall apart against her will.

"That's more like it. I'm gonna eat this pussy and there's nothing you can do about it. You're helpless and at my mercy, Mercy. What do you think about that?"

A whimper is all I get in response. That's okay. Neither of us needs to talk for this. I situate myself between her legs, using my nose to separate her wet folds. Her scent is heavy in my nostrils, the scent of a woman in need.

Time to sate that need.

Not bothering to slowly introduce her to the pleasures of

oral sex, I wrap my arms underneath her ass to circle her hips and dive in, licking a firm line from opening to clit.

"Amos!" she squawks, thighs clenching around my head as she tries to squirm away.

How cute. But not a chance.

I growl against her clit and drag her back against my mouth, running closed lips up and down her slit. Turning my head slightly, I grab her labia between my teeth and bite down lightly before adding more force.

"Ah..ah...ahhhh!" Her cries are music to my ears.

I release my bite, moving to the left and up to suck her clit. At the first hint of pressure, Mercy digs her hands into my hair, almost yanking it out by the roots, and yells. Yells her lungs out. Good thing we're out in the middle of nowhere.

"Ohmigod ohmigod ohmigod ohmigod—"

Sounds like I'm doing my job correctly. But we're just getting started. Separating her lower lips, I lick the skin on the left side of her clit. Usually one side is more sensitive than the other. I move to the right. Her legs jolt and her fingers grab on even tighter. *That's the spot.* I spend long seconds there, teasing up and down with the scrapes of my tongue, then go back to her clit and suck it hard into my mouth. I pop off, then grab it again.

Then I repeat. Just like she repeats my name.

"Amos. Ohmigod, AmosAmosAmosAmos..."

She's almost there. Dipping back down, I suck her clit with steady and rhythmic sucks. Releasing a hip, I bring a finger to tease her entrance, and she loses it.

"AMOS!" Mercy screeches as her orgasm rips through her. I don't let up, forcing her to ride it until *I* say she's done. She shrieks and squirms, grabbing my ears and trying to force me off.

I lift long enough to grit out, "You're not going anywhere. Be a good girl and give me more." Tightening my grip on her hips,

I suck, lick, and bite her tender folds until my face is drenched in her desire and her wails turn hoarse from crying out.

With one last long lick, I give her reprieve. She looks freshly claimed, both sets of lips red and swollen, but looks are deceiving. There's more.

Time for that sweet pussy to deep throat my cock.

CHAPTER 23

MERCY

I have no words for what this man has just done to me. *La petite mort.* The little death. This is an orgasmic crime scene. I throw my arm across my face and try to drag air into my lungs. I can't move my legs.

Voluntarily, that is.

They're spasmodically twitching and lewdly showing all the hidden secrets that aren't between us anymore, I'm sure. I can't bring myself to care. All I want is more of what he just gave me. I *need* it.

Amos is right—it was stupid to fight the idea of us together. He just shattered my world and pieced me back together. And the night's not through.

"You still alive, babe?"

This man. "Barely," I gasp out.

"Take a quick breath. We're not done yet." He doesn't give me much time to recover before he squeezes my pussy lips together, forcing my wetness to bubble up. His hands frame my mound, thumbs rubbing circles on the outside of my labia. Suddenly those not so innocent thumbs thrust lightly into me.

"Ooooh..." I let out a long moan. Oh, God. Did I say I

wanted more? I don't know if I can take it. Just having his thumbs in me feels so deliciously amazing. I weakly prop up on my elbows to stare down between my legs, needing to see what he's doing to me.

"You want to see your man claiming your body, baby? Watch these fingers."

I shudder as his thumbs run slow, sweet circles over my clit, then open my mouth on a silent exhale when they thrust with more force than before into my wet cunt.

His thumbs slowly slide back out, swirling in my wetness. With no warning, his wrists rotate and the index and middle fingers of both hands take the place of his thumbs. "Yeah, look at this sweet pussy taking these fingers. She's a hungry kitty."

Now it's a little tighter with a bite of stinging pressure. Four fingers inside me. Not all the way, but more than what's ever been inside me before. Which, other than tampons, has only been two of Amos's fingers. I'm not worried yet, though, because it still feels so good.

Dragging them out of me, he palms my entire pussy and squeezes the lips tightly together. A finger from the other hand traces the tight seam before digging in to tickle my clit where it's hidden, forcing a long moan from me.

Down the seam. Up to tickle my clit.

Again.

And again.

Changing tactics, he releases my pussy and alternates between using his thumbs and other two fingers to tease me, thrusting softly and then deeper, more forcefully. Showing me exactly what he's going to do to me with his cock.

I hope I survive it.

With a sweet kiss to my clit, Amos wipes his hand on the bed and reaches over to the nightstand, taking out a bottle of lube and nothing else.

"No condom?"

Those arctic eyes drill into mine. "No condom. There's never going to be anything between us. If it happens, it happens. If it doesn't, then it doesn't. Simple as that. You hear me, woman?"

My heart drops into my stomach before flying away. Could we really make a baby on our first try? I don't want to get my hopes up, but wouldn't it be a miracle if—

The *snick* of the lube opening draws my attention back to this moment. This is really happening. My breathing picks up as I watch the bottle drizzle liquid over his cock. With firm, sure strokes, he rubs it in, even swiping over his swollen balls. I'm so focused on that huge red cock that I don't even realize the lube is poised over my clit until I feel the chill of it.

I flinch. "That's cold."

"Sorry, baby girl. We need to make sure you're as wet as can be so the friction doesn't hurt you."

I'm glad he's thinking about things like this, because that never occurred to me. He spreads it on and around my pussy, paying close attention to my entrance. When he raises up and scoots closer, I fall back to the pillow and cover my eyes with my hands. I'm such a chicken, I know, but I don't think I can watch this part. At least not this first time.

"Mercy," he drawls. "Open those eyes, kitten. Nothing to be afraid of."

"I can't. I-I can't." *Calm down, Mercy.*

I feel his thighs against the inside of mine, then a smooth warmth lightly rubbing my cunt.

"Just the tip, babe. Just the tip for now." Back and forth he rocks, letting the head lightly pop in and out to get me used to the sensation. "Gonna go a little deeper." The pressure quickly grows more intense as he works himself further into me. Suddenly my heart starts to pound in worry instead of arousal.

"Amos, it's not going to fit," I wail. "Oh, why did I have to get abducted by a man with such a big penis? I'd be happy with a small one. I can't do this, Amos. You're going to split me in two! Get off! Get. Off!" I slap his shoulders and kick my feet against the bed, but then I realize I'm not thinking this through. It will be much worse to have to start again after having gotten this far. Better just to do it. I grab him tightly and tug him back down to me, wrapping my thighs around his waist. "No...never mind— just...just get it over with. Ram it in hard. Now. Just do it."

My nerves are getting the better of me. I'm so shaky. No, the bed is shaky. Why is it shaking? He's not thrusting. I can't take the suspense. Warily, I open my eyes and see Amos's huge shoulders heaving up and down. The big bastard is laughing at me.

"It is *not* funny," I fume. "Just you wait until I get my turn with you and want to stick a carrot up your ass."

"Baby, you're right...it's not funny. I'm sorry. I know you're worried, but I swear it's all going to be okay. I *will* fit. Your body was made to stretch inside." A hard kiss lands on my lips. "And for the record, I'd totally let you stick a carrot up my ass. Because it's you. And as long as you used lube. Maybe. Now, I think we were right about here." He grabs my hands and pulls them over my head. "These stay here for now."

Fingers lightly swirl over my clit before spreading my lips apart. When he gets the tip situated and poised to thrust, his hands slide up my body, up my outstretched arms, to wind his fingers through mine as he lowers down on top of me.

Words can't explain how good that feels. My small hands swallowed in his gigantic ones. The heat of his palms. His fingers separating mine. The weight of him—oh, *God*, the warm *weight* of him—pressing me down into the mattress.

A guttural moan slips out of me as his hips move forward, forcing my clenched cunt to open. It's almost unbearable, this tension. It seems to take forever. I wasn't expecting the almost nauseating feeling as his cock slides into me, though. "A-are you all the way in yet?"

I don't think I can take any more. I'm so full.

"Almost, baby. A little—*mhmm*—more. Like, two inches."

Just how big is this man? I don't remember it being twenty inches! That's what it feels like, at least. "Amos," I pant. "I can't take any more. No...no more. You're gonna get stuck and we'll have to call an ambulance and—"

His mouth moves to my neck. What is he doing? Oh, he's just kissing me. *Yes, please.* I shut up and let my head fall to the side. Then he does a double assault. *Pffft!* His lips suction to my neck and blow a raspberry against me, while his hips use the element of surprise to force those final inches inside my resistant body.

"Ooooooh..." I moan like I'm dying as my tight muscles throb around his cock. I swear I feel my pulse in my clit.

"There," he croons onto the top of my head. Tall guy problems. "Now I'm all the way in. Are you okay?"

That is an excellent question. I wasn't expecting him to do that. "I think so. That was somewhat sneaky of you, wasn't it?"

"It worked, didn't it?" He lightly rocks back and forth to get me used to the motion. "How's this feel?"

To be honest, it stings a bit. Plus I feel so stuffed. So full. Too full. But in a strangely good way. "I don't know yet. Try...try moving some more," I breathe out.

He smoothly drags himself out to the tip. "Good?" he rumbles.

Good. "Keep going. More."

He backs almost completely out of me and then slams forward.

"Oh!" I jolt. That was unexpected. He does it again, and again, and again.

"I have to tell you something," he rasps thickly. "Something important."

"What"—*thrust*—"is it?"

"My...vow to you."

How are we having a conversation while he's doing this to me? "Right now?" *Gasp.*

"God, Mercy. It feels like the"—*grind*—"first time. Like the very first time. Yes, right now. Later"—*pump*—"we'll get married before a judge, but I've got to say this to you now."

"What are yo—married?" He's really bringing out the marriage talk *now?*

Halting all motion, he gazes down at me, breath heavy and cock pulsing deep within my throbbing pussy as his hips and hands pin me down. "I'm telling you that I'm marrying you right here and right now with the words I'm about to speak. This is more than tonight, Mercy. It's forever."

My heart and eyes soften with the emotion he's drawing to the surface. *He means it.* "Oh, Amos. I...I feel it, too."

He leans down and brushes my mouth, making me gasp at the sensation that floods my center as his hips settle. "You are my woman, and I am your man. With this marriage, I lay a claim on you stronger than the heat of the sun or the pull of the moon. I vow to you darkness will never fall without the press of my lips upon yours or your body knowing the comfort of my touch." As if he can't help it, his hips move and he grits out over my yelp, "Though I've captured your body, you've taken my heart. This is what it means to be a Shay."

Before I can process fully what that means, he gives me more of his weight and pumps fiercely into me. A rigid dichotomy from his hands tenderly holding mine.

In. Out.

In. Out.

"More," I moan.

Mouths hovering but not touching, each breath is shared between us. I inhale his essence. He inhales mine. Our bodies slide together, learning the feel of each other. Every time he bottoms out inside me, his groin rubs deliciously against my clit. So deliciously. I may get another orgasm out of this.

"You gonna come one more time for me, kitten?"

He's a mind reader. "I...I think so," I pant between his movements.

"Yeah, you're gonna come for me. Gonna come all over this cock that's splitting this pussy open, getting my wife ready to be bred."

A hand slides down to my clit to rub firm circles. The stimulation, along with his words, tips me over the edge. *Wife. His wife.* I want to be bred by my husband. I want to give him a baby. Never in my life have I felt more feminine than now, with his massive strength surrounding me and manipulating my body at his will. I give in unreservedly to him, opening myself and my heart as an orgasm shoots through me like lightning. There's no escaping the sensations running rampant through me or the emotions that well up and break through the dam of my heart. *I love you. I love you...*

"Ohhhh, Amos...I love you," I gasp brokenly into his mouth. I can't believe I said it, but it's true. Oh, God, it's so true.

At my declaration, his hips falter between thrusts, then pound even harder. "Mercy, my sweet wife...I'm gonna come— love you—so much—" Tensing up and groaning deeply, he gives five slow, forceful thrusts, burrowing his cock as deeply as he can while his cum shoots out. When his muscles relax, he collapses on top of me, dick still swallowed by my pussy.

His gasps ruffle my hair but his weight on top of me is just what I need. Now that everything is over, I feel vulnerable. Even more than when every bit of me was on display. As if I'll crumble and fade away if he doesn't anchor me to the earth.

"I need to clean you."

"No. Not yet." I grab his shoulders and pull him back down to me. "I...just stay like this for a little bit." My voice is thick with the tears trying to escape.

He hears it. Of course he does. "Baby girl, are you okay? Did I hurt you?"

My Amos. "No, it was beautiful. So beautiful. I couldn't have asked for a more perfect first time. But I don't know what's wrong with me."

"I've got you, baby. You're safe with me." Gently, he drags his cock out of me, a rush of fluid leaking from me when he does. He rolls us to our sides, pulling my leg over his thigh and wrapping his arms so tightly around me. We don't talk, content to just stay wrapped up in each other. My need to cry dies out with each passing second.

In the silence, it hits me—this, *this* is what I've always wanted. What I've spent so many lonely nights shedding tears of sorrow over.

I have it now.

A man I love.

A man who loves me.

The foundation of a family.

Pulling Amos closer to me, as close as I can, I hide underneath his neck, just breathing in the scent of him.

Life was meant to be lived like this.

CHAPTER 24

MERCY

3 MONTHS LATER

"*W*ake up, baby. I've got something for you." A finger traces over my lips, making them twitch.

"It better not be dick," I mumble groggily, eyes still closed. "After last night *and* early this morning, I don't see how you can get it up anymore."

Amos's low laughter rumbles as he lightly scratches my back. "You sore? I'll kiss it all better."

No. I give this man an inch, and he'll give me *his* inches. Every. Single. Blessed. One of them. "Don't even think about it."

I may put up a good protest, but I don't really mean it. Three months of absolute bliss and I still can't get enough of him. The man can't get enough of me, either. I swear, he's so insatiable it's a wonder I'm not permanently bow legged from our bedroom activities. Erm...and kitchen activities. And the family room. And the reading room.

Activities in general, I'd be better off saying.

"Come on," he cajoles. "You don't even have to get out of

bed. Don't kick, though...you'll knock it over. Just sit up. I brought you breakfast."

My nose comes awake before the rest of me. *Is that...* "Bacon and"—*sniff*—"potatoes?"

"Close. Hashbrown casserole. Topped off with an iced caramel latte. Happy birthday, baby."

My sweet husband. Well, *husband* as the Shay tradition perceives it. His bright blue eyes lock onto mine when I finally drag them open. "Aww, Amos. That's so sweet." His scruff scratches my palms when I cradle his face. "You spoil me too much even when it's not my birthday. Wildflower bouquets, breakfast in bed, books... But I love it. Thank you, baby."

Sitting up, the sheets fall from my naked body as I pat the spot beside me. "You're not going to make me eat by myself, are you?" After all the love he gives me, it's impossible for me to feel self-conscious about my body anymore. Not now that I know firsthand just how much the sight of any hint of my bare skin turns him on. Especially when it's covered in his cum.

A delicious throb pulses in my center. I love it when Amos shoves his cum back in me, using his fingers as a plug so it can't escape. Or when he collects it on his fingers and traces my nipples and clit with it. Or when he growls out a command for me to open my mouth so he can feed it to me. *Shiver.*

"Of course not. Hold this." A wolfish grin shows his teeth as he smirks and puts the tray on my covered thighs. God, a shirtless Amos with gray sweatpants that hug his bulge is enough to tempt a nun.

Good thing this man is all mine. That includes his unwavering Shay fidelity.

"Guess what?" The mattress dips as he climbs in. "Connor and I will be finished this week with the deck. He's almost done with the arch, too."

"Is he really? Mhmm, this is so delicious. He's so talented," I manage around a mouthful. And not so intimidating once I got to know him a little better. "I love that dining room set he made."

An amused grin crawls over his face. "Don't you remember what that means?"

What *what* means? My gaze must be as blank as my fuzzy head feels. "Cut me some slack. I'm still half asleep!"

"Remember what we're building the deck for?"

Our wedding ceremony. We could have held it on the porch because it's definitely big enough for the small handful of people we're planning for, but we both wanted it to happen overlooking the back yard. Between the weather not cooperating and the hot tub being on backorder, it's taken a little more time than we thought. And now that it and the wedding arch are almost done—

"Oh, my God!" I sputter, choking on my latte. The *wedding* arch. "Next week. We're getting married next week!"

"Damn right we are," he chuckles smugly. "I'm locking you down every way I can. There's no getting away from me now. And then we get a year-long honeymoon. Speaking of...the rings are ready. Want to go with me to pick them up?"

These Shays really take their honeymooning seriously.

"Yeah, of course." I can't wait, really. Gulping down the rest of the food, I chase it with the latte until the straw gurgles. "Let me get dressed right quick."

"Wait. You have something on you." He moves the tray to the foot of the bed.

I don't recall dropping food on me, but I look down anyway. "Where?" I frown. There's nothing there.

"My mouth. Right...here."

"Wha—? Ooh." My confusion turns into pleasure as his hot mouth wraps around the tip of my breast. I grip his hair and fall back against the headboard. "Amos," I chuff, "I'm not complaining—much—but the rings?"

His teeth nip me. "They'll wait for the next little bit. Would you do something for me? I know it's your birthday, but I've been thinking about this for a while."

"Oh, Lord." There's no telling what's about to come out of this man's mouth.

"I bought you a present"—*suck*—"but I don't know if you'll like it."

The sight of him practically inhaling my breast makes me forget all about my soreness. I'm foolishly hoping the extra heaviness and sensitivity in my boobs is because I'm pregnant (it's been six weeks since my last period), but I'm not telling him until I know for sure. "What'd you get me, baby?" I breathe out. "I'm sure I'll love it because it came from you."

"An electric breast pump."

"What?" Did he just say what I thought he said?

His big hands heft the weight of my globes, calmly thumbing the areolae as he stares into my soul. "How would you feel about inducing your milk?"

"For you or for a baby?"

A faint grin tips his mouth. "You know me so well. How about we start with me and then a baby?"

"Let me get this straight. You want these"—I jiggle them in his face—"to start producing actual breast milk so you can drink it."

"Yep."

"Then *if* we have a baby, adopted or biological, you'll back off so he or she can drink."

"Actually, your body's capable of making enough for the both of us. Supply and demand, you know." His eyebrows waggle. "We demand, you supply."

"Oh, my God!" I nervously laugh before sobering. "Oh, my God. You're serious. Why, though?"

"It's a kink I want to do with you. I've never had these thoughts about anyone else—just you. And don't you agree that feeding your husband from your body is hot as hell?" He brushes a taut nipple with his lips. "The closeness and bonding of skin to skin with eye contact?"

I can't deny the zing of arousal that shoots to my clit when I think of the times we've done just that. Shifting to relieve the throbbing pressure, I blurt out, "Do you realize how committed we both have to be for this, if it's even possible? With my hormones so out of balance, it may not be, even taking supplements. And if it is, how long do we do it? And any kids...what about them? *Hang on, kids. Daddy's thirsty and needs Momma to make him something to drink. In the bedroom.* What if they grow even more ginormous and need emptied every hour? Quit laughing! I'm being serious. Stop—put me down!"

Amos manhandles me so I'm astride him. "Valid points, Mercy. Valid points. You're right—it may not be possible. But if it *is*...God, baby, that'd be so hot. I'm committed and prepared to learn if you are." A gleam of lust shines in his arctic eyes. "And I'm more than willing to milk those sweet tits day and night. As often as I need to so I can drink you down."

That *does* pique my curiosity. And libido.

"Mhmm," he groans as something else occurs to him. "We can even use the pump when we're having sex and change the settings so it'd be like someone sucking both nipples when I'm inside you. But that's as close as we're ever going to get to having anyone else in our bed."

He doesn't have to take that warning tone with me because one man—*this* man—is enough. More than. But I'm not focusing so much on that part.

He wants to milk me.

Milk me. Heat courses through me at the imagery that evokes. "Can I think about it?"

A calculated look twists his features. *Uh-oh.* This means some serious Shay compromise is about to hit the table. "Tell you what. You sit on my face and let me tell that pretty pussy happy birthday with my tongue, and I'll let you think about it while you're up there. Fair enough?"

I know a lost cause when I see one. "Fair enough."

"Fantastic." His huge hand gives me a smack on the ass as he slides down. "Now sit, woman."

I should have known better, though, because as soon as his mouth makes contact, all thoughts divert to the magic he's creating between my legs.

Dang it.

∾

"CAN'T STOP LOOKING AT IT, CAN YOU?" ONE HAND ON THE wheel, Amos gives me a crooked glance.

He's right. We tried the rings on in the store just to make sure they'd been sized correctly and now neither of us wants to take them off. "They just feel so right."

"Are you sure you want just a plain band? Money's no object and it's not too late for you to change your mind. We can delay the ceremony if need be."

"I'm a simple person, Amos. I'd be happy with no ring at all." I twist my hand this way and that, admiring its minimalistic beauty.

"Hell, no," he growls, snatching my hand and tapping the ring. "You must be out of your ever-loving mind if you think either of us is walking around without one."

"We've been doing it until now," I wryly point out. "And I think your hand on my butt is a bit more noticeable than a band."

"Oh, it is. But what about for me? I think you'd like looking at me and seeing I'm wearing something that marks me as yours and only yours. What if some woman slides her eyes up and down all this godlike masculinity—"

"I'd claw them out," I blurt, unable to contain the very real jealousy that small imagining conjured up.

"You vicious little devil, you."

"You sound almost proud."

A chuckle leaves him. "Hell, yeah. I kinda like the thought of you protecting what's yours. Not that you'd ever need to," he adds on.

Happiness compels me to lift his hand to my mouth for a kiss. "I love your hands. So strong and big."

"These old things?" he scoffs. "They're beat up and rough."

"They're perfect *because* of the roughness. It turns me on knowing what these hands are capable of."

That gets his attention. "Oh, yeah?"

"Yeah. And when I look out the window to see you shirtless, sweat glistening in the sunlight, and watch you cut and hammer all that wood for the deck, it makes me want to drag you inside and suck you off."

The truck swerves. "Damn, woman. I'll get sweaty for you any—wait a minute! I'm not the only one taking off his shirt. You get worked up seeing my brother's chest?"

"No!" I rush to soothe him. Well, maybe a little, but Connor doesn't hold a candle to his older brother. Not to me, at least. "I'm saying you building things with your own two hands gets me worked up."

He settles back down, eyes narrowed. "I'll build any damn thing you want. Love to build. When I was a kid, Mom and I would make the coolest houses with blocks."

"From what I saw at their house, you probably could have been a halfway decent artist if construction didn't work out," I tease, smirking when his ears turn a little red.

"Yeah, she loves those drawings."

"You really love her, too, don't you?"

"All the way. She's been my mother for forty years now."

I wonder if his birth mom dying when he was just a baby is

why he's obsessed with my boobs. Maybe he had to wean too early. That brings something to mind. "Were you jealous when you learned you were going to have a sibling? Especially since you'd had her to yourself for those first few years."

"Not at all. We were all so excited when she got pregnant with Connor. And when he made his way into this world, all three of us fell in love with him. Growing up, he could be a pain in the ass, but that's the way it is with all siblings. As far as I'm concerned, he's my full-blooded brother. Period."

"Did you worry that Corina loved him more since he was her first birth child?" I've often wondered if I'd subconsciously treat my children differently if I managed to have a biological child after adopting one.

"Never," he affirms in a resolute tone. "She showered the both of us in love." He shifts in his seat, laughing as he apparently thinks of something from his childhood. "Also disciplined us the same amount. But there's something about the heart of a parent—mother or father—that expands and lets more love in for their children, no matter how those kids come to be. And I have no doubt that any kid we get lucky enough to add to our family will be loved just as equally by both of us."

"You're right, I know you are, but I secretly worry that I'll do it and not even realize it." And that would kill me. I grimace at the sudden pang in my abdomen. "Can you drive a little faster, baby? I don't feel too well all of a sudden."

Immediately, the truck smoothly accelerates. "You okay? Do I need to pull over?"

"No, but I think we really need to get home soon." I have a feeling I know what it is, but I'm praying that I'm wrong. *Please. Please let me be wrong.*

He squeezes my knee. "Ten minutes or less, baby. Hang on."

When we make it within seven minutes, I'm out of the truck as soon as he stops beside my car in the driveway. "You can get the door for me later. I gotta..." I pant as I run up the steps and hurriedly press my thumb to unlock the front door. Dashing to the bathroom, I sit on the toilet and pull down my underwear.

Red marks.

My period.

I'm not pregnant.

No.

I fall back against the toilet, a cry of anguish leaving me.

"Mercy!" Amos bursts into the bathroom, looking wildly around for the source of my distress. "What's the matter?"

Throat tight with misery, I tell him as tears trail down my face. "I'm not pregnant. I hoped... God, I'd hoped because my breasts were so heavy and I hadn't had a period in six weeks. But I knew it was too soon to even think about it. Why, Amos? Why won't my body do what it's supposed to do?"

I'm about to have a breakdown on the toilet with my pants and underwear down at my ankles.

"Oh, baby." Sadness written all over his face, he kneels beside me and hugs me, heavy hands petting my hair. "I don't know, but it's gonna be okay. Let it all out now because I've got you."

Now that he's holding me, I unleash all my tears onto him, soaking his shoulder. When my eyes run dry, I listlessly move back and reach for some facial tissue. "I need a tampon."

Searching for a sign that I'm okay for the moment, he nods. "I'll get it for you."

I don't argue. Can't even find it in myself to stop him from cleaning me, putting fresh underwear on me, and carrying me to the bed. When he crawls over me and kisses my abdomen, bitterness bubbles up. I don't want him kissing me there and reminding me of what could have been. "Let's look at the adoption website now. Can you get the tablet?"

His tone is careful as he cautiously pulls it from the nightstand. "Why don't we wait a while before we do this?

"No," I say sharply. Too sharply. I soften my reply a bit. "I need to do this now. Please, Amos."

Silently, he pulls up the website we bookmarked a few weeks ago and clicks around. I grab his forearm. "Look at that little boy. Isaiah, twelve years old. He loves books and is searching for his forever family," I read aloud. "Carly and Christopher, three-year-old twins. They love holding hands and being held, playing with each other. Waiting for their forever family."

Amos murmurs in sympathy.

The more we look, the more my heart breaks. Soon, the tears I thought were all dried up come back with a vengeance. "Why is this so hard? It seems like we're practically shopping for the perfect child. Why are there so many options? This site lets you filter by age range, race, gender... They're human beings, not commodities! How many of these kids get picked over because someone doesn't like the way they look? If they'd only go and get to know them—" Words turn into broken sobs. "It's not fair. I look at these poor kids and just want to take all of them with us. How are we supposed to say 'I'll take this one but not that one' knowing that they all just want a family, too?"

"Mercy."

Raw emotion roughens my voice as I stare blindly at the images on the screen. "How can we take just one and leave all the others behind?" *Like I was.*

"Up you go." Amos bends and wraps me around him as he carries me through the house and outside. He settles us in the swing chair and wraps a blanket around me, the comforting gesture soothing my body but not my heart. Not yet.

"I'm sorry. I'm so sorry, but my birthday makes me even more overwhelmed. I didn't think it would still affect me this way because this one is different with you here, but I was so wrong."

"Don't apologize, baby." He gives me the sweetest kiss ever

and touches our foreheads together. "I'm not saying this to make you cry more, but if you want us to see a doctor for fertility treatments, we can do that. I don't care how much it costs. Whatever your decision, I'll support you, but know this— you're more than a womb, Mercy. Your worth isn't dependent on being a mother, regardless of how you become one. And you're right. Those kids are more than a picture on a page with their entire personalities reduced to a few descriptive words. But we need to go about this the right way, and that's standing together no matter what we choose."

Fertility treatments. Would I be setting myself up for heartbreak by reaching for the unreachable? I'm not sure which would make me more disappointed—trying and failing or not trying at all.

Arms tighten around me as a small chuckle rumbles through his chest. "Huh. Just thought of something."

"What?" I sniff against him, breathing in his scent that still sends flutters through my stomach.

"It's a good thing you didn't call the police on me, because if you'd sent me to jail, I wouldn't pass the adoption background check."

The outrageousness of his statement breaks me out of my funk, forcing a reluctant peal of laughter from me. "Oh, Amos... Only a Shay. Only you."

Never in my wildest dreams would I have believed it if someone had told me how drastically my life would change in three short months. But I wouldn't trade it for anything.

Amos is my world now. Protector of my heart.

*N*ervous jitters cause my nails to snag my elegantly simple wedding dress. Maybe lace isn't the best fabric to trace imaginary patterns on, but I need something to do with my hands. I don't know why I'm so anxious.

Actually, I do. Although I've become more confident in some things, it's only because Amos brings it out in me. Withdrawing into my inner shell when other people are around is still my instinctive reaction, and I don't think that's ever going to change. But with my protective husband at my side, I don't need to. Any minute now, he'll open the door and take me by the hand, leading us to the exquisite wedding arch Connor carved for us where we'll become one in the eyes of the law.

That's what makes me edgy. Not getting married, no, because I'm more than ready for that. I have no doubts, no second thoughts, no regrets. It's the walk there that's getting to me. Somehow I lose all ability to function correctly when the spotlight's on me. I can already see myself tripping on my own feet like a newborn giraffe in front of everyone, as if I haven't been walking for thirty-some-odd years.

"Mercy?" A tap on the door and then Mitchell's head

appears. He and Corina have been such a mom and dad to me these past months and I love them like I would my own parents. "Can I come in?"

"Of course." I smooth my dress around my knees and self-consciously tame the nonexistent flyaways on my high bun. "Is...is Amos coming for me?"

Mitchell speaks, warmth infused in his kind, gray eyes. "That's what I wanted to talk to you about, sweetheart. Would you allow me the honor of escorting you on my arm? I know I'm not your father, but it would mean the world to me to walk with you for such a momentous occasion."

Don't cry, Mercy. Don't cry. Furiously blinking back the tears threatening to escape, I manage to get my words out past the knot in my throat. "There's nothing I'd like more."

His offer settles something deep within and brings me inner peace. Was I subconsciously mourning the absence of my father in this pivotal moment of my life? Perhaps. But as I place my hand around this man's strong arm and allow him to guide me from my bedroom, all I feel is a sense of rightness.

At the soft opening strains of music, Mitchell pats my hand with a comforting touch before pushing through the open french doors to the deck. Then with confident steps, we walk together to where the man who abducted me in the name of love impatiently waits for me underneath the arch.

He barely spares his dad a glance, having eyes only for me as his hands settle low on my hips, fingers brushing the curve of my ass. "Sweet Mercy...you take my breath away."

Butterflies running rampant in my stomach, I duck my head in bashfulness and take in his appearance in return from underneath my eyelashes. He looks sinfully amazing with his hunter green shirt and brown tweed waistcoat. Leather belt loop suspenders with decorative brass O rings run down his wide shoulders and attach to his dark jeans that encase his muscular legs. And to top it all off, he smells so...so...*masculinely* decadent.

My nostrils flare as I discreetly inhale as much as I can without being obvious. God, it's like I'm breathing in his very essence and letting it seep through the walls of my lungs to become one with my body.

Amos doesn't let me look down for long, though. His thick finger tilts my chin up so our eyes meet. "Head high, baby, because your beauty is something to be proud of."

A smile slowly spreads his lips as my shoulders square up. "Good girl. Now let's get married."

Our captivated gazes fuse together, the words of the minister fading into white noise as the ceremony commences with his parents, brother, and photographer as witnesses. Time blurs, then the bonds of matrimony tighten even more securely around us with an invisible chain of sweet promise as the minister says, "I now pronounce you man and wife. You may kiss the bride."

"Mine. All mine," he growls before dominating my mouth, his tongue staking claim. My knees buckle in weakness from the force of his invasion and I grab onto his thick arms for balance. Breaking away, his hot breath heats my ear. "You and me, baby. Soon as everyone leaves, we've got a private appointment. In the bedroom," he adds with a hiked eyebrow.

My heart stutters its next few beats at the dark pledge in his words. *I can't wait.* He's my man—my husband—and I can't wait to give myself to him as his legally wedded wife. "Would it be rude of us to escape now?"

Before he can answer, his family surrounds us with a flurry of well wishes. "Little sister," comes Connor's carefully supervised hug and gentle kiss to my cheek.

"Hey, hey..." Amos protests. "Your lips and hands don't belong near my woman. Enough already." Playfully shoving Connor away, he embraces me from behind, erasing his brother's touch by kissing the same spot. "Keep it up and you'll find yourself banned from the food."

"Oh, no!" Connor's deep, mocking tone matches his expression. "Mercy, you gonna let him treat me like that?"

I tilt my head back on Amos's chest and bat my eyes. "Baby, don't be mean to your brother. He's the only one you have. And as for you..." I narrow my gaze on said younger brother. "I'm thinking you're not as innocent as you make yourself out to be, so don't come looking for help from me."

The black tattoos on his neck flex with laughter as Mitchell throws an arm around his shoulders. "She's got you there, son."

Smiling fondly at her little family, Corina pulls Amos—and me by extension—down to give him a motherly kiss. "My handsome boy—"

"Favorite," he interjects with a smirk. She stops with a silently raised parental eyebrow until he gives a small grimace. "Sorry, Momma. Go on."

"Finally getting your bride. And she's a beautiful one, too, inside and out." Corina lifts his hand from my waist and drags mine to rest in it, folding our fingers together. "Always hold on to each other, no matter what storms life brings your way. Because as long as you have each other, you can make it through anything."

"That's right." Mitchell wraps an arm around her waist and kisses her silvery blonde hair. "Anything."

A look of veiled longing covers Connor's face as he glances between his parents and us. I recognize it well because I wore it far too often for far too many years. On his last pass, our eyes catch. His façade falters, exposing the vulnerability underneath the sad smile he gives me. His gruff insults hide his loneliness just like my quietness did mine. While I hope he finds someone, I also hope he tamps down the Shay intensity and takes it easy on the poor woman. She'll be in for a healthy dose of culture shock, otherwise.

"Well," he announces loudly as he tucks away his vulnerability, "while y'all smother in all this love floating around, I'll be eating all those barbecue mini dicks."

"Ha," Amos snickers. "You like the taste of dick, do you?"

With a flip of his middle finger, Connor ignores him and moves to the crockpot keeping the cocktail sausages warm. "Call me when you cut the cake. So you know, I restrained myself from licking the icing. Just for you, Mercy."

A laugh leaves me at his absurdity. Like our wedding, the cake is simple, too. A chocolate chip red velvet bundt cake I made yesterday with cream cheese icing drizzled over the top. Mhmm...just the way I like it.

Leaning back, I make myself comfortable in my husband's strong arms as I take in the activity around us. Receptions have never been my thing at the few weddings I've attended. And though mine is small, it's still awkward because *everybody* knows what happens after people get married.

The wedding night.

Or afternoon, in our case. Regardless, everyone knows what shenanigans the bride and groom are itching to get to as soon as the last guest leaves. *I* never could stop myself from imagining any newlyweds doing *the deed*, so I'm pretty sure the thought is in everyone's head. And isn't it just lovely knowing that his parents know what their precious child is about to do to me?

Well, maybe not *exactly* what we're going to do. I will literally die from embarrassment if I see even a hint of a smirk or laugh, but so far, so good. Even from Connor.

A flash takes me by surprise, and I turn my head to take in the cheerful photographer. "That was absolutely perfect. Sorry —I just had to take that one before either of you moved. Ready for more?"

Amos gives my waist a warm squeeze. "Of course. Where do you want us?"

"How about we start at the arch and move on from there?"

Here we go. I'm not a fan of having my picture taken, but this is a once-in-a-lifetime event. Before I can stifle it, a quiet laugh escapes me because that statement is even more true when marrying a Shay.

A feeling of belonging overtakes me as Amos kisses my temple and moves us back to the wooden arch. I've been caught and claimed, but I wouldn't have it any other way.

THE FLOOR CERTAINLY LOOKS DIFFERENT FROM THIS ANGLE, I muse as Amos carries me through the house. Caveman style, with me draped over his shoulder and his hands simultaneously too close and too far from my center as he holds me in place.

His legs seem different, too. Longer and stronger. Watching them in motion sends a bolt of lust through me and tempts me to run my hands over his ass that is *right there*. When my fingers creep over his belt and lower down, his own slide up my thigh and gently tease me through my panties. A little squeak escapes me as I trap his roaming hand between my clenched thighs. "Amos!"

"Couldn't wait until we got to the bedroom, could you?" he rumbles as he crosses the threshold into our room. Kicking the door shut, he slides me down his body with aching slowness, then toes his shoes off. Purposefully advancing, he forces me backwards. "Now...what did I promise you? Oh, yes. You, me, and a bed. And here we are."

My heart thumps in anticipation with every footstep as he prowls towards me. When the backs of my legs hit the mattress, I shiver, feminine awareness sending icy tingles to my fingertips before settling back down in my stomach. There's just something about the heavy intent in his eyes...the flash of his secret smile he aims at me that has my hormones in overdrive.

Slightly intimidating, too, when I take in our stark differences. His masculinity to my femininity. His hard body to my softer one. He'd never hurt me, I know that now, but knowing he could pin me down without any struggle on his part and do wicked things to me causes a rush of desire to flood my panties.

"Right where I want you. Don't move."

I'm not scared, but I *am* completely turned on beyond belief. We've made love countless times these past three months, but this moment holds heavy tension because now we're married in all the ways we could possibly be. Breaths turning shallow, I greedily watch as his fingers deftly remove his lust-inducing suspenders and unbutton his waistcoat. Shrugging it off, his shirt buttons are next. In and out, they weave lazily through the buttonholes and reveal the dusty coating of hair on his chest.

"Wait!" I blurt. "Don't take it off." Suddenly, *I* want to be the one to take charge. Amos is a giver, for sure, but now I want to do something to him.

Something that's been on my mind for a while.

Something he hasn't asked me to do since my first few days here.

He freezes, then cuts a predatory grin my way. "And why not, kitten? I'm not opposed to us keeping our clothes on, but we'll have to get a little creative."

I swallow hard against the nerves making their grand entrance. Deep down, I know he's not going to make fun of me or laugh at my efforts, but it doesn't make it any easier to make that first move.

"Clothes will be coming off, but not just yet." Looking around the room, my eyes catch on the bedroom bench. *Perfect.* I drag him (only because he allows it) to the foot of the bed and push his chest. "Sit here."

"Yes, ma'am." His crooked smirk and teasing tone put me more at ease. Legs spread wide, he leans back a little to rest his elbows on the bed. "Now what?"

"Stay there and don't move. Don't touch." *Keep it together, Mercy.* As I pull my dress over my head, I hear his harshly indrawn breath.

"Sweet Mercy..."

Clad in just my lingerie, I watch him raze my body with fiery eyes. I do this to him. *Me.* Mercy Calla—oops. Mercy Shay. The sight of me causes his chest to heave in restrained lust. His fingers to twitch as he fights the instinct to reach for me. His pants-covered bulge to thicken in anticipation of having his way with me.

But I'm going to have my way with him first.

Tossing him a saucy smile, I lower to my knees between his open legs and trace my fingernails up and down his massive thigh muscles.

"Baby," he groans, "are you trying to kill me?"

"Of course not. The night wouldn't be any fun with you dead. I just want to do something for you before we do anything else."

His nostrils flare and his fists create creases in the bed blanket. There can be no doubt as to what I'm referencing, especially with me in this position of submission. "Yes. Do it."

Unbuckling his belt, I pull his zipper down in slow increments, the heady feeling of being in control almost making me dizzy with feminine power. Is this what he feels when we make love? I could get addicted to this. "But I can't unless you do something for me first."

"Anything." Amos stares through heavy eyelids. "Anything you want."

We'll see if he means that. "I...I want to...put my mouth on you." Blood rushes to my cheeks. I have no trouble giving him my body now, but ask me to say dirty words and my tongue twists into knots.

Heated interest crosses his face. "I'm all yours. Suck me dry, baby girl. There'll be plenty more to replace it before the night's through."

My blush darkens. Better go ahead and get the rest of it out. "But I don't want you to get hard. Not yet."

At his disbelief, I keep going. "You know my mouth is small and you're...you're big. Too wide and too long. My only hope of swallowing more than the tip is when you're"—I duck my head—"soft."

"Well." A bark of laughter rings out above me as he looks down in amusement. "That's not what I expected, but I'll try. *If* you give me something in return."

"What?"

"I want to use the breast pump on you tonight."

My mouth curls up. I've been thinking more and more about that lately since he first brought up the idea. "Deal."

"All right. Give me a minute." Tilting his head back, he inhales deeply several times, shrugging his shoulders back and forth. "Do you know how hard it is to will a boner away with only the power of thought?"

I stifle a giggle and add a bit of throatiness to my voice. "But don't you want to see how much you can stuff into my mouth?"

"Mercy." A moan of misery leaves him. "Not helping."

"Sorry." *Not sorry.* I rest my head against his thigh and lightly caress his calf through his pants. It takes a few minutes for him to fully relax, but when I feel the tension dissipate, I reach for the band of his briefs.

From the corner of my eyes, I see him leaning back onto his elbows, breathing deeply and steadily as I work the material down and tuck it under his balls.

And there it is—the organ and its associated parts that bring me to the heights of ecstasy day and night. I nuzzle my face against its softness and inhale his scent. Clean, yet earthy. "What are you thinking about?"

"Definitely not thinking how close my wife's mouth is to my dick." There's a slight pause. "Or that it's our wedding night and she wants to swallow me down instead of riding my face and drowning me with her honey."

His gravel-coated words send a flood of wetness through me. I know what he's doing, the sly fox...giving me an out if I need it. I love him all the more for it, but I really want to do this. And now...now there's been enough talking. I grip him and engulf the head of him in my mouth, making him jolt with a deep, low groan. Sucking lightly, I run my nails over his heavy sac, making it jump as a twitch runs the length of his shaft.

"Kitten," he grits out through a huff, tendons flexing in his neck, "how the hell am I supposed to stay soft when you do things like that?"

"Do it for me. Please." Rolling my tongue around him, I open wider and move further down until I meet the warm skin of his groin. When I feel him thicken, I pull off with a pop and lay him against his thigh. "Ah-ah-ah. Calm down."

"Mercy, sweet temptress." His eyes promise retribution, but he throws his head back, the salt and pepper curls on his chest heaving with every breath.

For long minutes, he fights his reaction and lets me play with him. It's not fair of me, I know, but I can't help teasing him. Pressing just his tip to me like lipstick, I trace the curve of my mouth with it. "Mhmm...you taste so good. I want you to paint my lips with your cum. Like you did the night you took me."

But a beast can only be taunted for so long before being provoked into action. And my last line was the tipping point.

"That's it," he growls. The fists holding so tightly to the bed release their grip and grab my hair, pulling down so my gaze meets his. "You've had your fun. Now it's time for me to have mine. Up."

Breathless, I stand with him as he gently yanks. That does surprisingly good things to me between my legs.

"Undress me," he commands as he shrugs his shirt the rest of the way off. Quickly, I pull down his pants and briefs. "Good girl. Stay there."

He moves to the closet and comes back with a machine and a bottle of lube. The beat of my heart picks up as I remember his words. *I'm more than willing to milk those sweet tits.*

Placing the pump on the bed, he turns to me with the lube and a dark smile. "I did a bit of research and I think this one is the best. We can always try another if you don't like it. Now,"— he pops the cap—"time to put this on those sweet nipples. Pull your bra down and hold it for me."

I obey, dragging the lacy cups down and waiting for his next move. Lust glazes over his eyes as he looks between the pump and my breasts. "Amos, this is so crazy. But I like it."

"It's *our* kind of crazy. We can do anything we want in our house. Just the two of us." Squeezing a drizzle over his finger, he smears it over an exposed nipple and areola before moving to the other. "Don't want you getting chafed. Keep the cups down; you're gonna need them for extra support."

Throwing a glance at me, he asks, "Ready?"

At my eager nod, he rubs the clear flanges over the tips of my breasts to coat them and then presses down to set the suction. Gently pulling my bra back up, he reverently kisses the slope of my chest. "Good thing it's wireless. Tubes would just get in the way."

Needing to stabilize myself with all the excitement building inside of me, I latch onto his thick forearms and watch his thumb hover over the power button. "Do it," I whisper through a secret smile.

"It's going to be on the lowest setting first to stimulate a letdown, so let's see how you like it." Eyes dancing between mine and my boobs, he turns the pump on.

My fingers flex tightly around him as it comes to life and the first bit of suction pulls my nipples in soft, quick pulls. This feels...nice. More than, actually. We both look down in wonder, amazed at the sight of my nipples being drawn up and down in rhythmic motion. My jaw drops in pleasurable awe. "This is what it looks like inside your mouth."

"That's hot, baby. So hot." Pure sex drips from his voice.

Seems I'm not the only one turned on by this. Suddenly, the suction slows down and deepens its pulls. I let out a breathy moan, my knees going weak. "Ooh...Amos."

"Now it's in expressing mode and it'll stay on this one until we change any settings again. Do you like it?"

"Yeah. It...it feels so much the same *and* so different than when you do it."

"Good." His hands fall to my hips and drag my panties down. "Now, let's see how this feels when I'm inside of you."

I carefully fall back onto the bed, not wanting to break the steady suction on my breasts. Casting my eyes toward him, I crook my finger. "Come here, lover, and make love to me."

Amos straddles me, supporting himself on one arm and rubbing his cock through my wetness. *"Lover."* He tastes the word on his tongue. "I like that, Mercy. Your lover. Your one and only."

With no warning, he thrusts inside me, forcing a gasp from my lips. "Yes," I hiss out, reaching a hand up to make sure he didn't jar the flanges loose.

"There you go, baby. Look at you, getting those sweet nipples sucked while my big cock moves in and out of you. Mhmm, you take me so good, Mercy. Grip me so tight. God, baby...you're choking my dick."

Words get stuck in my throat, unable to leave me as he drives broken gasps from me with his forceful thrusts. All I can do is hold on and enjoy the sensations warring for dominance in my mind.

Over and over, the tension builds between us as the pump sucks my nipples and his cock hits that sweet spot deep inside me. Higher and higher until it threatens to burst in release. I close my eyes, unable to bear the sight of the pump of his expression for fear it'll send me over the edge too soon. "A-a-mos," I manage to get out.

"Yeah, baby?" he growls. "You about to come?"

My answering moan makes him move harder and deeper, gripping my hips tight enough to leave marks for me to find in the morning.

"That's my girl. Come on, let it go for me. Give it all to me. Come on...come on..."

I can't hold it back any longer. Giving into the pleasure, I yell out his name as lightning courses through me. Vaguely, I can hear him grunting out his own release.

Knocking the still-pumping flanges from my breasts, he collapses onto me with heavy breaths and buries his face into my neck. "Damn, Mercy. I love you, woman. You hear me? You have my heart, my cock, and all of me."

Wrapping my arms and legs around him, I choke on a laugh at his ticklish mumbles as I try to regulate my own breathing. "I love you, too, Amos. I love you, too."

And I do, so much more than I thought would ever be possible.

EPILOGUE 1

MERCY

1 YEAR LATER

"*M*ercy!" Amos bellows from upstairs, a hint of despair coloring his tone. "Help!"

"Coming!" I yell back. Keeping my snickering to myself, I grab another apple slice. A quick unlatching of the baby gate guarding the stairs and then I'm headed to Leila's room to rescue my poor husband. Crowned with a headful of chocolate ringlets and bright blue eyes, little eleven-month-old Leilani joined our family three months ago by adoption and has both Amos and me completely wrapped around her chubby little fingers.

Sweet as she is, though, her dirty diapers are *not*. Especially when she's teething like she is now. We quickly learned the importance of keeping diapers and wipes in more than one room, but our supply downstairs has been depleted. Good daddy that he is, Amos offered to change her since I did the last one.

Following the pungent aroma, I turn into Leila's room and

immediately lose my battle with laughter. A mountain of balled-up dirty wipes litter the changing table—even the floor —and a baby clad in a crooked, backwards diaper chews on a set of toy keys as her daddy dry heaves to the side with his shirt over his nose. While he's jumped headlong into fatherhood, basic diaper changing is still something he struggles with, let alone ones such as these. He gets an *E* for effort, though.

"You all right, babe? What happened to her outfit?" I manage to get out through my tears from both the smell and my laughter.

Adjusting his shirt, he winces as he raises his head. "How— I repeat, *how*—something so cute"–he pauses to smile tenderly at a babbling Leila—"can produce something so foul, I'll never understand. It was all the way up her back, Mercy. Almost to her neck. I barely got her onesie off without getting it in her hair. Now, which cream am I supposed to use again?"

"The one in the purple tube. It's medicated and should help clear up her rash sooner."

When he reaches for it, a thought stops me. This new parenting gig is a little hard to get used to. "Wait! Since she had a blowout, though, let's give her a quick bath. Wipes are good, but I'd rather her go to bed super clean."

"Good idea," he says with a grimace. Gulping a huge breath, he picks her up and heads to the bathroom with outstretched arms as Leila giggles at me over his shoulder.

TWENTY MINUTES LATER, THERE'S WATER AND BABY SHAMPOO ALL over the floor, Amos, *and* me, but Leila's freshly bathed and dressed for bed. Head tucked against her daddy's shoulder, her mouth opens wide in a sleepy yawn as her tiny fingers gently pat his back.

Just like he's patting hers.

I swear, seeing this man of mine with a baby in his arms makes me want to throw him down and ride him until neither of us can move anymore.

Later. Time to put this little girl to bed first.

One thing I adore about our nighttime routine is reading to her. Young as she is, she absolutely loves books. And though some people may say she's too young to have a favorite, I'd have to disagree. The minute her eyes snap onto *Are You My Mother*, she'll squeal with glee and clap her hands in excitement until I read the title and open the book.

And tonight is no different. Corina's remarked in amazement before how it was Amos's favorite book, too, and that Leila's enough like him to be his blood daughter. To me, that was just the perfect sign that little Leilani was meant for us.

Joining them on the oversized glider a thoughtful Connor made just for us, my heart melts when my baby reaches for me from her daddy's lap. "Will you hold the book, babe? Looks like she's gonna be a Momma's girl tonight."

He drops a short kiss on both of our heads and holds us as he opens the book. "Anything for my girls."

His girls. What a picture we make, the both of us ensconced in the circle of his strong arms. Leila nestles against me, resting her curly head on my swollen breasts (yes, with the help of Amos, the pump, and hormonal supplements, these boobies make milk that he guzzles every chance he gets) and sucking her two middle fingers as I begin to read. Near the end of the book, her eyes begin to droop but she's still focused on the colorful illustrations.

"*Do you know who I am?*" I read aloud. Unbidden emotion hits me and I choke on it. Sometimes my new reality slams into me so hard and I can't believe I really have a husband and a baby.

Everything I've ever wanted, and they're both with me right now.

A happy tear escapes me with a sniffle, catching Leilani's attention. Looking up, she pulls her wet fingers from her mouth to pat me softly on the face. Wry amusement mixes with my happiness. *It's the thought that counts.*

Warm lips press against my temple. "I know, baby. I know," Amos soothes.

And he does. He understands. I see it in his eyes.

Getting myself together, I carry on, and by the time I finish the last word, she's passed out. I carry her to the crib her grandpa made for her and gingerly lower her down onto her stomach while Amos turns on the baby monitor. She lets out one of those sweet baby sighs and tucks her legs underneath her, little blanket-covered tush high in the air.

He bends down to press a soft kiss to her curls. "Goodnight, princess. Momma and Daddy love you. Come on, kitten. Let's go to bed."

Amos tugs my hand with his whisper, but I trip on something.

My blue rabbit.

"Wait." Picking it up, I place it on the glider, turning it just a bit so it sits evenly in the middle. Touching its floppy ear, I speak to it like I did all those years ago. "Watch over our baby girl, okay? Keep her dreams safe." With a final boop to its cloth nose, I turn and bump into Amos. "Sorry."

"It's fine. I just had to look at her one more time. She's so cute when she's sleeping." Drawing me to his front, his arms encircle me from behind, his chin lowering to rest on my shoulder as we stare down at our little sleeping miracle. "You thinking what I'm thinking?" His whisper is so quiet, Leila doesn't even stir.

Tilting my head back on his chest to look at him, I whisper back. "There's no telling with you. What are you thinking?"

Eyes serious, Amos cradles my cheek. "I'm thinking this

house still has three empty bedrooms, and Leilani needs at least one older brother to protect her."

Emotion wells within me and happy tears make their appearance once again. This sweet man of mine knows just what to say. We'd briefly tried some non-invasive fertility treatments, but they made me so sick that Amos put his foot down and told me it was killing him to see me like that. Ever since then, we've focused on building our family another way.

"That's exactly what I was thinking, too. I haven't been able to get Isaiah off of my mind." His profile still shows active a year and a half later.

Amos nuzzles my ear and grazes my nipple with a thumb. "Know what else I'm thinking?"

"I think you're probably feeling a bit thirsty." I grind my ass against his thickening cock. "Am I right?"

The warm breath from his grin tickles my neck as he squeezes a heavy breast, forcing a light trickle of milk from the tip. "Let's go, wife. Time for a read and feed."

He's in for a treat tonight, because I'm reading from a spicy, sexy book.

It's going to be a good night.

EPILOGUE 2

AMOS

2 1/2 YEARS LATER

"Thanks for making this, Uncle Connor." Isaiah opens his bedroom door so we can wrestle the elaborately hand-carved dragon bookcase through the doorway.

"You're welcome, bud," he grunts out. "I'm sure you'll get it filled up with books in no time at all and then I'll have to make you another one. Maybe you can help me, too. And down on three. One...two...three."

When the heavy wooden bookcase makes contact with the rug, Connor straightens and reaches for the hem of his shirt as he huffs, "Damn. Lugging that thing up the porch steps and upstairs is enough to make a man break a little sweat. Even with it being chilly outside."

"A little out of shape, are we? Hey—shirt down." I cast a furtive eye around and move in front of him, nodding to my fifteen-year-old son. "Isaiah, watch the door, will you?"

"Sure thing, Dad." His lanky form travels closer to the

"Dude, what's wrong with you? I'm only trying to wipe my face." Standing frozen with his stomach halfway showing, my baby brother's confusion is written all over him.

"Blocking the view. Mercy might be around," I mutter.

He grins as he catches on. "What—you don't want your wife getting a peek at all this muscle?"

My curse is muffled by a screech that rivals a pterodactyl's as Leila streaks past her brother into his room. "Unka Connor! Safe me, Unka Connor!"

Connor's shirt drops as he swoops down to pick up his niece. "You're safe with me, princess! But who am I *safing* you from?"

"Leilani Shay..." Mercy calls out from the hallway. "Where are you?"

The little fugitive cracks herself up laughing and buries her head into her uncle's chest. "Hide me, hide me!"

Connor turns with her just in time as Mercy peeks her head in. "Hey, guys. You haven't seen a little girl running around here, have you? She was supposed to pick up her toys downstairs before lunch, but she ran away instead."

All three of us men look stupidly at each other in attempted innocence before a muffled giggle makes Mercy peer suspiciously in Connor's direction. "Uncle Connor, are you hiding someone from me?"

He coughs and glances at her over his shoulder. "Well..."

Before he can stumble through an explanation, Leila pops up. "Here I am, Mommy!"

Little troublemaker will do anything if she thinks there's even a remote possibility of making us laugh. "Leilani," I interject, "go put your toys up like Momma told you to. You hear me?"

"Okay, Daddy. You come with me, 'Saya?" Wiggling her way down, she bats her baby blues at Isaiah. She's loved her big brother from the minute we brought him home a year ago.

"All right," he grumbles softly as he holds her hand. "I'll help you *this* time, but you've got to do it yourself next time. You got that?"

"Okay," Leila solemnly promises. We'll see how long that sticks.

When they leave, Mercy snuggles under my arm for a quick hug. "Little toots is a mess. Are you staying over for lunch, Connor? I'm making barbecue chicken wraps."

"Thanks, Mercy, but I can't today. Got to get home and feed Toto and Bagheera. *And Rosanna*," he mumbles under his breath.

"Aww. Give them hugs from me, will you?" Mercy smiles softly and kisses my cheek before backing up to the doorway. "I'd better make sure Leila isn't driving poor Isaiah crazy."

"Rosanna." I prop an elbow on the dragon's snout. That's new. "Picked up another one on your delivery trip last week, huh? Is this a dog or a cat?"

A secretive smile covers his face. "Kitten. The sweetest one I've ever had. Has two babies that came with her, too."

"What does ole Baggy think about her? I've never seen a cat more jealous than him." It's true. He doesn't like to share Connor with Toto. Poor dog's been nose-swiped by his feline friend's claws too many times.

"Bagheera," he emphasizes, "is pretty fond of her. Follows her around the house and brings her dead animals as presents. And Toto loves her, too."

Animal corpses decorating his hallways. Hilarious. "Appetizing."

"At least I find them before they smell." Connor grunts in disgust.

"Better get her spayed before her next heat, especially with Bagheera around. Cute as they are, I'm sure you're busy enough without a passel of kittens underfoot."

A weird chuckle passes through his lips. "Oh, I won't be getting her spayed. Not when I plan on breeding her myself."

What is he talking about? Then it hits me. No...it couldn't be. "Rosanna's not a cat, is she?"

"No, but she *is* a kitten. My kitten."

No. Not good. "Con, we can't both call our women *kitten*. Just no way. And I called Mercy that first, so you're gonna have to change."

Silent challenge dances in his eyes.

Damn. He's not going to back down and neither am I. "Fine. But when we're all together, we use something else. Agreed?"

"Agreed." We shake on it to seal the deal.

"Wait a second. You said two babies were with her. Human ones?"

If his smile were any bigger, it'd split his face. "Well, they're not exactly here yet. She's pregnant with twins."

"Twins? And they're yours?"

"They will be, if I have my way."

And we both know he will. I've never heard of any Shay ever taking a pregnant woman, but I'm so proud of him. My baby brother not only finds his woman, but also gets a ready-made family. "Well, I'll be damned. Look at you becoming a dad like me. She must not be from around here."

"No, she isn't." Connor turns serious. "I happened to catch her at just the right time."

"Good timing?" I cock an eyebrow at him.

"Yep." That secret smile comes out again. "Good timing."

How about that? June's just bustin' out all over.

"Goodnight, princess." With one last kiss to her petal-soft cheek, Mercy and I back away and close the door. Passing the two empty rooms reserved for ten-year-old Fenley and her five-year-old twin brothers Malachi and Maddox, we knock on Isaiah's door and wait for permission to enter.

"Yeah," I hear faintly.

Cracking it open, I see our son sprawled across his bed, nose buried in a thick book. "Mom and I just wanted to tell you goodnight."

"Oh," he says with a slight smile. A few months shy of living with us for one year, and he's still surprised that we do this every night.

"Mommy!" Leilani hollers. "I'm thirsty. Can I have some juice?"

"I'll be there in a minute, baby!" Mercy raises her voice before crossing the room to hug Isaiah. "'Night, Isaiah. I love you. Love you so much."

He leans into her hand as she ruffles his hair. Typical teenager, he struggles with shows of love and affection in front of people, but here and now with just us? He eats it up. Doesn't even shy away at her kiss on his cheek. "'Night, Mom. Love you, too."

I catch her hand on her way out and brush a kiss across the top. After we both watch her leave the room, Isaiah sits up and looks at me with a curious expression on his face.

"Something on your mind?"

"Yeah." I can see him trying to formulate his thoughts into words. "You and Mom love each other so much. How'd you get her to marry you?"

Not expecting that question, I choke on my surprise. *Damn, son.* But once it passes, pride takes its place.

Now I have a son to teach.

Moving to sit beside him on the bed, I throw my arm around his shoulders. "That...is a story for another day. But for now, let me tell you what it means to be a Shay."

A NOTE FROM THE AUTHOR

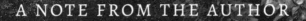

*M*any, many, ***many*** thanks to Alexis, Veronica, and Ashley. They say it takes a village to raise a child, and I definitely needed some help with this book baby. These girls fine-tuned my words and kept me motivated throughout the release of both *Caught* and *Claimed*. Seriously—they're the absolute best!

Thank you to Rachel for your help when this was only a novella and giving me an idea on expanding the word count.

Now, about this Claimed & Tamed series of mine...

I love musicals and eighties love songs. Always have, always will. Not so much the newer musicals, but the older ones from decades ago? Oh, yeah...I can sing along with most all of them! I'm a terribly old soul. You may have found several Easter eggs referencing different musicals and songs in this book.

When I first saw *Seven Brides for Seven Brothers* as a teenager, I was immediately intrigued by the plot—isolated men hungry for the company of a woman after their oldest brother marries, so each remaining brother abducts one from town. Though the movie was very tame in that regard, I was fascinated with the history behind it—the rape of the Sabine women, the story of which was briefly brought to life by the song "Sobbin' Women." (One of my absolutely FAVORITE songs!)

Years later, that (and the song "Into the Night" by Benny Mardones) birthed the idea of the Shay men. Men who live by their own set of standards and have twisted morals and logic. Men who claim their women with or without her permission, but do it from a twisted place of love. (Hot to some people—*cautiously looks around and raises a hand with a cheesy grin*—in fiction, but definitely not in real life. **Except in the case of CNC**) Men who have no qualms with steamrolling their women because that's secretly what their women want done to them, even if they don't know they do.

Yet.

While Amos and Mercy's story isn't for everyone—and really, no book will EVER be a perfect fit for everyone (that's the beauty of our uniqueness)—I hope it finds its way into the hands of those who are looking for it without traumatizing those who weren't.

I know several readers were disappointed by the shortness of Mitchell and Corina's story, but it did its job as a prequel. Their abbreviated journey was needed for Amos and Mercy to have theirs. I actually wrote *Caught* (Mitchell and Corina's story) when I was halfway done with this one and decided to release it just to see if people would like the general idea of a gentle, yet relentless, kidnapper.

And it turns out some of you do! I hope you enjoyed seeing them in this book and knowing they're really and truly deeply in love forty years later. Mitchell didn't have a whole lot to say in this book, but that's because Corina needed more of a voice since their story was only from his POV. (With the exception of the very last chapter)

Can I just add that I love how much of a Momma's boy Amos still is even as a grown man? <le dreamy sigh> And did I not warn you in the back of the prequel that he has **NO**

CONCEPT OF PERSONAL SPACE? Sure, he has some unique kinks, but never would he hurt Mercy. And, if you think about it (as my alphas and I discussed late one night), Shay men are already enamored of the female reproductive system because they're all about family. Make a family, take a family, make the family bigger, etc. All about knocking their women up. His woman's on her period? Meh, what's a little blood?

But in the case of Amos, well, his birth mom died. So his focus, while including the need to build a family, expands to include the breasts—those beautiful things that (for some) nourish babies and are a symbol of femininity. Maybe the lack of a mother figure in his early childhood prompted him to pay extra attention to a noticeable body part that intrigued him. Or maybe that was just his personal kink. (Believe it or not, preferences form early.)

Back to Mercy—some readers may wonder why she's still a virgin at her age. While the past few decades have seen many sexual liberations from so-called "taboos" passed down from generation to generation, there's one stigma that almost doggedly remains: that of virginity. What some people don't realize is a virgin status that extends beyond what most people would consider the "normal" age is more common than one might think—whether you believe virginity is a social construct or not—and it can happen for a variety of reasons, as Amos mentioned in chapter 9, and more. Beyond the somewhat stereotypical religious reason, there's also mental trauma, childhood trauma, low libido, social anxiety, low self-esteem, previous assault, emotional abuse, body insecurities, and **many** other factors which can contribute to a delay in the intimate sharing of bodies.

Whatever the reason may be, it happens, and Mercy is a representation of that.

Other readers may wonder why she didn't try to run away. Why she didn't put up more of a fight.

Well, it's said that when put in certain situations, people will either experience a fight or flight reaction. There's also a third reaction: paralysis. Mercy is shy, unconfident, and not going to run away when she knows she has absolutely no chance of success. She's too smart for that, and she's not going to rock the boat when it comes to conflict because she'd rather stay on the boat in choppy waters than jump ship and risk drowning.

Especially since there's no lifeboat on board.

And she's not wearing a lifejacket.

And she doesn't know how to swim.

I think I'm losing it on the analogy part, hahaha.

Moving on.

Becoming a certain age doesn't magically enable a person to do something overnight. Some people will *always* be shy and awkward and find it hard to stand up for themselves or make small talk.

There will *always* be older virgins who think they're going to live life alone and die without knowing what it is to feel the intimate touch of another person. (Though some may actually **prefer** this.)

There will *always* be women who feel every dooming, pulsating beat of their biological clock with every fiber of their being and become terrified that life is passing them by.

There will *always* be women who immediately burst into tears when seeing wedding invitations, pregnancy announcements, baby shower announcements, or teenie tiny baby clothes, and have an overwhelming wave of depression crash over them with no way of fighting it off.

There is an estimated five to ten percent of U.S. women of childbearing age (and many more worldwide) who have PCOS and struggle **so hard** to get pregnant while dealing with extra things this syndrome brings: excess body/facial hair, adult acne, terrible cramps, long periods, short periods, **no periods**, an increased struggle to lose or maintain a healthy weight... The list goes on and on.

All these things are just facts of life.

It sucks and it hurts, but I hope that giving voice to them gives hope that you're not alone. There are others going through the same thing, maybe even someone close to you. And while it may not seem like a consolation to know that, hopefully it gives you the virtual hug I'm intending. I'm a sap, I know.

Moving on again.

As for who's next, it's Connor and Rosanna.

Connor, oh Connor. This muscular, tatted, animal-loving man is going to do some *hot* things to his woman, let me tell you that. What are some of those things, you ask?

Well...let's just say he's obsessed with becoming a dad by **any** means—fair or foul. And, as with all Shays, boundaries don't mean much to him.

Moving on for the last time.

Writing is hard stuff, y'all (pardon my Southern). At least for me. And it's made me tip my hat in respect just a little bit more to my fellow indie authors. If you don't leave reviews, I hope you'll consider doing so for books you read in the future.

And if you've made it to the end of this long note from me, I love you for sticking with me to the bitter end. That right there sounds kinda like some Shay loyalty. <wink>

Lastly, if there are any typos, I apologize. I'm only hooman! <wink wink>

Okay, I'm done now.

ALSO BY M. L. MARIAN

ABOUT THE AUTHOR

M. L. Marian has no clue what to put here. She sees other authors with really cool bios, but there's nothing cool about M. L. Marian. She's just an antisocial hermit who comes out of hiding long enough to put a book into the world and then scurries back into seclusion.

She would like to remind you, however, that kindness doesn't cost a thing (except for when it does) and loose lips sink ships. Whatever that means.

Subscribe to her newsletter at https://mlmarian.com/newsletter/ for all the latest updates!

facebook.com/mlmarian

instagram.com/m.l.marian

tiktok.com/@m.l.marian

Made in the USA
Columbia, SC
28 December 2024

0972296a-ca41-4986-b022-aa71373bac18R01